"LOVE KILLS
INDUCES GENUINE
SWEATY PANIC! . . .

A paranormal caper that the most hardened skeptic can enjoy . . . A WITTY, SCARY INVENTION"
—*Newsweek*

"A novel of terrifying realism . . . should be read by every woman who lives alone"
—Gay Talese

"READ IT AND SQUIRM! . . . The whole thing works beautifully . . . WHOLLY IMAGINATIVE, EERILY CONVINCING!"
—*Chicago Sunday Sun-Times*

DAN GREENBURG

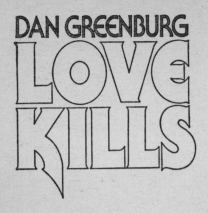

LOVE KILLS

PUBLISHED BY POCKET BOOKS NEW YORK

POCKET BOOKS, a Simon & Schuster division of
GULF & WESTERN CORPORATION
1230 Avenue of the Americas, New York, N.Y. 10020

Published by arrangement with Harcourt Brace Jovanovich
Library of Congress Catalog Card Number: 77-92056

ISBN: 0-671-82756-1

First Pocket Books printing July, 1979

10 9 8 7 6 5 4 3

Trademarks registered in the United States and other countries.

Printed in the U.S.A.

FOR SUZANNE

For helping me with the technical part of the research for this book I would like to thank: Sgt. Morton I. Hofstein of the New York Police Department; the officers and detectives of the Third Homicide Zone in Manhattan; the men of the Ninth Precinct in Manhattan; Charles Honorton of the Division of Parapsychology and Psychophysics, Department of Psychiatry, at Maimonides Medical Center in Brooklyn; and Dr. Michael Baden, Deputy Chief Medical Examiner of the City of New York.

I am also indebted to the following marvelous people for their editorial suggestions on the manuscript itself: Betsy Nolan, Lee Frank, Ivan and Jeannette Kronenfeld, Erica Spellman, Lynn Nesbit, Sam and Leah Greenburg, Mildred Newman, Bernard Berkowitz, Harry Stein, Elizabeth Johansson, Art Mandelbaum, Merice Mills and—most of all—Carol Hill and Suzanne O'Malley.

that the Commissioner decides to give you a break.

The way Max got his shield was to pull an elderly couple out of a building on Avenue A that was, as the

were sufficiently impressed with him, he could get him there to a special Homicide squad.

So now here he was in Third Homicide. He had learned as much as you can learn about being a homi-

1

Linda Lowry, possessor of the third best set of breasts in her graduating class at Hunter College, unmarried though she could have accepted any of several proposals of marriage from perfectly presentable albeit prematurely balding men, unlocks the three police locks on the door of her fashionable East Side studio apartment, hears her phone ring for the seventh time, and enters the last half-hour of her life on earth.

In her haste to get to the ringing telephone she lets the heavy steel door to the apartment thunk closed behind her without locking it from the inside as she usually does. On the eighth ring, silently cursing her answering service for not picking up on the third ring as they're paid to, she scoops the cherry-red receiver out of its cradle and claps it to her ear.

"—owry residence," says the bored nasal voice of the woman at the answering service.

"It's all right, I've got it," says Linda, sitting down on the unmade bed in the sleeping alcove and exposing an expanse of shapely and much-sought-after thigh in the process.

"Oh, *there* she is," says the bored nasal voice to the caller in a tone which suggests it was Linda and not she who was deficient in the phone-answering department and then clicks off the line.

"Linda?" A familiar male voice.

"Oh, hello, Arnold," says Linda audibly exhaling and

1

adopting the voice she reserves for perfectly presentable albeit prematurely balding men.

Downstairs the man with the vacant look in his eyes and the flowers in his hands enters the marble-floored lobby of the apartment building. Although it is a bitingly cold December night, the man's hands are perspiring slightly, dampening the paper around the stems of the fresh-cut flowers.

"Help you?" says the uniformed doorman to the man with the flowers.

In reply the man points to the card stapled to the wrapping paper. On the card in green type it says, "East Side Florists" and in felt-tip pen it says, "Lowry."

The doorman steps to the house phone on the lobby wall and presses one of the brightly polished brass buttons.

Inside the small automatic elevator the man with the flowers stares stonily ahead until the elevator comes to a halt and the doors jolt open. The man alights from the elevator and turns without the slightest hesitation to his right and walks silently down the carpeted hallway and stops before the door with an empty nameplate and the number 13B. The man presses the buzzer and waits.

A moment later the door is opened. Linda Lowry is holding the receiver of her phone in her left hand and stretching the coiled cord as far as it will reach to the door.

"Arnold, hold on a sec," says Linda into the phone. "I have to get some change for the delivery boy."

Linda walks back to the bed, puts down the receiver, and goes to the sideboard to get her purse. As she does so the man enters the apartment and shuts the door softly behind him.

"Here you are," says Linda brightly, turning back toward the door with two quarters in her hand and sees that the man has entered the apartment and shut the door behind him.

Oh my God, she thinks, the adrenaline pouring out of her adrenal glands into her bloodstream, Please don't let this be what I think it is, please don't—not after how good I've been all these years, never opening the door to anybody I didn't know till just this once, sometimes even sending away legitimate callers because I suddenly got bad vibes from them, only to forget myself because the door wasn't already triple-locked and make one mistake and have it turn out to be the real thing. Maybe he's just after money. Please let him just be after money.

The man in one swift motion steps to the bed, replaces the receiver in its cradle and disconnects the third presence in the room.

"Listen," says Linda, wondering if the man can hear the unsteadiness in her voice, wondering if it's better or worse if he *can* hear the unsteadiness in her voice, "if it's money I don't have all that much but you are certainly welcome to all of it, every penny. I also have some jewelry you might like. I didn't buy it myself, but frankly I think it's expensive."

Linda starts to turn around to get her purse to give the man what money she has, deciding not to mention the roll of twenties at the bottom of her underwear drawer, but the man steps forward and blocks her movement with the hand in which he holds the flowers.

It's *not* the money, she thinks with a sudden flash of queasiness—Oh my God it's not the money.

2

It is the rookie detective's first visit to the city morgue, and the two older plainclothes cops are kidding him about it.

"Hey, Max," says the one named Jerry Mahoney, "you really never seen a stiff before?"

Max Segal shakes his head. He is twenty-five, blond, slim, and only a set of too-big teeth stand between him and serious handsomeness—a sort of younger Jean-Paul Belmondo.

"You aren't going to faint on us now, are ya, Max?" says the one named Larry Cassidy, who decides that this is one of the funniest things he's said all week and explodes with laughter until he gags and Jerry has to pound him on the back. Max manages a strained smile.

The city morgue in New York is a fairly modern building right across the alley from the psycho ward of Bellevue Hospital at 30th Street and First Avenue. The morgue deals with all sudden, unnatural, and unattended deaths.

On the street floor of the morgue are ordinary offices. On the basement floor below is where they keep the bodies. Of the ninety thousand corpses a year that New York has to handle, about thirty thousand of them pass through this building. Seventy-five to eighty percent of these bodies have some sort of identification on them when they roll in. Roughly twenty-five percent of them are autopsied.

4

When a body is autopsied (or "postmortemed" or "posted") the first step is to slice the scalp across the top of the head from ear to ear and roll the face right down like a rubber mask. Next, with an electric saw the top of the skull is cut off like the top of a jack-o-lantern, and the brain is taken out and dissected.

Then a deep Y-shaped incision is made in the torso, with the arms of the Y extending toward the shoulders and the base of the Y extending toward the groin. The flaps of skin are peeled back and the abdominal cavity is opened up. A part of the rib cage must be removed with the electric saw in order to get at the heart and lungs. The heart, lungs, liver, kidneys, stomach, and intestines are lifted out, examined, and dissected, leaving the body a hollow shell.

Small samples of some of the organs are saved for examination under a microscope, along with a bit of blood and, occasionally, the contents of stomach and bladder.

The autopsy findings are dictated into the formal autopsy report by the doctor, and the body is reassembled by a morgue attendant. In the New York City morgue this is usually done by an old crone called the Seamstress. She loosely stitches the skin of the corpse together with a long curved needle and a few yards of wet white twine, in the same loose overhand stitch you may have used to make moccasins from kits in summer camp.

When the corpse has been sewn back together it is returned to its refrigerated numbered "box"—a sliding tray resembling a large filing cabinet drawer. Bodies in the morgue are transported to and from their boxes on stainless steel rolling carts known as "meat wagons."

The basement floor has blue-tiled walls and a double-tier of stainless steel boxes. The halls of the basement are kept spotlessly clean, but there is nonetheless the faint stench of rotting meat.

Jerry and Larry lead Max downstairs to show him around and run into the Medical Examiner. From the way they greet each other Max figures they must have gone through about half a dozen wars together.

"This here's Max," says Jerry, pounding Max on the back. "It's his first day in Homicide."

"Hey, Max," says Larry, reinventing his previous witticism in all its glory, "you aren't going to faint on us now, are ya?"

Larry has to be pounded on the back again, whereupon Max is treated to his first bona fide example of morgue humor.

"They bring a stiff in here yesterday," says the Medical Examiner grinning in anticipation, "I swear to Christ his shvantz is about a foot long. One of the morgue men turns to me. 'Doc,' he says, 'I got a shvantz just like *this* guy's.' 'That long?' I say. 'Naw,' he says, 'that *dead*.' "

Jerry and Larry are on the floor with convulsions. One more like that and they are going to have about three coronaries apiece. Max smiles faintly, already sorry he's come, wondering what he's even doing there, dreading the imminent confrontation with his first actual corpse which, as he's guessed, is not long in coming.

"So, Max," says the M.E., "this is your first day in Homicide, is it?"

"Yessir," says Max, briefly reconsidering the "sir." True, the M.E. is a doctor, but from what Max has seen so far it looks as though the guy might be just a shade too ghoulish to rate an out-and-out "sir."

"We brought Max to the morgue so he could see his first stiff in private, among friends, instead of out on the job," says Jerry, draping an arm around Max's shoulders. "That way, if he feels like tossing his cookies it won't be so embarrassing, eh, Max?"

"Or if he faints," adds Larry, wheezing out one last death rattle from his earlier masterpiece of levity. "You'd be surprised how many cops faint at seeing their first stiff."

"Right, Max," says the M.E. "As a matter of fact, *lots* of men faint when they see a stiff. But no women do."

"Fascinating," says Max with a thin attempt at sarcasm that escapes all present.

"Well, Max," says the M.E. with a wink at the two older homicide cops, "I suppose you're anxious to begin. Let's see now, what can I show you first? Anything in particular you're dying to see?"

Max shakes his head as the M.E. scans the cards attached to the fronts of the closest boxes, looking for something amusing.

"You like tattoos, Max?" says the M.E., grabbing a box handle and pulling it open. The box, like a giant file drawer, slides toward them, revealing the naked body of a longish-haired blond man in his early twenties which is covered with ornate tattoos.

Holy Christ, thinks Max, there it is, my first corpse. Max neither faints nor tosses his cookies. Rather, his first reaction is surprise that the corpse is *(a)* so lifelike and *(b)* not set up the way they are in the movies and on TV. In the movies and on TV if you saw a corpse in a morgue it was covered with a sheet and nothing peeked out at you except a pair of bare feet, which were the first thing out of the drawer, with a tag tied to one of the toes. In real life the head comes out first, as in birth, and there is no sheet—just the plain body, naked, with a few articles of clothing balled up at the feet.

Max is amazed that the tattooed guy looks not dead

but sleeping, as though he'd gotten a little hot and woozy and lay down for a fast nap in one of the refrigerated drawers and would any minute now stretch and yawn and put on his clothes.

"What about those tattoos, eh, Max?" says the M.E.

"Howya feelin', Max?" says Larry, giving him a poke in the ribs. "Not going to pass out on us, areya?"

Max shakes his head. How he is feeling is not at all. The thought that he is looking at a young man about his own age who had probably not planned on lying here dead tonight and that it could very well be Max himself in the drawer, with the M.E. pointing out some of his more amusing physical characteristics, is one that Max has thus far managed to keep at a wholly intellectual level.

That, thinks Max, must be what makes Larry and Jerry and especially the morgue attendants and the M.E. so relentlessly perky about this ghastly place— they no longer look at a corpse and see themselves in the drawer. I'm terrified of catching my death of death, but they've been vaccinated. They've conquered death in some weird way—they fucking *own* it.

"What did this guy die of?" says Max.

"Overdose. He was a junkie. See the tracks on his arms?"

The M.E. picks up one of the tattooed guy's arms, points out the track marks, then lets the dead limb drop to the drawer. It bounces as it hits. The gesture jars Max, who had thought you treated the dead with respect, junkies or no.

"How come you can raise his arm?" is what Max chooses to say instead. "I mean I thought it would be stiff from rigor mortis."

"Stiffs aren't stiff for long," says Jerry.

"Rigor mortis is a transitory condition," the M.E. explains.

"C'mon, Doc," says Larry, "show us some others. Max is getting bored here."

"Yeah, Doc," says Jerry. "Max wants to see some *broads*. Right, Max?"

"Sure," says Max. "Let's see some broads."

"I've got a real honey here," says the M.E. with another wink, and slides out a tray containing a naked lady.

3

Babette Watson, age twenty, proprietor of a pair of huge Fabulashed tragic eyes into which more than one hapless college sophomore has stumbled and drowned, lies in bed in a drowsy haze.

Babette has found that if she relaxes until she is nearly asleep but not quite, then sometimes she can tune into snatches of disembodied conversation. The fact that these snatches of conversation have from time to time turned up in Babette's actual wide-awake life, with people speaking the sentences as though they were making them up right on the spot, was the disquieting part, and it wasn't exactly what they called *déjà vu* either, as far as Babette could tell.

Déjà vu, if Babette understood it correctly, was the feeling that you knew what somebody was going to say at the moment they said it or a split second before, as if you had some vague memory of having had the same conversation with that person in the past. A psychology instructor in school had told her the effect was caused by a kind of double or mirror input into the brain at the moment of perception, and she'd let it go at that. She supposed it was a fairly common phenomenon, but it didn't describe her own experience at all, not by a long shot.

Wisely, Babette has never told anybody about such things.

Babette's first realization that she had supernatural awareness came with her father's death. The night he died so horribly she was jolted out of a deep sleep to find him standing at the foot of her bed, looking down at her, wearing his black rubber fireman's turnout coat, his face smudged with soot and filth, smelling terribly of burnt rubber. One moment he was standing there, gazing down at her with love and sadness, the next he had vanished.

Babette had turned on all the lights. She could find him nowhere. But the stench of charred rubber persisted for a long time. Two hours later the call came, informing them of his death.

Her mother told her she'd been dreaming and made her promise not to tell anyone about what she thought she'd seen. Babette knew that she had not been dreaming, but she didn't tell anyone about what she'd seen after she told her mother, and she was sorry she had told even her.

She felt her father's loss more keenly than anyone could have known, and she didn't want to desecrate his memory by talking about him or about the visitation on the night of his death.

Like most little girls, Babette thought her father was a hero. Like few little girls, she was right—her father was one of the bravest men in the city of New York and he had medals to prove it. Like even fewer little girls, Babette still thought of her father as a hero when she

grew up. The communication that Babette had shared
with her father was on such a level that they spoke in a
kind of shorthand. Indeed, one was always finishing the
other's sentences and each always seemed to know what
the other was thinking. The older Babette grew the more
her mother resented the special sort of communication
she had with her dad.

After his death Babette appeared to recover quickly.
Her mother and her friends marveled at how little she
spoke of him, how quickly she got back into the swing
of her schoolwork and her other routines. Some felt
Babette's apparent lack of mourning was almost callous.
What they didn't understand was that Babette had little
reason to mourn the loss of a father since he was still
with her. She felt that she had somehow absorbed him.
Absorbed his strength, his courage, his decency, his
resiliency.

Her schoolwork improved markedly. She seemed un-
usually level-headed and self-assured for her years. She
was able to grasp difficult concepts that others her age
would not understand until they were older, if at all.

Young men her age and those several years older
were irresistibly drawn to her. To their dismay, they
were unable to penetrate her aloofness. Despite her
longlegged dancer's body, creamy skin, perfect teeth,
sculptured buttocks, and a yard of honey-colored hair,
Babette was possibly one of the last certified virgins in
the entire city of New York.

Not that Babette wouldn't go to bed with a man if
the right one came along, but she felt the right one never
had. Possibly part of the problem was her Catholic
training. Probably part of the problem was that Babette
had never felt she'd known anyone, aside from her
father, who was a real man, a man who was brave, but
also sensitive and soft when it was appropriate to be so.

All she'd known thus far were boys in college, and they weren't men at all.

The only grownup man she knew—and the notion that anyone would call him a grownup was amusing—was Freddy, her stepfather. At least Freddy was old, that much you could say for him, although not much else. Particularly how he behaved with her when her mother was out of the apartment and the two of them were there alone and he had been on one of his disgusting drinking sprees.

Not that Freddy would ever make an actual pass at her. Although with Freddy you truthfully never knew. How her mother ever ended up with Freddy after being married to someone like her father was a mystery to Babette. She supposed it proved that her mother, at bottom, was more like Freddy than the man she'd married first.

Babette lies in bed and feels herself drifting, just drifting. She feels she is about to tune into another one of her precognitive visions. The first thing that comes through is a faint, silent picture of a woman brushing her long, straight, dark hair, just brushing it the way that Babette does her own, in very long strokes. The next thing Babette gets is a line or two of music. Old-fashioned romantic music, with a woman's voice singing something you could barely make out, like ". . . a blackboard high above you . . ."

A blackboard? There it was again: ". . . eyes a blackboard . . ." No, not eyes. Maybe it was: ". . . skies a blackboard . . ." *Skies* a blackboard? What? Drift, just drift and you'll get it.

". . . The sky's a blackboard high above you . . ." That's it: The sky's a blackboard. Now there's something else. A knocking sound, like the knocker on a front door. Now . . . a man. A man in a dark coat.

Something is wrong with the man. Something about him is terribly wrong. What could it be? But . . . no, now it seems to be OK. Nothing wrong. Two people dancing. Holding each other and dancing. Beautiful, oldtimey music: "Starting with the A-B-C of it, Right down to the X-Y-Z of it. Help me solve the . . . something something . . . help me solve the mis-to-*ree* of it . . ." What? Mis-to-*ree*?

A blurred bright object shimmers and comes into focus. Round. Shiny. Little bright-colored dots like . . . flowers. Yes, flowers. Little bright-colored flowers under a shiny round thing made of glass. What is it?

". . . Starting with the A-B-C of it, Right down to the X-Y-Z of it, Help me solve the mis-to-*ree* of it . . ."

Something else. Also shiny, also round. Two things. Both shiny, both round, both gold-covered. What? Focus. Looks like . . . a dark square space near the floor. A fireplace. Yes. And the shiny, round, gold-colored objects? Andirons. With . . . what is that that's splattered on them? Nail polish. No . . . looks like . . .

". . . Did you say I've got a *lot* to learn . . . Well, don't think I'm trying *not* to learn . . . Since this is the perfect *spot* to learn . . . Teach me tonight . . ."

The shiny round thing again with the tiny little flowers under it. Like a paperweight or something. Right, a paperweight. And the andirons. Gold and round and shiny on top with little specks of stuff on them. Brown? Brown stuff. Not nail polish. No. Looks like . . .

". . . One thing isn't very *clear,* my love . . . Should the teacher stand so *near,* my love . . . Graduation's almost *here,* my love . . . Teach me tonight . . ."

The woman. A name . . . is it Waverly? No. Beverly. Beverly something. Beverly what? Macklin. Beverly Macklin. Something bad is about to happen to Beverly Macklin.

The man. What is it about the man that's wrong?
His face. Can't see his face. His clothes . . . dark. Black?
Dark brown? Spotted? Dark brown spots. A coat with
dark brown spots, a fur coat. What animal—a leopard?
No. Not a leopard . . .

Brown spots on the andirons, not on the coat. No,
first on the andirons, then on the coat. Then . . . then
on the andirons again. But what is it that's wrong with
the man?

". . . Starting with the A-B-C of it, Right down to
the X-Y-Z of it, Help me solve the . . . Help me
solve the . . . Help me solve the . . . Help me . . .
Help me . . . Helllllllpppppp!!! HELLLLLLPPP!!!
HELLLLLLPPPPPP!!!"

Babette's mother rushes into the room what is it are
you all right who's killing you are you all right my God
she's asleep but her eyes are open BABETTE!

"Whew. Hi, Mom."

"Hi, *Mom?* Screaming 'Help' like that and then just
'Hi, *"Mom?"* What was that *screaming?* Dear God, I
thought you were being murdered in your *sleep!* Are
you all *right?* Were you having a nightmare or what?"

"Yes. A nightmare."

"But all that *screaming.* You're all *right?*"

"Yes, I'm all right."

"You're *sure?*"

"I'm sure."

"You're really *sure? Dear God,* you scared me half to
death. A scream like that, I thought for sure you were
being murdered in your *sleep.* Was it a nightmare or
what?"

"Yes, a nightmare. I'm OK now, Mom. Really. I'm
sorry I screamed."

"You're *sure* you're all right? You're really *sure?*"

"Sure I'm sure."

"Well, all right then. Scared me half to *death*. I thought for sure you were being murdered in your *sleep*."

Babette's mother leaves the room, muttering to herself, relieved it was only a nightmare and not Babette being murdered in her sleep. But Babette's heart is pounding so loudly she's sure they can hear it way out on the street, because she knows that whatever she just had, it definitely was not any kind of nightmare.

4

"I've got a real honey here," says the M.E. with another wink, and slides out a tray containing a naked lady. The naked lady is about sixty-five or seventy, with a huge fat hill of a stomach and collapsed breasts, a stern hawked beak of a nose, and a dyed blond pompadour so well shellacked with hairspray that not one strand has fallen into disarray throughout the entire normally hairmussing procedures of dropping dead and being carted off to the morgue and stripped of clothing and filed away under *D* for *Dowager*. Max sees great potential for a terrific hairspray commercial.

"How did this one die?" says Max, dully aware they could be looking at his mother.

"Heart failure. She dropped dead right in the middle of Fifth Avenue. Right in front of Saks."

As they've been chatting and the M.E. has been showing off his stock, various Black and Hispanic morgue workers have stopped, lingered briefly with smug, vaccinated smiles, then gone off about their favorite morgue activities. Now a new one, a white guy with a disquietingly depraved leer, has joined them for some fun.

"Let's see, what can I show you next?" says the M.E., looking around his showroom. "I know—we got a bunch of people in last night from a nightclub fire in the Village. Want to see some?"

"No!" says Max as the M.E. begins sliding open another drawer, for suddenly it is beginning to get to him, a vague queasiness and an unsteadiness in the knees; and the thought of having to look at a horribly burned body—what some cops he knows call "roastietoasties"—is more than he can bear just now.

"It's OK," says the M.E. with unexpected gentleness, "this gal wasn't burned at all—she died of smoke inhalation."

Max allows himself a fast peek at the chunky middle-aged woman in the drawer, sees a black face and vaguely assumes she's a Negro, then notices that she's white from the neck down. Max is temporarily disoriented—perhaps she'd participated in some macabre minstrel show in the doomed nightclub?

"Their faces get black from the smoke," the M.E. explains, sensing Max's puzzlement.

"Hey, Doc," says the depraved-looking morgue man, "why don't you show them the torso?"

"The new torso or the old torso?" says the M.E., sliding the black-faced woman back out of sight.

"What's the difference between the new torso and the old torso?" says Max and is instantly aware that he doesn't wish to know the answer.

"The new torso has a chain wrapped around its penis," says the morgue man with a wet gleam in his eye. "The old torso's penis was chopped off with its limbs and head."

"Fag homicides," says Jerry. "The fucking river's full of 'em."

"Yeah," says Larry. "You don't even find out about most floaters during the winter months. But the minute warm weather sets in the ripe ones start popping to the surface all over the place."

"Max, you're going to love it in Homicide," says Jerry with a smile.

"Hey," says the M.E. "I have just the thing for Max. They brought it in about an hour ago. I don't know why I didn't think of it sooner."

The M.E. goes to an upper-tier drawer, opens it with a flourish, and steps back proudly. Inside Max sees an extremely attractive young woman with blond hair, a good slim body, well-shaped breasts, a dark-colored pubic thatch, and a deep cut and bad bruises on her throat.

"What precinct they pick this up in?" says Jerry, giving her a professional once-over.

"The Seventeenth, I think. An apartment house on East 46th Street," says the depraved-looking morgue man.

Larry checks the name on the drawer.

"Linda Lowry," he says.

"Some terrific-looking chick you were, Linda," says Jerry sadly. "What a fucking waste."

Max is looking very hard at the pretty young woman with the well-shaped breasts and the dark-colored pubic thatch, struggling with complex and not wholly appropriate emotions. There is a terrible sadness, which is the first real emotion he has allowed himself to feel here. There is an urge to cover up the body and to shield it from the depraved-looking morgue man. And there is also the disquieting but inescapable realization that, no matter how much he may hate the thought of it, looking at the naked dead girl's body is causing Max to have fantasies of a romantic nature.

5

Linda Lowry starts to turn around to give the man what money she has, but the man steps forward and blocks her movement with the hand in which he holds the flowers.

It's *not* the money, she thinks with a sudden flash of queasiness—Oh my God it's not the money.

"Take them," says the man.

"What?" says Linda.

"Take them."

The man extends the flowers to her.

"They're for you," he says.

She looks at the man uncomprehendingly and slowly takes the flowers from him.

"I hope you like them," he says in a flat, toneless voice. "They cost ten dollars."

"*You* bought these?" she asks, still trying to figure it out. "For me?"

The man nods.

"Open them," he says.

She tears open the wrapping, her hands shaking just a little, and takes out the flowers and forces a thin smile. "They're . . . very nice," she says. "Thank you."

"They're anemones," he says. "Your favorites."

"How did you know that?"

"I know a lot about you, Linda," the man replies. "Where you work, what time you get there, where you eat lunch, what time you get home, what you have for dinner, what you do when you think you're alone—I've made quite a study of you. I even know what color underwear you have on. Beige."

A cold oil slick passes rapidly over her body at these words. Her eyes dart to the windows with their undrawn blinds, and beyond them to the darkened windows directly opposite in the building across the street. So that's it, she thinks, he lives across the street and he's been watching me, God knows how long, when I've been dressing, undressing, maybe all through the warm summer months when I wore hardly anything around the apartment.

The thought of having been watched while doing intimate things for that long a time makes her flesh crawl, but she is now slightly reassured—peeping toms never do more than peep.

"What do you want with me?" she says, a tone of authority creeping tentatively back into her voice.

"A date."

"A what?"

"A date," says the man. "I want to date you."

He unwraps a flat square package and produces a 78 rpm record in a worn liner.

"May I put this on the phonograph?" says the man.

OK, it's clear what we have here, she thinks smartly. It's a crazy person who's fallen in love with me from afar. All I have to do is be firm and get him out of here immediately.

"Get out," she says in a hard voice. "I'll count to ten and if you're not out of here by then I'm calling the police. One . . . two . . . three . . ."

She advances slowly toward the phone on the bed.

"Please don't do that, Linda," says the man. "Please don't."

". . . four . . . five . . . six . . ."

She reaches the phone and starts to pick it up, and then she hears the click and turns around to see the man has reached into a pocket and produced a switchblade knife, the kind they used to sell years ago that clicks open when you press the button, and all of her confidence runs out of her like air from a balloon.

"Oh please," she whispers, "oh no, please don't . . . I'll do anything you say, only please don't hurt me. Please put that away. I'll give you anything you want, anything. What is it you want?"

"A date," says the man. "I told you. All I want is a date. And a chance to get to know you."

"OK," she says, nodding rapidly, "whatever you say. Tell me what to do."

The man extends the record album in the worn liner to her.

"Put this on the phonograph," he says.

She takes the album and moves to the table where she has the stereo, and takes the record out of its liner and puts it on the spindle.

"See? I'm doing just as you told me, I'm putting the record on the phonograph just like you told me," she says, and turns the machine on. The record falls onto the turntable and the arm moves into position. A hiss of static, then an orchestral introduction, and the once-familiar voice of a singer in the fifties begins to sing:

Did you say I've got a lot to learn?
Well, don't think I'm trying not to learn,
Since this is the perfect spot to learn,
Teach me tonight . . .

"April Stevens," says the man pleasantly, as if Linda's chief concern at that moment might have been in trying to place the name of the singer. "Do you remember her?"

"Uh, oh, yes. I think I do."

"She looks a little like you, in a way."

"Mmmmm."

"Care to dance?"

"What?"

"I *said* do you care to dance?"

The thing to do is humor him, she thinks, humor him and wait for the right moment. You'll get out of this yet. Wait till they hear about this at the office—a peeping tom pervert who forces his way into your apartment and brings you flowers and makes you play April Stevens records on your stereo at knifepoint, all so he can ask you to dance with him.

Starting with the A-B-C of it,
Right down to the X-Y-Z of it,
Help me solve the mist-to-ree of it,
Teach me tonight . . .

"I'd *love* to dance," she says. "Provided you put that thing away."

The man thinks this over, nods, closes the switchblade, and puts it in his sportscoat pocket. He takes off his overcoat, starts to put it on the bed, then stops.

"Here OK?" he says.

"What?"

"I *said* is here OK? To put my coat? And don't keep saying, '*What?*'"

"Oh, yes, sure, the bed is fine."

"If you prefer, I could hang it in the closet."

"Oh, no, the bed is fine."

The man folds his overcoat neatly in half, tucks the sleeves inside it, and puts it down on the end of the bed. She tries not to stare at the pocket of the sportscoat he is wearing, where he dropped the knife.

"You really have a nice place here," he says, looking around.

"Thanks."

"Very nice. You do it yourself?"

"What?"

"Don't keep saying, 'What'!" snarls the man, suddenly furious. Then he recovers and repeats, as if to a child who refuses to listen: "I *said,* did . . . you . . . do . . . it . . . yourself?"

"Yes," she replies. She has a sudden wild thought that it's the apartment and not her he's been peeping at through his binoculars, and all of this is an elaborate scheme to find out the name of her decorator.

"I like how you don't have the furniture right up against the wall," the man says, looking around approvingly. "Most people just shove their furniture right up against the wall, but you have it standing away from the wall so it can breathe. I like that."

"Good."

"I do the same thing with my own."

"Really?"

"Yes."

The sky's a blackboard high above you,
If a shooting star goes by
I'll use that star to write "I love you"
A thousand times across the sky . . .

The man holds out his arms to her.

"Shall we trip the light fantastic?" he says.

With a shudder she moves toward him till he is holding her, and she begins to dance with him. She is trembling slightly. He holds her closer, perhaps mistaking her trembling for desire, and places his cheek next to hers. He smells of Old Spice shaving lotion. He is not as bad a dancer as she thought he'd be. He is not even bad-looking. Why doesn't he approach women in the normal way?

"You dance well," he says.

"So do you," she says.

"I ought to," he says. "I didn't go to Arthur Murray for a whole season for nothing, you know."

Oh, God, that's priceless, she thinks, Arthur Murray. She makes a mental note to work this into her story at the office. She moves her arm on his back ever so slightly. A little lower. A little closer to the pocket with the knife.

"Well, they certainly taught you very nicely at Arthur Murray's," she says.

"The first course I won for free. The rest I had to pay for. I learned everything—the foxtrot, the box waltz, the bunny hug, the tango, the rhumba, the samba, even the conga. They don't do the conga too much anymore, though."

She moves her cheek provocatively against his and drops her hand a little closer to the pocket with the knife.

"You know," she whispers into his ear, "you're a very attractive man."

"Thank you," he says, his voice getting softer. "And you're a very attractive woman. You don't know how I've planned this moment, Linda. You don't know how nervous I was. I had no idea how easy it would be."

"You should have simply called me," she says. "Why didn't you just call me on the phone? You didn't have to force your way in here at knifepoint."

"I didn't think you'd agree to go out with me," he says. "I thought I had to do it this way."

"Well, you were wrong," she says, and stops dancing, and slides one hand up to his face, and moves her lips to his, and kisses him. She's astonished at how smoothly it's going. Like taking candy from a baby. She should have been an actress.

Both of his arms go around her and hold her tight as he returns her kiss, closing his eyes.

One thing isn't very clear, my love,
Should the teacher stand so near, my love.
Graduation's almost here, my love,
Teach me tonight . . .

She holds her breath, drops her hand into his sports-coat pocket, closes it swiftly over the knife and whips it out, pressing the button and clicking the blade out, ripping his pocket in the process.

With a surprised cry he lunges at the hand holding the knife and blood spurts from the heel of his palm.

With his other hand he slams her hard against the wall with all his might. The shock of the blow causes her to drop the knife, which clatters to the parquet floor. He swoops down to pick it up in his bleeding hand and then, breathing hard, his face bright red with rage, he moves toward her.

Oh no, oh God, oh no.

6

Jerry and Larry and Max are ready to leave the morgue. The receiving doors at the far end of the hall open and a Black morgue attendant enters, trundling a stainless steel meat wagon ahead of him. On top of the meat wagon is something wrapped up in a green rubber sheet. Out of the end of the green rubber sheet is coming a thin red line of blood.

Max is torn between a horrid fascination to see what it is that is wrapped up in the green rubber sheet and a deep yearning to turn away and beat his ass out of there.

What is wrapped up in the green rubber sheet is a "fresh one," a victim of a car crash. The morgue attendants pull out a drawer, slide up the meat wagon, and begin unwrapping the body. The body is that of a man in his late fifties and it is clad in comical-looking long underwear. The head is all wrapped up in sheets. As the morgue men unwrap the head Max turns away. At the instant he turns away he hears Jerry and Larry gasp.

"What happened?" says Max.

"The guy's head just came off," says Jerry.

Max starts walking rapidly down the hall in the direction away from the body clad in comical longjohns and no head. Jerry and Larry and the M.E. fall in behind him, wanting to know if he is OK, wanting to know if he wishes to stop off in the men's room to wash up. What Max wants most to do is get the hell out of there, but he also feels a powerful urge to try to wash off the rancid film of death which feels like it's covering his skin.

They troop into the men's room and Max splashes cold water on his face and rubs his closed eyelids and pushes the soap dispenser above the sink and cannot believe the slimy red gore which has plopped out into his hands.

The M.E. glances at Max's hands, then at his stricken face, and chuckles.

"That's iodine. We put it in with the soap to prevent infection."

They walk upstairs to find that a pre-Christmas party is in progress in one of the ground-floor offices. Twenty or thirty ordinary-looking clerical people are in the process of drinking ordinary vodka out of ordinary paper cups, joking and flirting with each other in an ordinary way, and dancing to ordinary recorded Christmas carols only ten feet above the relentless awfulness of the floor below.

Max walks shakily into the party, flashes a plump secretary an uncertain smile, grabs a bottle out of her hands, and gulps down six or seven gigantic swallows of vodka. Jerry and Larry and the M.E. explode with laughter and pound Max on the back.

Hours later Jerry and Larry drop Max off at his two-room split-level apartment on East 19th Street. Max triple-locks the door from the inside and turns on a light in the ground floor living room. Then he walks downstairs to the basement bedroom and he turns on a few more lights. Then he turns on every light in the apartment. Hey, Max, you aren't afraid, are you? A homicide cop with a snappy snub-nosed gun and a bright gold shield? No, I'm not afraid. What would I be afraid of?

Max thinks it might be nice to hear some music, so he puts a record on the stereo. Then he thinks it might also be nice to get the news, so he turns on the radio. Then he thinks that it might be a little less lonely if the TV were playing, too, and turns it on as well. With all the lights on and all the sound, Max crawls into bed.

7

With his left hand the man grabs Linda by the front of her blouse and with his right hand he holds the blade against her throat, as the blood runs freely out of his palm and onto her beige silk blouse.

"Bitch!" he hisses at her. "Dirty stinking scheming bitch!"

"I'm sorry," she whispers, "please don't hurt me, please don't. I'll do anything, anything, please please please please please."

" 'You should have simply *called* me,' " he mimics, " 'Why didn't you just call me on the *phone?*' "

"I'll do anything," she whispers, "anything."

"Get me a first-aid kit. And take off your clothes."

"Anything. Anything you say. I'll make it up to you for doing that, I swear to you I will, I swear it."

With the man continuing to hold her at knifepoint Linda backs into the tiny bathroom, gets the first-aid kit out of the medicine chest and gives it to him. Holding the blade against her adam's apple, he somehow manages to stop the blood. She helps him bandage the hand that holds the knife.

"And now take off your clothes. Stinking rotten bitch."

She nods and unbuttons the blood-stained blouse and pulls it out of her skirt and takes it off and drops it on the floor of the bathroom. Her mind is racing all over the place, desperately trying to come up with another plan.

"Faster," he says.

She nods and hurriedly unzips her skirt and lets it fall to the floor, and steps out of it and out of her shoes, and pulls down her half-slip and lets that drop as well. He is staring at her bug-eyed, the sweat standing out on his face, and she is beginning to think that if she goes along with it and doesn't make any more mistakes she will get off with maybe just a slight rape. A slight rape and a permanently stained pure silk blouse.

"Pantyhose," he says with disgust. "I *hate* pantyhose."

She quickly pulls down the pantyhose and steps out of them. Maybe when I take off my bra and panties, she thinks, he'll be so bug-eyed and sweaty he'll be too flustered to touch me.

"What would you like me to take off first," she says in as provocatively husky a voice as she can muster, "my bra or my panties?"

He looks at her without speaking and swallows dryly. "Bra."

She reaches behind her and unhooks her bra and slips out of it, being careful not to let her neck press too hard against the blade of the wicked-looking knife, and drops the bra on the floor.

His breathing is getting very heavy, she notes.

She forces herself to smile at him and runs her tongue over her lips, and hooks her thumbs inside the waistband of her panties and begins to pull them down. Just then the telephone rings, and both she and the man start violently, and the blade of the knife goes into her neck and blood starts squirting out of her.

"Oh my God, *no*," she says softly, realizing what has happened, seeing a reflection of herself in the mirror with blood spurting out of her neck, seeing the man's face frozen in horror, seeing now how it is going to be.

The man drops the knife and places his hands around her throat in panic, trying to stanch the blood, choking her in the process. The phone continues to ring. The blood is running all over both of them and she can't breathe and blackness is beginning to spread over her like a warm blanket and all she can think about is how the phone is still ringing and why doesn't the damned service pick it up and the last thought she has is surprise that your life doesn't suddenly pass in front of you in a rush after all.

It is not until the woman goes limp in his hands and slumps to the floor that the man realizes what he has done. He kneels over her on the bathroom floor, which is now covered with blood, and he feels for a pulse and it is so weak that it is hardly there at all, and he begins to cry.

"Linda," he says softly. "Oh, Linda, I'm sorry. I never meant for this to happen."

He cradles her head in his arms and bends to kiss her and then he cries some more to think what he has done, even though she probably deserved it. Even though she probably really deserved it for pretending to be glad to be dancing with him and for saying he was an attractive man and for kissing him like she meant it when all she wanted was to take his mind off what he was doing and grab his knife and get rid of him.

How often he's dreamed of holding her in his arms with her breasts against him, and now here he is with her in his arms with her breasts against him, only it's on the bathroom floor instead of on the bed and both he and she are covered with blood and she is probably dead. It isn't fair, he thinks, it really isn't fair.

"Oh, Linda, I love you," he whispers, and means it.

8

"So, Max, I hear you had a great time at the morgue last night."

The big detective with the thick neck and forearms and the pockmarked but pleasantly rugged face and the plaid sportscoat opens the door of the dirty metallic-green Plymouth and slides inside on the passenger's side.

"Yeah," says Max, "I had a ball."

Max can think of about eight hundred people he'd rather be stuck with as a partner in Homicide than this guy Caruso they've stuck him with, even including Jerry and Larry, who are not exactly winners but at least better than this guy Caruso. What it is that has made Max hate his new partner immediately upon meeting him is the remark which Caruso made about how Max got his shield.

The way you get the gold shield of a New York City Police Department Detective is not by taking any exam like you do for sergeant or lieutenant or captain but by hanging around in the job for about a hundred years, doing tough assignments in tough precincts in uniform, sucking up to your captain and hoping he'll recommend to the Commissioner that you be promoted, and hoping that the Commissioner decides to give you a break.

The way Max got *his* shield was to pull an elderly couple out of a building on Avenue A that was, as the

30

firemen put it, "fully involved with flame," before the
fire apparatus even rolled up on the scene.

Max had never thought of himself as a hero before
that day—even now whenever anybody said he was,
it made him terribly uncomfortable and embarrassed—
and if someone had told him the day it happened that
he was going to be running into burning buildings and
pulling out elderly people, he would have told them
they were out of their tree.

But Max did save those two old people's lives and he
did get to be on "Eyewitness News," and then the Commissioner gave his big-deal speech and Max was promoted off a recent assignment on a uniformed foot
patrol in the Battery into plainclothes, with a gold
shield, and assigned to a precinct on the West Side. And
when Max didn't exactly jump out of his skivvies with
joy at that the Commissioner asked him what the trouble
was and wasn't he delighted and all, and Max, who
never knew when to shut up anyway, said that what
he'd really always wanted was to be in Homicide and
now maybe he'd be stuck in the West Side precinct
and being there might be really more of a liability than
an asset.

The Commissioner of course thought that was one
of the three funniest things he'd ever heard because
it was so ballsy and everything, especially for a kid
fresh out of the Police Academy, and so the Commissioner made a deal with Max: stay just six months
at the West Side precinct as a detective, take the six-
week C.I.C.—Criminal Investigation Course—training,
followed by the two-week Homicide School at the
Fourteenth Street Armory, and then, if his instructors
were sufficiently impressed with him, he could go from
there to a special Homicide squad.

So now here he was in Third Homicide, having
learned as much as you can learn about being a homi-

cide cop without actually being one, and having also thrown away a promising education in prelaw because he'd privately decided that he could do more for humanity behind a badge than in a courtroom. And the only dumb thing about all of it was that deep down inside Max knew that, saving old geezers or no, he'd probably never have gotten even the gold shield and the West Side precinct much less the berth at Homicide if the Commissioner hadn't seen Max on "Eyewitness News."

"Head down to 46th Street," says Caruso as Max kicks over the motor and puts the car in gear, "225 East."

Max does not mind driving. Max happens to *like* driving. What Max minds is Caruso not even *asking* Max if he minds driving, as if to make sure that Max knows that Caruso is the senior man and Max is so low on the pecking order, hero or no, that he doesn't even get *asked* about things like whether he wants to drive. And if Caruso had not said what he had said when he met Max, maybe Max would not have instantly hated him.

What Caruso had implied was that Max had gotten his shield not because he had pulled any old geezers out of a fire but because Max was a Jewboy and had important Hebe friends who were tight with the Commissioner. The one thing Max was afraid of getting stuck with—a fucking anti-Semitic dago bigot!

"This is it," says Caruso, and Max eases the Plymouth into a parking space beside the large modern apartment house with the sign EXECUTIVE HOUSE outside it and they get out of the car.

"Help you?" says the uniformed doorman to the two cops.

Max reaches inside his jacket for his shield, but

Caruso is already sticking his own in the doorman's face.

"We're looking for the doorman named McMartin," says Caruso. "That you?"

The doorman nods.

"Understand you were on duty the night of the Lowry murder, McMartin. That right?"

The doorman nods his head and sighs.

"Lovely girl, that girl," he says. "Shame to kill anybody as lovely as that."

"They've estimated the time of death at between 6:30 and 7:00 P.M.," says Caruso, taking out his notebook and a ballpoint pen. "You were on duty at that time?"

"Yeah. I worked from 4:00 P.M. till 12:00 midnight," says the doorman.

"Wrkd. 1600–2400 hrs.," writes Caruso in his notebook.

"And you told the patrolman who made out the initial report that the deceased came home on or about 6:00 P.M. and that she had no visitors all evening. Is that right?"

"That's what I told him," says the doorman.

"Dcsd. cmc. hme. 1800 hrs. no vis.," writes Caruso in his notebook.

"Now, there was no evidence of forced entry on either the windows or the door, so we assume that the deceased knew her assailant. Do you happen to know of anybody who might have had reason to kill the deceased?" says Caruso.

"Nope," says the doorman.

"Dsnt. knw. anybdy. wh. mght. hve. klld. dcsd.," writes Caruso in his little notebook.

"OK," says Caruso, "tell us something about this Lowry dame. What are your recollections of her?"

The doorman cocks his head, as if to slide all the

Linda Lowry recollections over to one side so he can scoop them up.

"She was a lovely girl," he says. "I don't know what else I can tell you."

"Did she have a lot of boyfriends?" says Caruso, pen poised to write either "hd. lts. byfrnds." or "Nt. mny. byfrnds."

"Boyfriends?" The doorman thinks this over. "Yes, I guess you could say so. She was a lovely girl. I couldn't tell you much about them, though."

"Why not?" says Caruso.

"I'm very discreet about my tenants. You *have* to be in my profession. The tenants go their way, I go mine. They think I don't notice who goes into an apartment, who goes out or when, but a doorman sees everything, don't you worry. Only I don't talk about it, because I'm discreet. I could tell you some stories, though, you better believe it."

"About Linda Lowry?" says Caruso.

"About everybody. But I wouldn't invade their privacy by talking."

"We could *make* you talk," says Caruso.

"What's *that* supposed to mean?" says the doorman.

"I mean we got ways to make you talk," says Caruso, slipping into something that had doubtlessly lodged in his throat after digesting one too many B-movie cop melodramas.

The doorman takes on a very feisty look, which impresses Max, since Caruso has maybe eighty to ninety pounds on the guy. Max decides to stop the doorman before he says something that will get him hurt.

"Caruso, you mind if I talk to him?" says Max.

"What do *I* care?" says Caruso. "Go ahead. Talk to him."

"I mean alone," says Max.

Caruso looks at Max like there was never anything

called the buddy system, where first a cop playing the bad guy really harasses somebody in interrogation, and then a cop playing the good guy takes over and makes friends with the harassed guy and proceeds to get whatever he wants out of him.

"What do you need to talk to him alone for?" says Caruso suspiciously.

"I'd just *like* to is all," says Max. "Is that OK?"

Caruso shrugs, then sighs.

"I'll go check out the super," says Caruso in a tone which suggests the doorman and Max are going to swap demeaning anecdotes in his absence, and sulks out of the lobby.

"I'd like to apologize for my partner," says Max. "He shouldn't have talked to you that way."

"He doesn't scare me," says the feisty doorman, not yet ready to give up his feistiness. "I've been threatened by much tougher guys than him. You want to take me downtown and give me the third degree, go ahead. I still wouldn't talk about the personal affairs of my tenants."

"That's very discreet of you," says Max.

"I'm discreet," says the feisty doorman. "Discretion is a vital part of the doorman-tenant relationship."

"You're very professional," says Max.

"I *am* a professional," says the doorman. "There's a lot more to being a doorman than opening the door for people, you know. Especially in *this* town."

"Oh, I know that," says Max. "*Especially* in this town."

"You have to decide who to let in and who to refuse admittance to. You have to make snap decisions about people that could be a matter of life and death. You get to be a pretty shrewd judge of character in this job, I can tell you that much."

"Oh, I can just imagine," says Max.

"You get so you can spot a guy coming in with a female tenant after they've been out on a date and you know whether or not the guy is going to score with her."

"How can you tell a thing like that?" says Max, who has never been able to tell such things, particularly about himself.

"Observation. You observe enough times how the female tenant behaves in the lobby with a guy she goes upstairs with who doesn't come down till the morning, and then you observe how she behaves with a guy who comes right down on the return elevator. It's not hard to figure out after awhile how long it's going to be before any guy going upstairs with her will be coming downstairs again. I got so I can call it within twelve to fifteen minutes."

"Whew!" Max shakes his head appreciatively.

"Yessir. I know if the guy is going to score before *he* does, and sometimes before the female tenant does herself."

"That's amazing," says Max, figuring he has now spent enough time salving the doorman's Caruso-burned ego. "Tell me, were you that accurate in predicting how long Linda Lowry's dates stayed upstairs?"

"With her it was easy," says the doorman.

"Oh? Why's that?" says Max.

"On account of how she acted with men," says the doorman.

"And how was that?" says Max.

"Oh, Linda was a bit of a tease," says the doorman, in a fondly reminiscent tone. "I don't mean it in a bad way."

Max flashes the doorman a huge wink.

"You sound like you've had some first-hand experience," says Max.

"*Me?* Nah. I'm just a *doorman*. Linda Lowry wasn't

about to make it with no *doorman*. But that didn't stop her from teasing."

"How did she tease you?"

"Oh, you know. She'd call you up to the apartment on the house phone to give you a package that was going to be picked up in the lobby and all she'd be wearing was her little underwear. You know. Stuff like that."

"Did she tease any of the other building staff besides you?"

"Oh, sure. All of them. But she didn't mean anything by it. It was just her way."

"That kind of teasing, though, could make a man pretty frustrated. And pretty mad. Maybe even mad enough to kill her."

"Oh, she wasn't killed by anybody in *this* building."

"How do you know?"

"How do I know? Because I know who killed her, that's how."

Max's breathing comes to a halt. He *knew* he was right to get rid of Caruso. If he hadn't, the feisty doorman and the belligerent detective would have escalated their confrontation into an ugly little fight. Instead, Max gets to wrap up the case his first shot out of the box—the doorman will tell him who the killer is, Max will go and arrest the guy, read him his Mirandas, maybe there'll be a scuffle, and then Max will bring him in, acting like there is nothing special about wrapping up a homicide your first couple days on the job. *Then* let fucking Caruso say Max got his shield because of Jewboy connections downtown. Ho ho!

"Who killed Linda Lowry?" says Max.

"A boogie," says the doorman.

"A *boogie?*" says Max, hoping he hasn't heard right. The doorman nods his head.

"*What* boogie?" says Max.

"Who knows?" says the doorman. "Who could tell

one from the other anyhow? For sure it was a boogie that *did* it, though. That's who does *all* sex murders—boogies. Ninety-eight-point-two percent of all sex murders are committed by boogies. They have the figures downtown, you could look them up for yourself."

"OK," says Max, "I think I'm going to go and find my partner now."

"Go right ahead," says the doorman. "And when you finally catch the killer, you just see if he isn't a boogie."

"OK," says Max, heading off in the direction Caruso had gone.

"They do all the sex murders—ninety-eight-point-two percent of them," says the doorman. "They have all the figures downtown. But don't take *my* word for it, look it up yourself."

"OK, I will," says Max. "Thanks for the tip."

Max disappears around the corner. The doorman stands looking after him, shaking his head.

Well, thinks the doorman, too bad he had to fib about Linda not having any visitors. It hardly mattered, though. The only one she had was the man who delivered the flowers, and most likely he came right down on the return elevator. He would have seen him, too, if he hadn't slipped downstairs for a nip of Chivas. Having that bottle of Chivas down there was what kept him going on this job. Nobody with half an ounce of heart would deny a man a nip of Chivas every so often on a job like this, especially at the holiday season.

Anyway, what did it matter if the cops knew about the delivery guy from the florist or not? He wasn't the killer, after all. He was a white guy. The killer was a boogie.

9

"Oh Linda, I love you," he whispers, and means it.

He lets the naked body of the young woman slump back down on the tiles, now sticky with blood. She's dead. She is definitely dead. And that, he supposes, makes him a killer.

A killer. So that's what he is. That's what he's probably been all along. Well. He had always known he was guilty, but never of what. Now at least he knew. It was a relief to know.

A killer, eh? Well, it wasn't much, but at least it was *something*. At least it was better than *some* things he could name. Like being an actor who couldn't even get a job, no matter how good he was.

How he hated the auditions, the "go-sees," the cattle calls, the going to read for parts and waiting in some crappy office for hours along with dozens of actors who did get the occasional parts, who didn't even have the talent that he had in his little finger. How he hated the unemployment office and the questions they asked you before they would even give you their laughably tiny unemployment checks. How he hated the temporary jobs he had to take to survive—waiting tables and bussing dishes and delivering packages. Even Helping Hand, the temporary employment agency which sent him out on these jobs, was terrible to deal with, despite the fact that it was supposedly run by and for out-of-work actors. People treated you like you were scum under their shoes or ignored you altogether as if you didn't exist, as if you were a zero, a cipher, a total void in the universe.

Well, that might be how people acted toward out-of-work actors or waiters or busboys or delivery boys, but it sure as hell wasn't how they acted toward killers. People looked at killers the way Linda had looked at him when he first took out the switchblade. "Oh no, please don't," she had whispered with that soft, scared look in her eyes. "I'll do anything you say, only please don't hurt me."

If only he could have kept that going, that look in her eyes of yielding, of softness, of cringing submission, of *respect*. If only he could have kept her that way and given them a chance to get acquainted and fall in love.

"I'll give you anything you want, anything. What is it you want?" she had said. "A date," he had replied like some asshole. *Why* had he said something as assholic as that? "A kiss to build a dream on," he could have replied. *"Respect,"* he *should* have replied.

What a romance they might have had, those two, if only things had worked out better. He had of course known what they might have together the instant he first saw her in the lingerie department at Bloomingdale's. He had admired her spunk in dealing with the rude salesgirl, making the girl's cheeks blush red. Standing next to her at the counter as the manager apologized for the thirtieth time and made out the sales slip it was so easy to read her name and address off her Bloomingdale's credit card that he almost didn't do it. A sporting gesture *that* would have been, as the hunter might let a rabbit loose who'd been too easily bagged, so sure was he that he would trap her eventually and that the hunt and the chase would prove amusing.

But then he'd caught a quick flash of the charge

card and the name and address had burned right into his eyeballs so deeply that he could even see the neat blue letters on the shiny silver background when his lids were shut, like staring at the sun too long. LINDA LOWRY it had said, 225 EAST 46 ST, and that is how it had begun for him. That is how his tragic love affair with Linda Lowry had begun.

Wait. That is *not* how his tragic love affair with Linda Lowry had begun. That is how his love affair with Beverly *Rachlin* had begun. It was Beverly *Rachlin* who had humiliated the rude salesgirl in Bloomingdale's lingerie department and then displayed her credit card to him as if she were making him a present of her name and address. Like old Mae West: "Why don't you come up and see me some time?"

No, Linda was not one of the almost two dozen girls he had started up with at Bloomingdale's. Linda he had discovered at the end of his binoculars, undressing prettily in a window on his very own street. It was embarrassing to make that kind of mistake about how you began an affair that had supposedly meant so much to you, although perhaps it was understandable when you were a guy who had as many women as *he* had.

The man begins tidying up in a leisurely manner, mopping at the bloodstains on his clothing with moist balls of toilet paper. What was it you were supposed to use on bloodstains? Cold water. Cold water, not hot. Hot sets the stain. And, oh yes, cornstarch. A few drops of cold water on each stain, then powder thickly with cornstarch. When the cornstarch is dry you rub it off and the stains are gone.

The man goes to the tiny kitchen area and begins to poke about for cornstarch. He reflects upon the months he has spent getting to know Linda Lowry. Studying her habits. Following her around the city from an unob-

trusive distance as she went to and from her midtown
job as a junior stockbroker. Waiting for her patiently
on streetcorners, observing her tirelessly through op-
tically perfect, high-powered German-made field glasses
from his apartment. Content to be noting things without the slightest sexual value if it went that way, recording each new discovery about her in tiny uppercase
letters in the section of his little looseleaf notebook.
which was headed LOWRY, LINDA, and then conceiving
and rehearsing and finally executing tonight's well-
thought-out maneuver. Looking back on all that planning and preparation, it hardly seemed worth the bother.
The date with Linda had been a definite disappointment.

Not that he hadn't enjoyed dancing with her—the
woman had been a feather in his arms as they'd danced
to the April Stevens record. And the necking was certainly more than he'd dared to expect on their very first
date, her kisses sweeter than wine. But then she had
gone and ruined everything by going for his switchblade. Why had she done that when they seemed to be
having such a good time together? That was the trouble
with women. Just when you were beginning to get to
know them they up and turned on you. If she hadn't
done that he never would have made her take off
her clothes, as much as he longed to see her nakedness up close after all these months, and he never would
have held his knife against her neck like that, much less
cut her.

The man finds the cornstarch and dabs it on the
bloodstains.

Well, it wasn't really his fault she got cut when you
thought about it. The phone had startled both of them
and then she had to go and shove her throat into the
blade. If the phone hadn't rung, she would be alive
now and he might have let her put her clothes back
on without even touching her on the first date. Assuming

that she apologized for the cute trick with the switch-blade, that is. No, it wasn't really he who had killed her. It was the person who had telephoned her, and it was Linda herself.

Well, in all honesty he supposed he had to accept *some* of the guilt for what happened himself. That was only fair. He was, at least technically, one-third a killer.

The man finishes dabbing the cornstarch on his cloth-ing and flushes the last bundle of reddened tissue down the toilet. He dries the dampness in his clothing with Linda's hair drier, being careful not to step on her body as he putters about the tiny bathroom. Then he changes the bandage on his hand, puts the April Stevens record back in its sleeve, wipes fingerprints off hair drier, phonograph, phone, first-aid kit, doorknob, and every-thing else he remembers touching. Then he forgets what he'd wiped clean and what not and does it all over again.

He lovingly pulls Linda's panties the rest of the way off and stuffs them in his pocket. He straightens all the picture frames on the wall so that they are absolutely horizontal. He crumples up the wrapping paper from the florist, puts the flowers in a vase on the table, puts on his coat, and walks to the door.

The flowers look nice in the vase. And they *are* Linda's favorites—anemones.

"So long, Linda," he says to the bare feet sticking out of the bathroom doorway. "Take care, now."

Nobody is in the hallway. The man walks noiselessly down the corridor to the stairwell and then down the steps to the street floor. When the coast is clear he passes back through the lobby and out to the street.

Outside the man checks his watch. Nearly seven-fifteen. Good. He still has time to slip across the street for a fresh change of clothes before going across town for his next appointment.

10

"Mr. Kupperman?"

"Yes?"

"Mr. Arnold Kupperman?"

"Yes?"

"I'm Detective Max Segal of Third Homicide."

"Oh, yes, Detective Segal, I've been expecting you. Please come in."

Max allows the short, prematurely balding man in the brown cashmere cardigan and tweedy slacks and imitation Gucci loafers to show him into the tastefully decorated if a bit pretentiously quaint apartment. Max has purposely waited till he was off-duty so he wouldn't have to bring along Caruso—his schmucky partner would be sure to antagonize Kupperman and queer what sounded like a fairly hot little lead.

"You said on the phone that you had some information about the Lowry case?" says Max, taking out a cigar and stripping off the cellophane, and sticking it professionally between his teeth.

"Yes, I do, Detective Segal. You see," Kupperman lowers his voice and allows a dramatic pause to elapse just as they do it on TV before catching up with the rest of his sentence, "I was probably the last person, other than her killer, to speak to Linda Lowry alive."

Max inadvertently bites through the end of his cigar. He watches Kupperman warily, waiting to see where he's going to go with what he's just said. It could be the lead he was hoping for, or it could be another set-up—another chance to be told that somebody knew who had killed Linda Lowry and that it was a boogie.

"When did you have this conversation with her?" says Max, surreptitiously spitting the bitten-off cigar end into his hand.

"Friday night. The night she was killed. About six o'clock."

With his other hand Max slips the cigar back into his mouth and pats his pockets for a match.

"Go on," says Max.

"Well, I had been dating Linda off and on for a couple of months, and I was calling her that night to see if she was free for dinner on Sunday. She had just gotten home from work when I called. In fact, the phone rang about seven or eight times and the service picked it up. I thought she must not be home yet and I was about to hang up without leaving a message, but then she picked up at the last second."

"You say you were about to hang up without leaving a message?" says Max, locating a pack of matches and striking one into his cupped hand, "Why?"

Kupperman looks sheepish.

"Well . . ."

"Why were you not going to leave a message?" says Max, inhaling, sucking the flame into the cigar, swallowing a big gulp of fetid smoke and nearly choking to death. Kupperman pounds his back and the color comes back into Max's face.

"Thanks, thanks. Tell me, why were you not going to leave a message on her service?" says Max, coughing.

"Well, the thing is that I'd called *before* and left one. A couple of days before. And she still hadn't returned my call, so . . ."

"So you didn't want the humiliation of having to

leave a second one. I understand," says Max with a smile.

Kupperman's face reddens. He smiles and nods. A guy who doesn't get his calls returned by attractive ladies doesn't have to feel too schmucky in the presence of a guy who swallows his own cigar smoke.

"Well anyway," says Kupperman, "she'd just come in from work, as I said, and we talked awhile. Then somebody came to the door and she went to answer it."

"Who was it?" says Max. "Could you tell?"

"Some kind of delivery."

"What makes you think so?"

"Because," says Kupperman, "she said, 'I have to get some change for the delivery boy.'"

Fabulous. McMartin, the boogie-suspecting doorman, swears that nobody visited Linda Lowry all night, and now here's somebody delivering something to her door at 6:00, a half-hour before she was killed.

"Was that the only interruption in the telephone conversation, getting change for the delivery boy?" says Max. "Or did the doorman ring up on the house phone to say the delivery was on the way up?"

"That's right," says Kupperman snapping his fingers, "the doorman *did* ring her up on the house phone."

"Perfect. And then what happened?" says Max, making a mental note to pound the doorman worse than Caruso would have.

"After the doorman rang her up? Well, we talked for a couple minutes, and then the delivery boy came to the door and she let him in."

"How do you know it was a delivery *boy?*"

"That's how she described him. She said, 'I have to get some change for the delivery boy.' So she went to her purse and got the change, and said, 'Here you are,' or something like that. Then there was this strange kind of silence, and then somebody hung up the phone. I

got worried and called the police—the 911 number—
but they were very rude and told me to call my local
precinct. I did that, but I don't think they took me
very seriously. I guess I should've gone over to Linda's
myself, for all the good it would've done—she was
probably dead by then anyhow."

11

You can learn a lot about a person from her garbage,
he thinks.

He stands across the street from Beverly Rachlin's
building and waits for her to deposit hers. Some of his
women, unfortunately, lived in buildings where the
tenants dropped their garbage down a chute to the
incinerator. Others had supers who collected it along
with that of other tenants before leaving it outside,
thus making it too much trouble to sift through for
information. But Beverly brought hers out herself, usually just before she went to bed. About midnight.

He pulls back the cuff of his overcoat sleeve and
checks his watch again: 11:55 P.M. She ought to be
coming out any minute now. On past pickups he has
discovered in Beverly's garbage, among the broken
eggshells, wet coffee grounds, empty cans and bottles,
crumpled Kleenexes and cigarette stubs and juicy
scraps of spoiled leftover food, such fascinating items
as: (1) empty cardboard cylinders from several Tampaxes, which enabled him to begin computing her

menstrual cycle; (2) a copy of *TV Guide* with certain program listings marked with a felt-tip pen, including several on both Friday and Saturday nights, which indicated she didn't have many dates on weekends; (3) empty envelopes from American Express and Master Charge with recent postmarks, indicating that she paid her bills promptly and probably lived within her means; (4) the torn foil container from a popular brand of birth-control pills, indicating that, although she wasn't seeing anybody regularly or seriously enough to occupy her Friday and Saturday nights, she was still hopeful enough and horny enough to keep taking the Pill.

The door to Beverly's building opens. Somebody comes out, but it's not Beverly. Perhaps she isn't throwing out her garbage tonight. After all, it's not something that she does every night. He slips his field glasses out of his coat and focuses on Beverly's apartment windows. The lights are on, all right. He checks his watch: 12:05. He hasn't seen her yet, but he knows she's home. When she's out she leaves a different light on—the timer turns it on at 6:15 and off at 1:15.

Ah, there she is now. He hurriedly slides the binoculars into his coat and begins walking. He sees her place a shiny plastic bag of garbage on the curb and scurry back inside the building. He decides to wait three minutes before picking it up.

He walks in and carefully locks the door behind him. He takes off his coat, hangs it up, and washes his hands. He spreads a plastic bag from the cleaners out on the floor, squaring it off parallel to the edge of the raised platform he often uses as a stage when he's rehearsing a part. He turns on the overhead colored spotlights he installed to light up his stage area. He puts on a pair of rubber gloves. Sifting through garbage might be messy work, he thinks, smiling, but it is certainly not undig-

nified, being a time-honored research technique of the
FBI and the CIA.

He takes Beverly's bag of garbage and shakes it out
onto the plastic bag from the cleaners. There is the
usual assortment of empty cans and bottles, leftover
food, et cetera, which he arranges into neat piles as
meticulously as if they were pieces of an expensive
jigsaw puzzle.

There are no Tampax cylinders, but a lot more
dirty Kleenexes—Beverly's period is over, he thinks, but
she's caught a cold. There are the remains of two mari-
juana cigarettes, an empty bottle of Kaopectate, and a
reminder card from the dentist—which tells him she
uses illegal drugs, suffers from diarrhea, and can afford
a dentist who has his office on upper Park Avenue.
There is also a letter postmarked Brookline, Massa-
chusetts, which seems to be from her parents and which
gives him further insights into her romantic and professional discontents.

The dossier on Beverly Rachlin is nearly complete.
Very soon now they will meet and she will learn of his
secret love for her which has burned so brightly it's
illuminated his study of her all these months.

12

"McMartin, you're in big trouble."

"Oh, hiya there, son," says McMartin, awakening
guiltlessly from an on-the-job snooze. "You catch the
boogie that killed Linda yet?"

"Don't boogie *me,* buster," says Max, adopting a tone Caruso is more familiar with than he. "You still sticking to the story you gave me that Linda Lowry had no visitors the night she was killed?"

McMartin looks at Max without blinking.

"That's what I told you before, young fella," he says.

"I *know* that's what you told me *before,*" says Max. "What I'm asking you *now* is whether you want to stick to that story, and accompany it to the slammer for withholding evidence and obstructing justice, or whether you want to tell me instead about the delivery boy that came to see her at six o'clock and probably killed her. Because I got a gentleman who says not only did Linda Lowry get a *delivery* while he was talking to her on the phone, but that *you* called her on the fucking *house* phone to tell her he was coming up in the *elevator.*"

Max melodramatically takes out a pair of handcuffs and unlocks them.

"Now, then," says Max. "Are you still sticking to your story or aren't you?"

The formerly feisty doorman regards the cuffs thoughtfully and sighs.

"OK. So I lied," he says.

"Oh, terrific. 'So I lied.' That's marvelous, absolutely marvelous. So because you lied we've been spinning our wheels while some maniac is out killing more women like Linda Lowry. You heard about the Rachlin case? The social worker on the West Side?"

The doorman nods.

"That was probably the work of your delivery boy. Thanks to you he's going to have time for a few more free shots like that before we get him."

"Oh, take it easy. You want to hear my story or don't you?"

"Tell me your story, McMartin. Tell me why you lied to an officer of the law and withheld evidence and obstructed justice. I want to hear about that, you ass-hole."

"You call me asshole and you don't get my story."

"I don't get your story and I'm taking you in and booking you, and letting you spend a while in the slammer, explaining to your fellow prisoners why it is that all sex killers are boogies."

The doorman sighs a gigantic put-upon sigh.

"OK, McMartin, I'm all ears. Tell me about the delivery boy. What did he look like? What was he wearing? What was he delivering?"

"I didn't get that good of a look at him, to be honest with ya. He was wearing a dark overcoat. And he wasn't no boy—he was maybe in his late thirties. And he was delivering flowers. He had this card on the flowers that said the name of the florist. East Side Florists, or East River Florists. Something like that."

"How tall was he? How heavy? What color was his hair? What color were his eyes?"

"I don't know, I have to be honest with ya. He was probably about average height. And I don't know if he was heavy. Maybe a little. And he was dark. Dark hair. And he had these sort of peculiar eyes."

"Peculiar? How do you mean peculiar?"

"Empty, kind of. Staring. A little spooky, if you ask me."

"You let somebody with empty, staring, spooky eyes up to see one of your tenants, eh, McMartin? One of the tenants in this building you're protecting with your professionally shrewd ability to make snap decisions about whom to let in and whom to refuse admittance to?"

"OK, lay off, willya? It wasn't *me* who killed her. I don't have to take no third degree from you about this either. I happen to have some rights, you know."

"How long was this man with the empty, staring, spooky eyes upstairs with Linda Lowry?"

"I don't know."

"You don't know? I thought you knew exactly how long everybody who went up in the elevator was up there. I thought you were an expert on how long people spent upstairs, McMartin."

"That's only on guys who date the female tenants. I never saw the delivery boy come down again. I was out on my break."

"Your break?"

"I . . . keep a bottle of Chivas downstairs. I went down to take a nip. You can tell my boss—he knows anyway. I figure the delivery boy musta come downstairs while I was in the basement."

"How long were you in the basement?"

"I don't know. Not long. Five minutes, tops."

"And then you came back upstairs?"

"Yeah. Then I came right back to the lobby. I never saw him after he went up in the elevator."

Max sticks his unlit cigar between his teeth, the way it's done on cop shows.

"Just tell me one more thing, McMartin."

"Yeah, what's that?"

"This delivery boy of yours. Was he a boogie?"

13

As great an actor as he might have been, thinks the man, he would have been an even greater detective. He stands counting subway cars, deciding it will be luckier today to get onto an even-numbered one than an odd. The train grinds to a halt and the doors open and the people inside the subway car push outside and the people outside push inside. Beverly Rachlin gets into the fifth car of the train. He gets into the sixth.

He has a natural ability to tail people without looking suspicious, he thinks, and he has an instinctive sense about the best way to gather information on them. The gathering of information on each of his women is far more than the minimum needed to gain entry to her apartment and have a date with her.

Hell, if that's all he cared about, he wouldn't need more than a day to research any one of them. Follow a woman around for only a little while and the chances are you can watch her write a check out to somebody. The chances are the check will have her name and address printed on the face of it and, since nobody considers a woman a good risk on a check, they usually demand she write her phone number on it as well. Nearly all of them do what they're told, and there you or anybody else who wants it has it all set out in front of them in black and white.

No, the research was designed to get a sense of what the woman was like, so that when he actually made the

contact with her, actually had the date with her, he'd
already know so much about her it wouldn't be like they
were strangers in the night. It would be like they were
old friends. Better to know too much than too little,
even if it takes more time.

He moves through the car, opens the door, passes
into the car where Beverly is standing hanging onto the
overhead bar, trying to read her newspaper. For example, here he is following Beverly up to the South
Bronx, to the area where she works. Does he have to
take the time to do this in order to gain entry to her
apartment? He does not. He already has the address, the
telephone number, her schedule of arrivals and depar-
tures down cold. He even has the means of entry all
worked out and rehearsed.

No, the only reason to follow Beverly up to the South
Bronx and tail her to either two or four of her cases—
even numbers are better there, too—is what separates
the men from the boys, the amateurs from the profes-
sionals, the dilettantes from the serious artists.

He folds his newspaper lengthwise very neatly along
the space between the columns of type and pretends to
be reading it as he finally moves into position alongside
Beverly. He notes with some satisfaction, when she
pauses in her reading to open her purse and pop a pill
into her mouth, that it is, just as he'd predicted, a green
and black capsule of Librium, 10 milligrams, that she's
taking it because of anxiety over the Hernandez case
she's visiting first, and that he knows not only the name
of the drug but the name of the doctor who prescribed
it, the pharmacy that prepared it, and the number of the
prescription.

Poor Beverly. So wracked by needless tension—tension that will melt from the warmth of his love once he
deems the time is right to reveal it. The time is close
at hand.

14

Max is half-sitting, half-lying on the queen-sized bed in Linda Lowry's apartment, his fingers laced behind his head, his cigar clenched between his teeth, frowning mightily and trying to figure it out. What he is trying to figure out at this particular moment in time is why in the name of Christ anybody would voluntarily smoke anything as vile-smelling and vile-tasting as a cigar.

Who *cares* if they seem to go with the name Max, and who *cares* if most of the detectives in Homicide smoke them, and who *cares* if they tend to make you look a little tougher than you are—if you still can't stand the smell and the taste after your sixth one, then it's never going to be your kind of thing. Max takes his cigar out of his mouth and throws it into Linda Lowry's trashbasket.

Max has been in Linda Lowry's apartment several times already, and experienced about the same degree of satisfaction he is experiencing now. None. The guys at Homicide have been over every square millimeter of this place. The Crime Scene Unit has photographed everything, dusted it for prints, and found nothing of any use.

Either Max or Caruso or one of their colleagues has personally interviewed the day doorman, the night doorman, the relief doorman, the super, the handyman. They are interviewing the tenants in the building, the members of Linda's family, Linda's coworkers at the brokerage house, and everyone in Linda's address book. They are interviewing everyone they saw at Linda's funeral. They are interrogating all known sex offenders, checking all mental institutions and correctional facilities for the criminally insane, interviewing every delivery boy who ever worked for a florist on the East Side, and what they have to show for all their efforts so far is nothing. Zero. Zilch.

If only, Max thinks, you could go back in time, in a time machine, and relive the event.

15

"Yes? Who's there?"

"Police Department, ma'am. May we speak with you a moment, please?"

Strong New York accent. Probably Brooklyn.

"What about?"

"A homicide case we're working on. We'd like to ask you a few questions about the deceased. May we come in?"

Not Brooklyn. Bronx.

"What case is this?"

"The Lowry case. Linda Lowry. Could you open the door a moment, please?"

"Lowry? I don't know anybody named Lowry. Was this case on the evening news?"

"Not yet. We're trying to keep it quiet until we check

out a list of suspects—which is where you might be able
to help us, Miss Rachlin."

"What are the suspects' names?" says Beverly Rachlin, reaching for a flowered dressing gown and slipping
it on over her underwear.

"Well, I have a list with me which we've been asking
the other tenants about, Miss Rachlin, but I'd prefer to
show it to you instead of talking through the door here.
Is that all right?"

"Well, I . . . What is your name, please?"

"Savage. Detective Savage, Third Homicide Zone."

"Do you have any identification with you, Detective
Savage?"

"Yes, ma'am."

"Hold it up to the peephole so I can see it."

A sigh from the other side of the door. Let him sigh,
thinks Beverly Rachlin. Anybody who opens their door
to someone just because he says he's a cop deserves
whatever they get.

The man outside her front door reaches into his coat
and pulls out a gold detective's badge and holds it up to
the peephole.

"OK, Miss Rachlin?"

"OK," she says. She unlocks the three dead-bolts on
the inside of her door and lets the policeman into the
apartment. She looks briefly into the hallway for his
partner, having thought he'd said, "May *we* come in?"
then realizes this was obviously another linguistic affectation of cops, like the editorial or royal *we*. She closes
the door behind him and relocks the three deadbolts.

"Sorry to have put you through such a hassle," she
says with a sheepish smile. "The way things are in this
city these days you just can't be too careful."

"Oh, don't apologize," says the policeman, "I couldn't
agree with you more. In fact, I wish more people were

as careful as you are, Miss Rachlin. It would make our job at Homicide a lot easier."

Beverly Rachlin nods, gives the detective the once-over, and draws her dressing gown around her a little more tightly. It's probably paranoid as hell, but for some reason this man gives her the willies. She wonders what is in the flat square package under his arm. She wonders whether the wound in his bandaged hand which is quietly seeping blood was sustained in the line of duty and whether the "alleged perpetrator" who inflicted it was one of her uptown cases.

"All right, Detective Savage," says Beverly Rachlin, toying briefly with the notion of offering him a hot cup of coffee or a roll of fresh bandage and then deciding against it, "let's see that list of suspects."

There is an awkward silence.

"I'm afraid there isn't any list, Beverly," the man replies.

16

SOCIAL WORKER SLAIN: 2ND SEX KILLING IN 2 DAYS

The nude body of a 33-year-old social worker, Beverly Rachlin, was found with a fatal head wound in her apartment at 328 W. 37th St. in Manhattan. The shapely, long-haired brunette was discovered by building superintendent Aldo Rienti, who was "shocked at the senseless killing of nice Miss Rachlin."

Rienti discovered the naked form of the comely Manhattanite while on a routine service call to repair a leaky faucet in the apartment of the deceased. Miss Rachlin was lying face down in a pool of blood.

Police stated that Miss Rachlin's body may have been sexually abused. The Rachlin case is the second sex slaying in as many days of an attractive Manhattan woman living alone. The previous victim was identified as Linda Lowry, 23, of 225 E. 46th St.

Authorities declined to speculate upon a possible link between the two crimes. Said Detective Salvatore Caruso of Manhattan's Third Homicide Zone: "We have no idea if these two homicides were the work of the same person, although in both cases the victims were attractive young single females living alone in Manhattan, and there was no evidence of forced entry on either the windows or the doors of both apartments. We assume both victims were acquainted with their assailants."

Frank McMartin, doorman at the 46th St. building, was "shocked at the senseless killing" of Miss Lowry. She was, he said, "a lovely girl, that girl," adding it was "a shame to kill anybody as lovely as that."

Babette Watson stares at the newspaper in her lap and rereads for the twentieth time the story about the murders of Linda Lowry and Beverly Rachlin. So *that's* what her horrible vision had been about. The premonition of disaster, the woman with the long, dark hair and the name like Beverly Macklin, the man in dark clothing that something was very wrong with—was that man the killer? She had seen them dancing. Had he progressed from dancing to killing, and if so, how?

Although this is by no means the first time that Babette has had visions verified by subsequent events, she is still unable to understand how one could ever know about something that was yet to happen.

A professor of hers had once talked about physicists' current preoccupation with the concept of time. About how our Western linear notion of time was in all likelihood false. About how perhaps the past, the present, and the future all exist simultaneously—whatever *that* could possibly mean. If they did exist simultaneously, though, then maybe you could move forward and back in time as easily as, well, the Concorde SST.

On New Year's Eve of 1976 the Concorde had a big private celebration on board at the Paris airport at 12:00 midnight. Then it took off and, flying westward at Mach-2 or whatever unimaginable rate of speed it flies, it caught up with midnight again somewhere in mid-Atlantic and had a second celebration. Then it landed in Washington, D.C. at 12:00, having traveled back into the recent past once more, and had its third and final New Year's Eve celebration of the night.

If the Concorde could time-travel, then maybe Babette could, too. And yet . . . and yet the whole idea of being able to see beyond the present bothered her. It bothered her a lot.

17

She thinks that there must be some mistake, that she did not actually hear the policeman she has just let into her apartment say what she has indeed heard him say. She prefers to focus instead on the fact that he has inappropriately addressed her by her first name.

"What did you say?" she says.

The man stares at her coldly.

"Please do not ask me what I said. What I said was that there isn't any list."

"There isn't any list?"

"That's right."

"Why did you say you had a list?"

"I needed to get inside your apartment to talk to you."

"Good," says Beverly, going to the door and beginning to unlock the locks. "And now you can go right back outside and think of something else to say. And while you're doing that I'm going to call your supervisor at the Third Homicide Zone and file a complaint on you, Detective Savage."

"Do you have a phonograph?"

"A what?"

"A *phonograph?*"

"*Yes,* I have a phonograph. What business is it of yours?"

The man swiftly unwraps the squarish package he carries and holds up the worn album liner.

"May I put this on your phonograph?" he says.

"*No,* you may not put that on my phonograph," says Beverly Rachlin with a snort. "Just what do you think you're doing here?"

The man looks at her impassively a moment.

"What do *you* think I'm doing here?" he says.

"Well, you *were* trying to investigate a murder case," she says, unlocking the second lock, "and now you *are* leaving."

"Wrong," says the man simply.

Oh, swell, thinks Beverly to herself, he wants to stay and make a pass at her. That's all she needs after a hard day of casework in the South Bronx, an amorous cop.

"Look, Buster," says Beverly in a tired, tough, no-nonsense voice, "I just came home from one hell of a tough day of work in an area of this city that would make you vomit just to look at it. I have a splitting headache and severe gastritis, I'm tired and filthy and I don't smell good. I am just about to pour myself a martini and hop into a hot tub for about two hours. If you're not out of this apartment in three seconds flat I am not only going to have you busted out of plain-clothes, I am also going to bust your jaw."

She scoops a glass paperweight with little bright-colored flowers imbedded in it off the coffee table and holds it menacingly above her head.

The man feels suddenly sleepy. Suppressing a yawn, he reaches into his pocket and withdraws the knife and clicks out the wicked-looking blade.

She looks at the knife as if she has not seen one be-fore and doesn't know what it is.

"Please don't make me hurt you, Beverly," says the man in a reasonable tone. "I really don't want to hurt you. But if you force me to, I will."

Beverly slowly puts the glass paperweight back down on the coffee table.

The red warning light which had been blinking un-heeded in her brain from the moment the man first knocked on her door is now joined by clanging alarm bells and police sirens. Only her extreme exhaustion had prevented her from realizing, first, that this man was not a cop and, second, that he was probably the one who had committed the crime he claimed to be investigating. Fortunately, she has had some training in handling psychos.

"I won't force you to do anything," she says pleas-antly. "And since neither one of us wants you to hurt me, you can put the knife away if you want to. How-ever, if it makes you feel better to have it out, then that's OK, too."

"Oh, no problem, Beverly," the man replies with

equal pleasantness, and closes the blade and puts the knife back in his pocket.

"Now what can I do for you?" she says.

The man again holds up the album liner.

"Will you put this on your phonograph?" he says.

"Yes. Yes, of *course* I'll put it on my phonograph."

He gives her the album. She takes it from him and goes to the phonograph and removes the recording from its sleeve and places it on the turntable and turns on the machine. The arm moves jerkily through its programmed movements and places the needle neatly in the first groove. Her mind is slipping into the same series of preprogrammed jerky movements, trying to select a recording of her own that can cope with the situation.

She hears a hiss of static, a brief orchestral introduction, and then the voice of a female vocalist begins to sing:

Did you say I've got a lot to learn?
Well, don't think I'm trying not to learn,
Since this is the perfect spot to learn,
Teach me tonight . . .

Teach me tonight? Perfect. The entreaty of the sexually innocent lamb to the experienced wolf. So *that's* how he sees us. All I have to do is be his teacher. All I have to do is be his mother.

"April Stevens," says the man pleasantly. "Do you remember her?"

"I think I do. She's marvelous."

"She looks a little like you, in a way."

"Really? Thank you. The woman on the album is very beautiful."

"Care to dance?"

"Love to."

That's the ticket, go along with it, anything he wants. He wants to dance? Perfect. I'll make him think he's Fred Astaire and I'm Ginger Rogers. He wants maybe a bite to eat? Terrific. I'll make like I'm Julia Child and he's Craig Claiborne. He wants perhaps a little after-dinner piece of ass? Gorgeous. I'll play Linda Lovelace to his Attila the Hun. It won't be the first time I've dropped my drawers to get myself out of a tight spot, and I doubt that it's going to be the last.

Starting with the A-B-C of it
Right down to the X-Y-Z of it,
Help me solve the mist-to-ree of it,
Teach me tonight . . .

The man folds his coat neatly and places it on the sofa, exactly parallel to the backrest, then holds out his arms to her.

"Shall we trip the light fantastic?" he says.

Oh, cute, very cute—*Shall we trip the light fantastic,* is it?

She moves into his arms. They begin to dance in time to the music. She is surprised to find that he can dance at all.

The sky's a blackboard high above you,
If a shooting star goes by
I'll use that star to write "I love you"
A thousand times across the sky . . .

"You're a pretty good dancer," she says. "Where'd you learn?"

"Arthur Murray. I took for a whole season."

She moves in a little closer and hugs his body to her own, very conscious of the pocket with the knife. It would be so simple to make a grab for it. Yank it out of the pocket, snap it open and shove it right into his hot little groin, the putz.

"You're a very sexy man, you know that?"

"Don't con me, Beverly."

"I wouldn't *dream* of conning you. I happen to think you're a very sexy man. You must have a lot of women."

"I do OK."

"I'll bet you do. I'm sorry, I didn't catch your first name. The last one was Savage, right?"

"No, that's just a pseudonym. My real name isn't important yet."

One thing isn't very clear, my love.
Should the teacher stand so near, my love?
Graduation's almost here, my love,
Teach me tonight . . .

"With all those women after you, what do you want with *me?*"

"I admire you."

"What do you admire about me?"

"I admire the way you handle yourself. How you don't take crap from idiots like some people do. You give as good as you get, that's what I admire."

"Why, thank you. But how do you know that about me? We've never met before, have we?"

"Maybe not, but I've been admiring you from afar, you might say. I know a lot about you, don't worry."

"Oh? What do you know?"

"Well, I know, for example, that you wear size 34-C in a brassiere and size 5 in panties. I know that you have a nervous stomach and a loose bowel and that Dr. Mandelbaum prescribes Librium and Combid for it. You want any more?"

"No. How do you know all this?"

"Observation. I've been observing you for quite a while now, don't worry."

"Have you? How?"

"The usual methods. Following you, listening to you talk to others, watching you through binoculars. The usual methods. Don't worry, I know what I'm doing."

"I'll bet you do."

So the little putz has been observing me, has he? Ugh. She shudders. Closer, move closer. Stroke his back. Breathe on his neck.

"When you watch me through binoculars," she says, "have you ever seen me naked?"

"Partly. Not for very long, though."

"Would you like to see me now? Not partly but completely? And for as long as you want to?"

She teases his face with her lips, lightly runs her fingers across the back of his neck.

"Yes. I'd like that very much. Darling."

She cups his face in her hands, brushes his lips with hers, then moves a few steps back, swaying in time to the music. She opens the front of her flowered dressing gown and gives him a flash of bra and underpants.

"Are you quite an experienced lover?" she asks.

"Sort of."

"Have you had hundreds of mistresses, women of all ages and descriptions, or do you specialize in a certain type?"

Approximating a stripper's movements, she continues to dance, teasing him with her open gown, then swishing it closed again, dancing close to him one moment, then whirling away.

"I guess you could say I've had all kinds," he says. "Although I tend to like strong women the best."

She unhooks her bra under the gown, continuing to sway with the music.

"Do you like them to seduce you? Tease you and taunt you and then pull off your clothes and have their way with you?"

"I . . . like to be in charge."

"Do you? Do you really? Or do you like it when they're aggressive and make you follow their direction?"

She slips the bra off her shoulders, withdraws it gracefully from under her gown, trails it under his nose and then whips it over her shoulder. She dances up against him, allowing little flashes of her breasts to peek out of the gown. She begins to unbutton his shirt.

"What are you doing?" he says.

"What am I doing? Why, what does it *seem* like I'm doing?"

He takes a step backward.

"Well, take it easy," he says.

"I thought you like strong women. I thought that's what you said you like."

"I do. But I . . ."

"But you *what*, lover?"

She moves to him again, runs her fingers lightly across his chest, unbuttons another of his buttons.

"I . . . like to be in charge . . ."

She toys briefly with the notion of going for the knife, then rules against it.

"Sure you do. Sure you like to be in charge."

She lets her gown fall open, exposing her naked breasts. She rubs up against him, still swaying with the music.

"I do . . . I like to be the one who . . . calls the shots," he gulps.

"Sure you do. Sure you like to be the one who calls the shots, lover."

The perspiration is pouring off his face, soaking through the armpits of his shirt. She has practically pinned him against the fireplace wall. It's perfect, she thinks. He's in the middle of the best wet dream he's ever had, and I have totally regained control. I can toy with him as long as I like before I let him off the hook. I might even let him think he's going to fuck me before I'm done with him.

"I . . . like to be in charge . . . I really like to be in charge," he whispers, finding it difficult to breathe.

"Sure you do, lover. Tell me about it."

She starts to pull his shirt out of his pants.

He reaches for something to fend her off with. His hand closes over a brass poker. He brings it down hard on her head. There is a sickening sound of metal against bone and she falls in a heap at his feet.

He stands there stupidly, watching the blood gush out of her scalp, and realizes that he has done it again.

No, it wasn't *he* who has done it again, it was *they* who have done it again. Women. Treacherous, deceitful women. First it was Linda, pretending to be attracted to him and then trying to get his knife. Now it was Beverly, seducing him and trying to make a fool out of him. Trying to make a mockery out of his ability to be in charge of things and out of the act of love and out of his feelings for her. All he'd wanted was to love her and cherish her and try to make a life for the two of them together.

What he really ought to do, what nobody would ever blame him for doing, was to never give a woman an even break again. To never give a woman a chance to hurt him or make a fool of him again. To never allow himself to be vulnerable to a woman again in any way.

That's what he really *ought* to do, but he knew that he wouldn't do it. What he would do was just probably keep right on going the way he'd been going, trusting women and being hurt by them. His love was too great to do anything else.

He gently tugs Beverly's panties off her body and stuffs them in his pocket.

18

Max parks the car on 51st Street across from the 17th Precinct and he and Caruso get out and walk into the station house and on up to the second-floor headquarters of the Third Homicide Zone.

It is nearly 4:00 P.M. Max has been working his first eight-to-four shift and is exhausted, partly because it has been a tiring but unproductive day out on the street with Caruso, and partly because sleeping with the TV, the radio, the phonograph, and all the lights on is not conducive to getting the best night's rest. Max yawns.

"Not keeping you up, am I?" quips Caruso, whose material, Max decides, is specially written for him by Larry Cassidy and Jerry Mahoney.

They enter the dingy suite of offices with the two-tone green walls and Max slumps down behind one of the depressing olive-drab steel desks with mismatching light green Formica tops. On the wall is a map of the area covered by the Third Homicide Zone—from the East River to the Hudson, and from 59th Street down to 30th on the East Side and to 14th Street on the West Side. Stuck into the map are thirty-six pins with different-colored heads, representing the eighteen "uncleared" or unsolved cases they are working on and the eighteen they have cleared and are in the process of following through the courts.

The city is divided into sixteen Detective Districts, five of them in Manhattan. Each district has a Homicide Squad. In the Third Homicide Zone there are about seventy homicides a year, which sounds like a fairly large number, and is, although not compared with the two hundred or so a year they get up in Harlem. Seventy percent of all homicide victims know their killers— everywhere but in the Third Homicide Zone, where it just so happens that the reverse is true.

The phone rings and the Lieutenant picks it up.

"Third Homicide, O'Malley."

The Lieutenant sighs and scribbles an address down on a piece of scrap paper.

"Gentlemen," he says, addressing the five other detectives in the room, "we just caught a fresh one."

Everyone groans in unison.

"The address is 328 West 37th Street, Apartment 1B. A female Caucasian was found, nude, with her head caved in."

"Hey, Lieutenant, it's practically four o'clock," says Caruso, pulling on his sportscoat.

"Caruso don't want to see no nude broads," says Mahoney. "Nudity offends him."

"Let's roll, men," says the Lieutenant, halfway out the door. "I want to take a good look at that crime scene before it becomes a Chinese fire drill."

"Hey, Max," says Cassidy, following him out the door, "two naked broads in two consecutive tours— you must be our lucky charm."

By the time Max and Caruso roll up at 328 West 37th Street, three sector cars with their dome lights going and the Crime Scene Unit have double-parked in front of the building and a small crowd of people is milling about. A sergeant from the Midtown South Precinct has sealed off the area with ropes and signs saying CRIME SCENE, DO NOT PASS.

Max and Caruso push past the people and make their way into the building.

The woman is lying face down in a pool of blood. A "95" tag addressed to the morgue has already been tied to her ankle by the first responding patrolman on the scene. The woman's shapely body is indeed nude. Blood is spattered over the fireplace, the brass andirons, and an adjacent glass coffee table. The two Crime Scene Unit men are busily at work, taking flash pictures of the body from all angles and carefully dusting the entire apartment for latent prints. The detectives begin making notes and sketches of the body and its location relative to the windows, the door, and various pieces of furniture.

Max feels slightly sick to his stomach at the sight of yet another recently alive woman who has been reduced to so many pounds of useless dead meat. Looking at the woman's naked buttocks stirs something dark deep within him, making him sicker yet.

"The M.E. will be here in about twenty minutes," says the Lieutenant. "The super was the one who discovered her. He says nobody else has been in here, so maybe we'll turn up something. The deceased's name is Rachlin. Beverly Rachlin. Segal, you OK?"

"Yeah, Lieutenant," says Max.

"Don't worry about Segal, Lieutenant," says Cassidy. "He's an old hand at stuff like this. In fact, he just told me he was sending out for pizza. What kind you want, Max, the mushroom-and-meatball or the pepperoni-and-anchovy with jimmies?"

19

Babette is on a crowded subway car, rocketing home from class. The roar and clatter of the train, though irritating to most of the passengers, is to Babette strangely soothing. It effectively screens out the full spectrum of sounds of the outside world and makes her feel snug and secure in her own little cocoon.

The rhythmic sound of the train and the swaying of the passengers has a hypnotic effect. Her vision blurs. The swaying passengers standing in front of her gradually take on the appearance of corpses hanging from trees, swaying in the wind. The advertising cards above them become their epitaphs. The first one says LOWRY. The second RACHLIN. The third one is harder to make out. It looks like MANTOFFLE. No. MANTUFFLE. No. MANTEUFFEL. There is also a first name. She can't make it out. There are other words and numbers. Dates of birth and death? No, more like addresses. Something with a 5 and a 3. 53rd Street. An address on 53rd Street: 124 East 53rd Street. Then, on the epitaph above the next corpse, a name that looks like MARLIN. Or possibly MARLON.

Lowry and Rachlin are murder victims, but who are Manteuffel and Marlin? And what is Marlin's other name? The subway train grinds and screeches to a halt. The vision abruptly ends. Babette feels sick to her stomach.

20

The man in the dark overcoat signals the bartender for a refill and tries to keep his ears tuned to the conversation two seats down between the attractive young woman with the reddish hair and freckles and the brunette with the short hair.

It is the redhead he's researching. Virginia Manteuffel. Phone company supervisor. Twenty-eight years old. Born and bred in Madison, Wisconsin. Came to New York three years ago to take it by storm. Has not exactly taken it by storm, but is doing well in a less-than-fascinating job. Bubbling Under the Hot Hundred, as they said in the record business. Could possibly hit the Top Forty if she ever becomes his steady girl.

"They think both girls were killed by the same man," says the brunette.

"How do they know it's a man?" says the redhead.

"Virginia, honestly. You don't honestly believe both of those girls were killed by a *woman,* do you?"

"Why not?"

"Why *not?* Because. I mean they were sexually *molested,* darling."

"So what?" says the redhead. "Haven't you ever heard of a woman sexually molesting another woman?"

The brunette sighs.

"Can't you ever be serious, Virginia? Most women I know won't even open their doors to people they *know* anymore, and here you are, joking about it."

"I'm not joking about the actual murders, Gloria. I think those are horrible. But I'm certainly not about to stop going out of my apartment or letting people into it just because some maniac has killed a couple of women. I can't live that way. I'd rather commit suicide than do that. How many people are there in New York, Gloria—eight million? Ten million?"

"Ten, I suppose. What's your point?"

"Two people out of ten million, Gloria. That's not such terrible odds, really, now is it?"

The brunette shakes her head. "Well, those may be good odds in Madison, Wisconsin, but in New York that attitude seems a little naive."

"Maybe so, Gloria, but that's the way I feel and I guess I'm stuck with it," says the redhead. "Listen, if I don't go and pee this minute, I'm going to float right out of here."

The man squares off his cocktail napkin with the edge of the bar and watches the redhead get down off the barstool and make her way to the ladies' restroom and go inside. He keeps looking in the direction she has disappeared and tries to envision her entering the little stall. Closing the door behind her. Putting paper down on the seat. Reaching underneath her skirt and pulling down her panties as she squats on the toilet.

He returns his gaze to the bar and the rows of bottles mirrored behind it and begins idly counting the bottles. He has always been fascinated by women urinating. How many times had he watched his mother or his sister sitting on the john, the underpants below their knees, the little trickle of urine running out of them from no place he could even see. He had never understood why at a certain age he was suddenly banished forever from the bathroom when his mother or his sister wanted to urinate, when before they seemed perfectly willing to share that intimacy with him, were even amused by his curiosity about the way they peed.

Well, being banished from the bathroom didn't stop him. He watched anyway, whenever they didn't close the door completely. And if they did, he could still listen.

The man pushes his shopping cart slowly down the aisle of the A&P, counting cans of vegetables and squaring off the untidy stacks, but keeping close tabs on Virginia Manteuffel who is farther down the aisle, trying to decide among several flavors of ice cream.

He brushed by her at least twice on this particular shopping expedition, close enough to smell her hair and to assess the contents of her market basket. He loves the smell of her hair, and identifies the shampoo as Herbal Essence. He does not approve of many or most of the items she has put into her shopping cart. The bread she has selected, for example, is made from bleached flour. The frozen orange juice concentrate she's chosen is heavy with artificial additives and refined sugar. After they start dating and fall in love, he will have to speak to her about the poisons she is pouring into her body and how she must take better care of herself so they can live a long and healthful life together.

He counts the number of items in her shopping cart. If there are ten or less, she will go through the express line at the checkout counter. If there are more than twelve it will be a sign that they are going to have a wonderful romantic relationship. There are thirteen.

He times his apparently random progress through the supermarket so as to put himself just behind her in line at the checkout counter. He relishes spending time in close proximity to her, even though she's not aware of him.

He notes the contents of her purse as she digs out enough cash to pay for her groceries. He notes the address she gives the checker for the delivery, but he doesn't enter it in his little notebook under the heading MANTEUFFEL, VIRGINIA, because that piece of information he has known for weeks.

This is the third consecutive Monday evening that he has gone shopping with Virginia Manteuffel. It is now time for them to meet.

21

It's about ten o'clock on an unseasonably mild December night. Max and Caruso are on their way back to Beverly Rachlin's building in the area known as Hell's Kitchen. A tenant whom they've so far not managed to find at home on previous canvasses of the building has agreed to talk to them. The tenant sounds as though he might have some useful information.

As Max cruises through the rundown industrial neighborhood he notices small knots of provocatively dressed Black women drifting out of doorways to the curb to peer into the unmarked police car. Caruso waves at the women and smirks.

"Hey, Max, you want to get your ashes hauled?" Caruso points his thumb over his shoulder. "Those girls specialize in knob jobs. They do maybe ten on a good night. At a pound a hit that ain't a bad night's pay."

Max shudders.

"Who'd ever stick his dork in one of *their* mouths?"
he says.

"Oh, you'd be surprised how many young Jersey hot-
shots drive all the way from Newark to do just that.
Saturday nights in summer the cars with Jersey plates
are lined up clear to the tunnel. Stop the car, Max."

"Why?"

"Just pull over and stop."

Max pulls over and stops. Caruso rolls down the
window.

"Hey, girls," Caruso calls.

"Caruso, cut it out," Max hisses.

"Why? I want to introduce you. Girls? C'mon over
here."

The hookers, who'd first drifted toward the car, then
made its occupants as cops and melted away, now drift
halfway back.

"This here is my new partner, Max. What do you girls
think of him?"

Two of the hookers, realizing that these are not vice
cops but homicide ones goofing around, approach the
car and peer inside at Max.

"Max, this here is Snow White and Tiny Alice."

Snow White wears a short white fur coat, a white
plastic rose in her hair, and pink plastic curlers. Tiny
Alice has braids and white knee socks and Mary Janes.

"Hi, sweet pants," says Snow White.

"Hey, my man," says Tiny Alice.

"Hello, girls," says Max, squirming in his seat.

"Max is a Jewish boy," says Caruso. "You girls ever
had a kosher hotdog?"

"My man, we's had mos' everything," says Snow
White.

"Max has heavy Hebe friends at City Hall," says
Caruso, "and he's tight with the Commissioner. We're
very lucky to have Max in Homicide."

"Jesus Christ," says Max.

Snow White and Tiny Alice study Max and nod sagely.

"Hey," says Caruso, "you girls hear anything about a woman on West 37th Street who got her head caved in the other night?"

The two hookers stare at him as though they haven't heard the question.

"A social worker," says Caruso. "Lived a couple blocks from here. Name of Rachlin. You girls hear anything about this?"

"She a white girl?" says Snow White.

"Right."

"My man, we don' know nothin' 'bout no white girl," says Tiny Alice, making Max feel sure she knew several Black girls who'd gotten their heads caved in on the night in question.

"Well, keep your ears open," says Caruso.

The hookers are clearly tiring of the conversation. Snow White picks up an imaginary telephone, pretends to listen, hands it to Tiny Alice.

"Alice, honey," she says, "they's a call for you."

"We got to go now, my man," says Tiny Alice.

"Good evening, ladies," says Caruso.

Max puts the car in gear and pulls away from the curb.

"What the hell was *that* for?" says Max irritably.

"Just spreading the word," says Caruso. "You never know what you'll hook when you go fishing. By the way, I suppose you know that those girls were both guys."

"What?"

Max is truly surprised.

"Oh, yeah, absolutely," says Caruso. "Four-fifths of the hookers in this area are transvestites. Most of the guys they blow never even know it. You should see how they dress in warm weather. With their blouses open and their tits hanging right out there."

"How do they have tits?"

"Hormones. And silicone shots. Snow White's going to have the operation in February. They'll cut off her cock and balls and put in a little plastic vagina. Five thousand bucks that costs, and guess who pays for it."

"Who?"

"The city. The taxpayers. You and me."

"C'mon."

"You think I'm kidding? Snow White is on welfare. She's classified as handicapped because she's a drug addict. Any of these jokers want the operation, all they have to do is find a shrink on the city's payroll who'll say that they're suffering from a 'sexual identity crisis' and that if they don't have a sex-change operation, they'll wind up in the loony bin, at the city's expense."

Max turns into Beverly Rachlin's block and finds a parking space.

"I can't believe the city actually coughs up five grand any time a Black transvestite hooker wants a sex-change operation," says Max.

"They do, though. Listen, I could tell you *lots* of stuff that would knock your socks off. Don't get me started."

Max and Caruso get out of the car and go into the lobby of the building. Caruso rings the bell.

"By the way," says Caruso, "I forgot to tell you. They found some prints in the Rachlin apartment that look like they match a few we found in Lowry's. On the poker that was used to bash her head in."

"Honest? That's terrific."

"What's terrific about it? They only have about two distinct fingers on one hand. You need at least four to trace anything, and that assumes the perp has a sheet on him somewhere."

The buzzer buzzes and they go inside. An elderly man sticks his head out the door of his apartment and looks down the hall at them.

"Are you gentlemen from the Police Department?" he calls.

"Mr. Weinstock?" says Caruso. "I'm Detective Caruso and this here is my partner, Detective Segal."

They go into Mr. Weinstock's apartment. It's a musty and depressing place. Weinstock, a widower, lives there alone. He wears a moth-eaten gray cardigan and house slippers and is very polite. He pours tea for them in fluted glass cups.

"Mr. Weinstock, Detective Caruso tells me you witnessed some interesting things the night that Beverly Rachlin was killed."

Mr. Weinstock shakes his head and sighs. "Such a terrible thing to happen to that young girl. Such a senseless way to die."

"What was it you witnessed, sir?" says Max, burning his tongue on the tea.

"I didn't think about it then, but the next day when I heard she has been killed, then it occurs to me that somebody was knocking on her door that night and saying they were from the Police Department."

Caruso takes out his notebook and his ballpoint pen.

"This individual was impersonating a police officer?" asks Caruso.

"It seems to me that this is what he said to her. I cannot be certain because the television set was also on, but he was outside in the hallway and the unfortunate Miss Rachlin lived just across from me. It seems to me that this is what I heard this person say."

"Do you remember anything else he might have said?"

"He said, if I am not mistaken, that he is investigating the killing of a young woman. The name escapes me that he mentioned, but—"

"Lowry? Linda Lowry?" says Max.

"That sounds correct, yes. Linda Lowry. I believe that was the name he used."

"Do you remember the name *he* used?" says Caruso.

"That I do not. I am sorry. It seems to me that I saw him show her some sort of identification, but exactly what he—"

"Identification? What kind of identification?" says Caruso.

"I am sorry. I do not know."

"A shield? A detective's badge?"

Mr. Weinstock shrugs and spreads his palms upward.

"I am truly sorry. I wish I could be of more assistance to you."

"Not at all, not at all, Mr. Weinstock," says Max. "You've been very helpful, and we appreciate it very much."

Max and Caruso walk back out to the car.

"Well," says Max. "Now we know the killer is into impersonating cops as well as delivery people."

"Not necessarily," says Caruso.

"How do you mean?" says Max.

"I mean," says Caruso, "that the killer may really *be* a cop."

22

"Miss Manteuffel?"

Pleasant voice.

"Yes?"

"Miss Virginia T. Manteuffel?"

Wholesome, Midwestern accent.

"Yes?"

"Miss Manteuffel, I represent the Kinsey-Pomeroy Institute of the University of Indiana. I wonder if I might come in a moment and chat with you?"

"What about?"

"Well, we're doing a survey similar to the ones which Dr. Kinsey conducted on human sexual behavior. Are you familiar with those surveys?"

"Well, sort of."

"This is a similar sort of survey, one concentrating on young single career women. I wonder if I might come in and chat with you and fill in a questionnaire? We're able to pay you an honorarium of ten dollars for your time, I might add."

He slides something under the door. She picks it up. It's a check for ten dollars bearing the imprint of the University of Indiana.

"May I come in and talk to you?"

"Well, I don't know. Will it take long?"

"Not at all. Not more than eight to ten minutes."

"The reason I ask is that I'm dressing to go out. I

couldn't spend more than five minutes, if that would help you at all."

"Five minutes is better than nothing, I guess. May I come in?"

"OK."

The door is unbolted and opened. The woman who ushers him in is attractive and has reddish blonde hair, freckles, a girlish body, small breasts, long legs. She wears a blue flannel robe and her feet are bare.

"Excuse my appearance," she says.

The man smiles, then enters the small studio apartment. He takes in the feminine frills, the gingham curtains at the window, the framed engravings of flowers on the walls, the polished-brass fittings on the antique hurricane lamps and other New England bric-a-brac.

"Nice place you have here. Decorate it yourself?"

"Thank you, yes."

"Well, I won't waste your time with small talk. May I sit down and begin?"

"Certainly."

The man takes off his overcoat and folds it neatly and places it on the sofa, then sits down and scans the large clipboard in his hand. The young woman sits down opposite him in a wingback chair and crosses her legs modestly under the flannel robe.

"All right, let's see here. You're a single woman, Miss Manteuffel, are you not?"

"Yes."

"Age . . . twenty-one?"

"Thank you, no. I'm twenty-eight."

"And your occupation is . . . ?"

"I work at the telephone company. I'm a departmental supervisor."

"Very well. Now then, since this is a sexual survey, we're going to be asking you some fairly personal questions. Your replies will be kept in the strictest confidence, of course, and any data that you supply us will remain anonymous."

"I understand."

"Good. First of all, Miss Manteuffel, are you a virgin?"

"No, I'm not."

"All right. At what age did you lose your virginity?"

"Nineteen."

"All right. And are you presently involved in a sexual relationship?"

"Yes."

"With a member of the opposite sex?"

"Yes. Of course."

Little frown lines appear on her forehead.

"All right. And about how many times a week now would you say you have sex?"

She blushes slightly, then replies in as offhand a manner as possible.

"Oh, I'd say about three times on the average."

"Fine. And do you usually have an orgasm?"

She flushes again.

"Most of the time. Listen, is there much more of this? Because I really have to run. I'm late as it is."

"No, there isn't much more. Do you achieve orgasm more with your partner's penis in your vagina, or with your partner stimulating your clitoris with his tongue?"

She stands up, her cheeks still flushed.

"Look, I hate to be rude, but I really didn't think your questions would be quite that personal, besides which I really do have to fly. I still have to put on my makeup and do my hair and finish dressing, and I—"

"I understand, I understand." The man smiles. "And I'm sorry if I embarrassed you. But this is a very important survey, and unless I am able to finish the last few questions with you I have to throw the whole thing out, you see. Won't you just answer the few remaining questions?"

"I don't know. How many more are there?"

"Well, let's see. Not more than three or four, but in the time we've already spent discussing it you could have finished."

She sighs a great, put-upon sigh and sinks back down in her chair.

"OK, what else do you want to know? Hurry up."

"All right. Our next question is in several parts and concerns masturbation. First, how many times a week on the average do you masturbate; second, how long does each session last; third, how long does it take you to achieve—"

"Look, I really don't want to answer any more questions."

She gets up.

"I understand. That question a number of women find particularly embarrassing."

"I'm afraid I'm going to have to ask you to leave."

"I understand. And I don't blame you."

The man merely smiles and makes no move to either stand or leave. The woman seems disoriented.

"I thought I asked you to leave."

"You did. And I will. As soon as we're finished."

"But we *are* finished. I told you that. I'm not answering any more questions. And I would appreciate it very much if you would leave right now."

"Now, now, don't get that pretty little head of yours all in a dither."

"I said I want you out of here *now*."

The man smiles, shrugs, and reaches into his pocket.

"Our first fight," he says fondly.

He withdraws a switchblade knife and clicks out the blade.

"Virginia, my love," he says, extending the knife in

her direction, "tomorrow at the office you'll have Gloria and Marcia rolling in the aisles when you tell them what a silly goose you were on our first date, but for now, where is your phonograph?"

23

Bright sunlight, so bright it could put your eyes out. Velez, the super of the building at 124 East 53rd Street, sticks his head back inside and accustoms his eyes to the much darker room. Sure is bright out. Cold, too, colder than a witch's tit. Better to be inside where it's warm, even if being inside means working and working is at a shit job like his, it's still better than being outside.

Velez walks down the narrow hallway of the building, past dozens of doors of nothing-needed-today-thanks, and stops at Apartment 4-G. Today is the day Apartment 4-G gets to stop having a leaky shower head and nice Miss Manteuffel will be so happy she will probably give him a tip even though Christmas is almost here and she's planning to give him twenty bucks and a bottle of booze which she does every year although she is not what you would call rich, still she knows how to make a person feel like they are more than a super, more than a greasy janitor, more than some kind of an animal with dirty hands and filthy, greasy clothes, which is what most tenants made you feel like.

Velez knocks at the door of Apartment 4-G, but there

is no answer. Not surprising. It's almost 10:00 A.M., and nice Miss Manteuffel is already at work.

Velez takes out his passkey and slips it into the lock and turns the knob of the door and opens it and is just about to go into the bathroom and fix the shower head of nice Miss Manteuffel and if there's time go through her laundry hamper and check out her soiled underwear when he notices that nice Miss Manteuffel herself is lying on the floor with most of her clothing torn off and her nice buttocks showing and a number of objects scattered around her including an antique mariner's compass and a heavy pewter ashtray and a gold Dunhill cigarette lighter that must have cost a mint.

Velez looks at the body of nice Miss Manteuffel and first he thinks about how sad he is that this has happened to nice Miss Manteuffel and then he thinks that he is glad to have at least seen what Miss Manteuffel's nice buttocks looked like naked at least once in his life before he dies, and then he bends down and delicately picks up the gold Dunhill cigarette lighter which must have cost a mint and drops it into his greasy green workpants pocket, because if nice Miss Manteuffel had known she was going to be dead before Christmas and not able to give Velez his Christmas money and his Christmas booze she would have wanted him certainly to have it probably on account of how nice she was, and then he squats down next to the body and takes a good look at her nakedness because what was the harm in that and she was dead anyway, and then Velez goes to the telephone and calls the police.

24

He stands at the window, scanning the buildings across the street with his binoculars, counting windows and looking over his women.

It is shortly before dusk on a December Sunday—a good time to see something, he has found. Most of his women have spent the greater part of their weekend alone. "All alone by the telephone," he thinks to himself. What was that from?

The promise of romantic adventure on Friday and Saturday nights which had enabled these women to get through the week has, by this time on Sunday, finally faded. Hope is dead. There is nothing for them to look forward to except the bleak prospect of Monday morning at the office and another full week of drudgery at jobs which most of them detest. At this hour on a Sunday afternoon the weekend, like their lives, could be viewed as one gigantic letdown, one colossal anticlimax.

The sun dips lower and lower in the winter sky. Shadows slant across parquet floors littered with Sunday papers read alone and glasses with the dregs of beverages consumed alone and the wrappings from unnourishing foods usually eaten in solitude—frozen TV dinners, canned ravioli, fattening chocolate cookies like Mallomars—lonely food.

Many of his women choose this hour to begin bouts of serious drinking. Some of them, he has noticed, choose it to begin bouts of serious masturbation.

88

Most of them do it with their hands. Wanda Polodin, an overweight brunette in her late forties, does it with a battery-powered vibrator, but her masturbatory sessions are as erratic as they are erotic and therefore hard to plan on. Only one of his women—impossibly young and innocent-looking little Pamela Marlin—never disappoints him.

He checks his watch: 4:50 P.M. Too early still for Pamela, but best to be prepared in case she decides to start sooner. Yes, there she is, lying on the floor in her quilted white bathrobe, reading the papers, listening to the unwatched TV which probably makes her feel a bit less lonely. From time to time her hand absentmindedly slips inside her bathrobe and goes between her legs, only to be discovered and withdrawn. Patience—it isn't time yet.

He remembers spying on his older sister when she was still his babysitter. Once he caught a glimpse of her rubbing herself in just that manner when she thought he was asleep. Then she caught him peeking and he didn't know which one of them was more embarrassed.

She hauled him into her bedroom, threw him down on the floor, straddled him with her knees, and spanked the daylights out of him. She was so mad she just kept spanking. He didn't cry, didn't even make a sound. Partly because crying was what babies did and he wasn't going to give her the satisfaction, and partly because he knew that when he started crying she would stop. He kept his mouth shut and the spanking went on.

She asked if he'd had enough. He didn't answer. His butt was numb, he had to go to the bathroom, but he refused to answer. Besides, his little thing had gotten stiff and he didn't want her to see it.

Again she asked if he'd had enough and still he refused to answer. Whether from his full bladder or the excitement of the spanking or both he didn't know, but suddenly he began to go to the bathroom in his pajamas. His sister was outraged and swore to tell their parents, but if she did they somehow never said a word.

Perhaps his sister should have treated him with more respect. Perhaps she would have had she known that it was largely due to him that she even remained alive. How many thousands of times had he counted the squares in the sidewalk as he walked over them, placing his feet exactly in the middle of each square and not on the crack, which, if he had not done so, might have caused his sister terrible pain and even death. Step-on-a-crack-break-your-mother's-back was a phrase he had modified to include all the members of his family, not only his mother, and particularly his sister, the moment he realized how fragile they were. How vulnerable to accident or to disease or to the effects of his own evil thoughts, which could cause them to shrivel and die if he let them continue for even more than a second and didn't cancel them three times each.

Oh, yes, had his sister only known what he was doing for her every day, even now, to magically keep her from certain death, she would have acted quite differently toward him, as would his mother and father and the kids in school and everybody else. That people—even strangers on the street—didn't have a clue how hard he had to work every single day of his life in order to keep them free from calamities was one of the great ironies of his life. But telling would have spoiled it. Besides, who would have believed him anyway?

25

PHONE COMPANY SUPERVI-
SOR, 28, IS 3rd SEX SLAYING
OF WEEK

The nude body of an at-
tractive 28-year-old woman
was found in her apartment
at 124 E. 53rd St. in Manhattan. The slim young redhead, a departmental supervisor at New York Tele-
phone, was identified as
Virginia T. Manteuffel. She
had been strangled by an
unknown assailant.

The body was discovered
early today by Angel Velez,
57, superintendent of the
building, who said he was
"shocked at this senseless
killing."

The Manteuffel murder is
the third sex slaying in the
past week. Previous victims
were Beverly Rachlin, 33,
of 328 W. 37th St., and
Linda Lowry, 23, of 225 E.
46th St., both in Manhattan.

Although causes of death
vary in each case, there is
speculation among police
authorities that the same
man may have committed
all three crimes.

Reading the story about Virginia Manteuffel in the
paper, Babette begins to tremble.

I could have warned her, she thinks. I could have
called her and warned her and today she might still be
alive. I had her address. I even had her telephone number, but I didn't call her because I couldn't bear the
prospect of sounding like a crazy person. Because I
couldn't bear the prospect of sounding like a crazy person, Virginia Manteuffel is not alive today.

Why am I so weak? Why am I so hopelessly weak? I
pray to God that my life never has to depend on some-

body's willingness to be thought a crazy person if they are as weak as I am.

Well, there is only one thing to do now. And if I'm too late for Virginia Manteuffel, then perhaps I won't be too late for this Marlin person and the others.

Babette timidly enters the 17th Precinct police station and is struck by the faint smell of urine. Two uniformed cops give her body the once-over as they pass her, which she does not appreciate. She walks uncertainly up to the desk. The policeman behind the desk looks at her expectantly.

"I . . . don't know who I want to talk to exactly," she says, "but I think I have some information on a murder case."

"Which murder case?"

"The . . . Manteuffel one. And others."

"Others?"

"Yes. The Lowry one and the Rachlin one."

"What kind of information do you have?"

"Well, just that they were going to happen, mostly." The policeman behind the desk appraises her coolly.

"Just that they were going to happen?"

"Yes. Are you the person I'm supposed to be telling this to?"

"Excuse me?"

"I mean is there some special person I should be telling this to, or are you the one?"

The policeman points upward.

"Right up the stairs," he says. "Turn right and go to the end of the hall."

"Thank you."

Babette climbs the stairs to the second floor and turns right. At the end of the hall is a door marked THIRD HOMICIDE ZONE. She enters.

There are several steel desks with nobody at them.

There are doors to two other offices. Out of one of the two doors comes a large man dressed in a plaid sports-coat. He seems surprised to see Babette.

"Can I help you?" he says.

"Yes. I have some information on a murder case. They told me to come up here."

"Which murder case you have information on?"

"The Manteuffel one. And others. Are you the person I'm supposed to be telling this to?"

The man smiles and nods and does a little fake bow.

"Detective Salvatore Caruso at your service," he says.

"Oh, hi. My name is Watson. Babette Watson."

"You have information on the Manteuffel case, you say?"

"Yes. And the Lowry one and the Rachlin one."

"What kind of information?"

He takes out a notebook and a ballpoint pen and begins to write.

"Well, just mostly that they were going to happen," she says.

Caruso looks up from his notebook.

"Just that they were going to happen?"

"Yes."

"And how did you get this information?"

"Well, I had a . . . you might call it a dream, I guess. About the Rachlin murder first. The night before it happened . . ."

"Yes . . ."

"And then again, the night before the Manteuffel one. I had a vision she was going to be killed, too."

Caruso's face is totally impassive.

"You had a *vision* she was going to be killed?" he says.

"Yes."

Caruso closes his notebook and puts it away.

"Well, thank you for coming in and telling us about it," he says.

"You're welcome. I also know about a killing that hasn't taken place yet. The name of the victim is Marlin."

"Marlin what?"

"Just Marlin is all I know. It could be Marlon, a man's first name, I guess."

"I see. Well, thank you very much."

"You're welcome. Detective Caruso?"

"Yes, ma'am."

"How are you going to follow up on this information?"

"Oh, we'll follow up on it, don't worry."

"But how?"

"In the usual way."

"I see. Tell me something."

"Yes, ma'am?"

"You think I'm a crazy person, don't you?"

"Yes, ma'am."

She stands there a moment longer, looking at Caruso, then sighs and turns around and walks out the door.

She feels like a fool. But it hasn't been as bad as she thought it would be. Perhaps if she talked to somebody higher up in the Police Department. Perhaps if she went downtown, to police headquarters, she could find a policeman who would take her seriously.

26

She gets out of the Lexington Avenue subway at the Brooklyn Bridge station, walks along the filthy underground tunnels embroidered with aerosol graffiti, and comes up onto the street at Centre and Chambers. Number One Police Plaza—what a ridiculous-sounding address for what is doubtlessly just another gritty governmental building painted inside in industrial cream and avocado.

"Excuse me, but could you direct me to Number One Police Plaza?"

"Go through the Municipal Building. It's on the other side."

She walks through the grime and draftiness of the Municipal Building and exits, not to more of the same but to a delightful, unexpectedly modern red-brick building with a tree- and bench-lined red-brick courtyard and landscaped sculpture garden—less a dreary headquarters for sour Kojaks and Columbos than a stylish San Francisco shopping mall.

Crossing the plaza to the main building, she feels an odd sensation, a prickling of the skin between her shoulderblades. She starts to turn around, and as she does she locks eyes with a young man about twenty feet behind her. He is blond, clean-shaven, and wears an olive-drab Army trenchcoat with the collar up. He seems startled and stops dead in his tracks.

Flashbulbs pop behind her eyes. Her knees wobble

and her calves threaten to telescope into her thighs. He is the most extraordinarily attractive man she has ever seen.

She turns away to hide the flush of red that must be enveloping her entire neck and face and starts walking again, then stops and turns around to see if he is following. He's not. His shoes have taken root in the red-brown brick. She turns away again, resumes her pace, but slower. He catches up with her, and suddenly she realizes she can't think of a single thing to say to him, not one. That's all right, let *him* start it—it's the man's job anyway, isn't it?

"Uh, excuse me, miss, uh . . ."

She stops and turns to face him, a yard away.

"Yes?"

Up close the effect is heightened geometrically. She sways unsteadily on her feet. Her cheeks are so hot you could fry eggs on them. Good Christ, what is *happening* to her?

A self-conscious grin on his face.

"Uh, I couldn't help noticing you . . . noticing you noticing *me,* I mean, and . . ."

She feels as though her forehead were plexiglass and he's been peering through it, reading her thoughts. Mortified, she wheels around and tears off across the plaza in the direction from which she came.

"Hey, *wait* a second! What did I say that . . . ?"

He takes off after her but she loses him in the lobby of the Municipal Building, tears of hot humiliation streaming down her cheeks. *I couldn't help noticing you noticing me!*

She nearly collides with an elderly man exiting from the revolving door and is once more out on the street. A taxi passes. Without considering the expense she flags it; it screeches to a stop, and she hops inside.

"Hey, *wait* a minute! Miss! Wait up!"

He bursts out of the Municipal Building and races up to the cab, but the driver already has it in gear. The young man throws himself across the hood. The driver slams on his brakes, stopping abruptly, cursing, shouting, gesticulating, and leaps out of the cab. A uniformed cop ambles over, listens briefly to the hackie, frowns, then turns to the young man. The young man reaches inside his coat and flashes something in the cop's face— a badge! The young man is a cop himself! The uniformed cop smiles, nods, and walks away. The hackie is subdued, but grumbling. The young man sticks his head in the door.

"Hey, what did you run away for? I have to talk to you."

The cabbie comes over.

"What about my fare, fella?"

"What *about* your fare? You didn't take her ten fucking *feet*—oh, sorry, miss—what kind of fare you *charging* here, by the *foot*?"

"Six bits. The drop on the meter. What about it?"

"You don't knock it off," says Max, "I'll drop *you*."

"Oh, yeah? You and what army, kid?"

"OK, pal, you got a choice," says Max. "Either get back in the cab real nice and without another *word*, or I am taking you in and booking you for harassing an officer of the law and obstructing justice."

The cabbie grumbles back into the cab and turns to Babette in the back seat.

"*You* wouldn't wanna settle the fare, wouldja, miss?"

"*No, she wouldn't. OK, you asshole*—sorry, miss—*you're under arrest. Get out of the cab!*"

"OK, OK, forget it. I'm going. You getting out here, miss, or what?"

Max is already pulling her out of the cab.

"I guess I have no choice," she says.

Grinning at all the trouble the guy has gone to,

Babette figures they're even now. The cab pulls away from the curb so fast it leaves an inch of rubber on the pavement. They stand looking shyly at each other. He's not really as handsome as she thought. His mouth is too wide and his teeth are too big. And yet . . .

"I'm sorry I caused all that," says Max, who is clearly not sorry at all, "but I couldn't let you get away. I told the patrolman you were a material witness in a homicide case. I don't think he bought it, though."

She giggles.

"My name is Max. What's yours?"

"Babette. You a detective?"

He nods. "Homicide. I'm older than I look."

"You look about twenty-five."

"That's how old I *am*. I thought I looked twenty-seven."

"You look twenty-five."

They giggle self-consciously, both aware they're not talking about what's really going on.

"Uh, well, Babette . . . Babette? Babette, I saw you walking across the plaza there and I . . . well, this really weird feeling came over me. I mean you really are some terrific-looking . . . woman."

She has to turn away.

"Thank you."

"Were you going into the building on police business?"

Suddenly she remembers why she came, and all the girlish shyness and self-consciousness dissolves.

"You know what you told that cop about my being a material witness in a homicide case? You may have been telling the truth."

27

To tell the truth, Max feels a little funny about having thrown himself across the hood of the taxicab. Not that he doesn't think it was one swell romantic gesture. It's just that starting off a relationship with something that theatrical places you under a lot of pressure to keep coming up with equivalent things on a fairly regular basis, and such a burden is exhausting even to think about.

The chick herself he still can't figure. In the looks department she is a definite 10. He loves her honey-colored hair, her big tragic eyes, her slim dancer's body. In the personality department he is projecting her as a probable 7.

They are sitting in a dark, gimmicky little bar in the City Hall area called the Convent, not far from One Police Plaza, and because it is too late for lunch and too early for happy hour, the waitresses, who are dressed like nuns, are leaving them pretty much to themselves.

Max is drinking a brandy stinger, his latest affectation, and Babette is working on a scotch and soda which, once she'd ordered it, made Max decide she was a lot worldlier than he'd pegged her to be. Max feels you can tell a lot about a woman from what she orders. He'd figured her for some mild, too-sweet drink with a tricky name, like a Harvey Wallbanger. The scotch and soda he would have to think about.

"So," says Max, swallowing the last gulp of his stinger and flashing their nun the sign for another round, "you think you're having precognitive dreams about homicides, do you?"

Babette nods her head.

"Which homicides?"

"The Lowry one and the Rachlin one. And then the Manteuffel one."

"What sort of thing was in these dreams?"

"A lot of strange images that had to do with where the murders were committed. Also some names."

"Names? What kind of names?"

"On the Rachlin murder I only got close—Macklin instead of Rachlin. But on the Manteuffel one I not only got the name perfectly, but also an address: 124 East 53rd Street. I looked it up in the phone book and there it was. I considered doing something about it, but then I chickened out. Then the next day I read about Virginia Manteuffel in the paper. I felt awful—I could have prevented her killing. I feel responsible for her death. That's why I have to find out if I can warn this Marlin or Marlon person whose name was in the vision, too."

"You say you had a vision of Virginia Manteuffel's name and address? *Before* she was killed?"

"Yes. The night before. If I had even just called her on the phone and *warned* her. Even that might have helped. But I felt foolish doing it, so I didn't call, and now she's dead. Because I was afraid of feeling foolish."

"Don't be so tough on yourself. Even if you had called her, she wouldn't have done anything. She would have probably assumed you were a nut and ignored you."

"Do *you* think I'm a nut, Max?"

"Well, no, not really. I think you're . . . what I do think is that you're probably a person who has a lot of natural . . ." He smiles and shrugs. "Look, Babette, I don't know you. You're a very pretty girl and you're very nice to talk to, and, well, very frankly, I guess I do think you're probably a nut, but I—"

"Then why are you even talking to me? Do you take every nut you meet to a bar and buy them drinks?"

Babette is getting very red in the face.

"Calm down, Babette, OK?"

Babette tries to stand up in the tiny space behind the table, but Max pushes her gently back into a sitting position.

"I said calm *down*, OK?"

"I'd like to leave now, if it's all the same to you."

"It is *not* all the same to me. Will you please wait one second here and listen to what I'm saying? Will you just please do that much?"

"What is it you want to say?"

"Look. I don't happen to be the most diplomatic guy in the world, Babette, but at least I'm honest, OK? Now, I'm sorry I said you're probably a nut—although, very frankly, I still think there's a chance that you *are*—however—"

Babette lurches to a standing position again and again Max pushes her down in her seat.

"—however, even if you *are* a nut, you're one hell of a gorgeous one and I'm enjoying the hell out of talking to you. And if it turns out that you're *not* a nut but somebody who has real powers of ESP—assuming that there are such things, that is—then maybe you and I can work together and catch the maniac who's killing all these women before he kills a whole lot more, OK?"

Babette just glares at him.

"OK, Babette?"

28

Dr. Tony Natale is a police shrink. He was not always a police shrink. He was once a common uniformed cop on foot patrol. Before that, at age sixteen, he was a longshoreman in Brooklyn. He got interested in people's heads—of cops as well as of "alleged poipetrators." He went back to school at night while he was a cop in the daytime, got his Ph.D. in psychology, and is now a genuine bona fide legitimate shrink. The only problem is he still sometimes talks a little like a Brooklyn long-shoreman. No problem. The fucking guy knows his stuff.

Into his office comes Detective Max Segal, a young blond Jewish kid who got made a homicide dick from pulling old people out of a fire. Interesting kid. He'll go far in the homicide racket.

"Hi, doc, thanks for seeing me."

"Sit down, Max."

Max sits down in a grubby overstuffed chair with the overstuffing falling out of it. One of the drawbacks of being a police shrink.

"Doc, the word is that you know a little about parapsychology. That right?"

"It's kind of a sideline of mine. Why?"

"OK. I have a friend, a girl about twenty years old. She's had some dreams that she thinks described a couple of these homicides before they happened. She also says she was warned about the Virginia Manteuffel case before it happened. She even got Manteuffel's address."

Natale soberly nods his head.

"Some people claim to get information from Ouija boards, too," says Natale. "Stuff that happens to be true but that they'd have no way of knowing. Most of the time they think it's spirits of the dead talking to them."

"They're not dealing with a full deck, these people, huh?"

"They may be," says Natale. "There are thousands of cases, reported by very solid citizens, of people getting clairvoyant stuff through dreams. Or automatic writing. Or Ouija boards. Or seances. Whether they actually get this stuff through spirits, like they claim, or through their own latent ESP is hard to say, though. You know what I mean?"

"You don't believe in *spirits,* do you, doc?"

"I don't believe in spirits. And I also don't *dis*believe. There's one hell of a lot of evidence that that kind of stuff might exist, though."

Max looks to see if the doc is maybe putting him on. The doc does not seem to be putting him on.

"Well," says Max, "maybe I'd believe in that kind of stuff if I ever saw it myself, but I never have."

"I don't think you'd believe in it even if you *did* see it," says Natale.

"No?"

"No. Most people don't. No matter how spectacular whatever they see is—a ghost, a UFO, or only a simple case of clairvoyance or telepathy—the thing is too threatening to them. To their belief systems, you know what I mean? So they go explain it away with some bullshit conventional explanation. Or they discredit it some way: 'I was drunk,' they say, or 'I was hallucinating.' Bullshit. They just don't have the guts to see what they really saw."

29

Another late Sunday afternoon, another free show in the buildings across the street. He scans the most promising apartments with his binoculars, counting floors and windows.

Pamela Marlin is merely lying on her bed, watching a football game on TV. It is not yet time for her date with herself. Wanda Polodin is not in sight. If she plans a session of sexual self-indulgence she has thus far given no indication.

He has no interest in ever meeting Wanda Polodin in person. For one thing, she is too old. For another, she is not good-looking enough. For a third, she is too plump. He has never cared for plump women. His own mother was a little on the plump side, which he'd never found attractive. And Mrs. DiPaolo, of course—she was plump, too. He has not thought about Mrs. DiPaolo for a long time.

He had always been a quiet child, always polite and well-behaved and good. But he never played well with other kids. It wasn't his fault. He would have liked to play with them, but they never seemed to want to play with him. He eventually stopped trying to make them like him and resigned himself to being a loner. It was not much fun being a loner at first, but after a while he began to see how stupid and petty the kids who'd rejected him were, and then he was glad he'd never had anything to do with them.

His parents were worried that he never seemed to have anyone to play with and so, more to satisfy them than anything else, he made up someone whom he called Lance Steel. He often told his mother he was going to Lance's house to play after school. Whenever his mother told him to invite Lance to play at *his* house, he made up elaborate excuses why his friend was unable to come.

When he started high school his parents were worried that he wouldn't go to mixers and dances because he didn't appear to be socially at ease. The best way to become socially at ease, they told him, was to learn to dance. He told them he didn't want to learn to dance. They insisted. He was too polite to refuse. The dance studios they talked to were all on the expensive side, but his mother had heard that a downstairs neighbor, Mrs. DiPaolo, had once been a professional dancer and occasionally gave dancing lessons to kids in the neighborhood.

His dance lessons with Mrs. DiPaolo were awful. First of all she lived in this stuffy, dark apartment that smelled funny. Second, she was overweight and used too much perfume and drank. Usually she didn't get started drinking till nighttime, but sometimes she began right after lunch, and by the time he got to her apartment after school she was potted. If she hadn't been overweight and a drunk, she might have looked OK. Her hair was dyed a fake shade of red that was almost pink, but she had large breasts and pretty good legs for a lady that old, he had to admit that. He figured she was at least forty.

What she'd do was put a record on her old Victrola, demonstrate to him at some length whatever step they were going to learn that day, and then have him do the footwork alone while she watched. The worst part was when he had to dance with her. He was embarrassed to even touch her, much less hold her as close as she said you had to hold your partner when you danced. He always held her as loosely as he could. But one afternoon, when she was looped, she insisted he hold her very close, and when he did, as much as she disgusted him, he found himself getting a boner.

He was very embarrassed. Not knowing what else to do, he asked to be excused and went to the bathroom. But when he closed the bathroom door he caught sight of her underwear hanging all over the place and his boner got worse than ever.

Hanging up in the shower were several pairs of panties, stockings, and brassieres. He walked over to inspect them, and that got him more excited than ever.

Mrs. DiPaolo must have wondered what he was doing in there so long. She knocked on the door and asked if he was all right. He said he was and flushed the toilet to show he was doing legitimate bathroom things. Then he noticed her laundry hamper and opened it to see what treasures it might contain.

When Mrs. DiPaolo finally pushed open the door, which he thought he'd locked, he was wearing a pair of her outsized panties.

She seemed as unsure about how to react as he was. At first she tried on shock, then anger, and then she just burst out laughing. Finally she stopped. She said it was all right with her if he liked her underwear, that she liked it all right herself. She said her late husband often wore it around the house to tease her, and sometimes he even wore it to the office underneath his suit as a secret way to keep her with him when he wasn't home.

He said he was very ashamed of himself and hoped she wasn't mad at him and wouldn't tell his parents what he had done. She said that not only wasn't she mad at him, she was flattered that he had done some-

thing reminiscent of her late husband. She told him
to come back into the living room just as he was and
continue his dance lesson. He said he wouldn't do that
in a million years. She said if he came back into the
living room dressed just as he was and continued his
dance lesson, she wouldn't tell his parents. Otherwise
she couldn't promise.

It was blackmail, no question about it, but what
could he do? He went back into the living room. She
put another record on the Victrola and held out her
arms to him. He was very uncomfortable, but he put his
left hand in hers and his right hand on her waist, and
they began to dance. She pulled him in close, so close
he thought he'd suffocate and, sure enough, he got
another boner, this one even worse than the last.

Mrs. DiPaolo thought that was pretty funny, too, but
finally she took pity on him. She told him she had a
remedy for his problem. She led him to the sofa and sat
him down. She gently pulled down the panties he was
wearing and took his penis in her hand and told him
how fine it was. Then, to his utter amazement, she
kissed it and slowly put it into her mouth.

When it was all over she went and started the record
over again. The record was then one of the Top Ten
Tunes on the Hit Parade. It was April Stevens singing
"Teach Me Tonight."

30

The doorman unlocks the door to Linda Lowry's sealed apartment with his passkey, then slips away. Max goes in first and turns on the lights. Babette hesitates outside in the hall, suddenly leery of what she might sense there in the dead woman's apartment.

"C'mon inside," he says.

"In a minute."

"Hey. You aren't afraid, are you?"

"Of course not. No. I don't know."

"There's nothing to be afraid of. They took the body away days ago."

"It's not the body I'm afraid of."

Eventually she does go inside. Looks around. Is surprised to find she has no immediate reaction to the place. It's just an ordinary apartment, really, nothing very special about it. Except that the woman whose refuge it was got murdered in it, of course.

She peeks into the bathroom. There are bloodstains on the floor and on the walls. Staring at the bloodstains, she gets a slight chill and then a vague flash of nausea.

"This is where they found her. Lying on the floor there."

"Mmmm."

Max takes his Sony TC-55 cassette recorder out of his trenchcoat pocket and puts it on the table.

"I thought it might be a good idea to get this on tape. In case you come up with anything. You mind?"

Babette shakes her head.

"The killer gained entrance to her apartment by posing as a delivery boy. From a flower shop. The doorman who let us into the apartment got a look at him, but all he can remember is his eyes. Vacant-looking eyes, he said."

Another slight chill. As if from a vent on the floor. Max turns the tape recorder on, looking dubiously at Babette.

"Her wound," says Babette. "The one she died of. Was it in the throat?"

Max looks at her.

"How did you know that? Was it in the papers?"

"Not that I know of."

Her eyelids flutter closed, then open.

"Also in her hand," she says.

"What?"

"He cut her in the hand."

"I don't think so."

"OK."

"I mean I'm not sure. I only saw her briefly. In the morgue. But the only wound I remember was in the throat."

"OK."

"Why did you say he cut her hand? Did you pick that up psychically or what?"

"I don't know. It's not important."

"Maybe it is. Can you try and see it again?"

"I don't know."

A slight unsteadiness in the knees. Maybe if she sat down a moment.

"I'm going to sit down."

She goes to the bed, considers it briefly, then sits. Nausea breaks over her like a wave, recedes.

Max, studying her face intently, sees it.

"Hey, Babette, you OK?"

"Yes. I just felt a little sick for a moment. It passed, though."

"Why don't you lie down for a minute?"

"It's OK."

"No, go ahead. We've got time."

"OK."

She swings her feet up and lies down on the dead woman's bed and lets her eyes flutter closed. Babette feels herself drifting, just drifting. Then: A snowstorm. A line of old-fashioned romantic music, and a woman's voice: ". . . Did you say I've got a *lot* to learn . . . Well, don't think I'm trying *not* to learn . . ." Little bright-colored flowers. In a shiny round thing made of glass. No. In a bouquet. ". . . Since this is the perfect *spot* to learn . . ." What kind of flowers? Tulips? No, they're . . .

"They're anemones," says Babette aloud, "your favorites. How did you know that? I know a lot about you, Linda."

Max stares hard at the young woman on the bed.

"Babette . . . ?"

The images are beginning to come faster and stronger now, rushing toward her like subway stations from the front of a train picking up speed.

"What do you want with me?" says Babette tone-lessly, then adds, "A date. A what? A date. I want to date you."

It's coming faster now, the images and the dialogue speeding up, banking, careening toward her.

"I'd *love* to dance," murmurs Babette, "provided you put that thing away . . . well, they certainly taught you very nicely at Arthur Murray . . . you should have sim-ply called me . . . you didn't have to force your way in here at knifepoint. I didn't think you'd agree to go out with me, I thought I had to do it this way. Well, you were wrong . . ."

Babette starts to scream. Max rushes to her, grabs her
shoulders as she jerks to a sitting position, babbling:

"Bitch! Dirty, stinking, scheming bitch! Please don't
hurt me . . . I'll do anything, anything, please please
please please please get me a first-aid kit and take off
your clothes anything anything you say I'll make it up
to you for doing that I swear to you I swear it and now
take off your clothes stinking rotten bitch faster what
would you like me to take off first oh my God no
noooooooooooOOOOOO!!!"

"Babette? Babette, snap out of it!"

Babette is screaming one long scream.

Max tries to hold her on the bed, but she wrenches
free of him with surprising strength. He tackles her on
the floor and pins her down, yelling her name over and
over again in her face until her eyelids open and she's
out of whatever she was in. Max holds her a moment
longer on the floor and then releases her.

"Babette, you OK? Babette?"

She looks nervously around her, trying to adjust to
her surroundings, and then collapses against him in
wracking sobs of anguish.

"Sssshhh. It's OK now, Babette, it's OK now.
Sssshhhhh."

Thinking: Jesus H. Christ, I really needed this! I
don't have enough trouble with sex killers, I really
needed to get involved with crazy chicks who think they
can see the past.

A voice outside the door:

"What's going on in there?"

Oh, perfect—the neighbors think another murder's
going on in here.

"Who's in there? What's going on?"

A banging on the door. Excited voices.

"What was it? . . . Did you hear? . . . A fight between

a man and a woman . . . Call the cops! . . . Somebody call the cops!"

Max hugs Babette briefly, then goes to the door and opens it. A ring of frightened faces backs away from the door.

"Who are you? . . . What's going on in there? . . . We're calling the cops! . . ."

"OK, simmer down now, will you?" says Max with mounting irritation. "Just shut up, all of you!"

"Don't talk to him! Let the cops talk to him!"

"I *am* the cops, you schmucks!" says Max, and reaches into his jacket and flashes his shield.

The crowd's clamor shifts down to a low mutter as they inspect Max's shield. The doorman appears, frowning.

"What's all the commotion?" says the doorman.

"Everything is under control, McMartin," says Max, turning around and reentering the apartment. "Go back downstairs and drink your booze."

Babette bends down and picks something off Linda Lowry's floor. It's a Maltese cross, the kind firemen wear, on a delicate silver chain.

"Damn," she says.

"What's that?" says Max.

"Something my father gave me. The clasp keeps breaking." She fastens it around her neck. "Max, I'm so embarrassed about the way I carried on before."

"Don't be silly," he says. "Don't be embarrassed either."

But he's embarrassed too. The way she carried on was unlike anything in his experience. Babbling all those weird things. To think he'd considered getting involved with her romantically. That was about all he needed, to be romantically involved with a crazy lady.

What if she wasn't crazy, though? What if what she

said came not from the head of a crazy person but from that of a genuine psychic? Assuming that there were such things as psychics, of course. What if she really had tuned in on dialogue that had taken place in this apartment a few days before? How could such a thing be possible?

Somewhere he had read that sound waves never die out, that they just keep vibrating outward farther and farther, fainter and fainter, just likes echoes, and if you could ever build an amplifier sensitive enough you could tune into all the words that had ever been uttered throughout the course of history. Where had he read that one?

"When I was on the bed, babbling," she says, "did I say anything that made any sense to you?"

"Well, yes, of course you did."

"Really? Like what?"

"Well . . . well, like anemones, for instance. When the body was discovered there were a bunch of anemones in a vase on the table there."

"There were? Honest?"

"Yeah. I mean I saw them. You could have read that in the papers, though."

"Why would I fake a thing like that?"

"I'm not saying you *did*. But you might have read it and forgotten about it, and then it came up in your . . . in your . . ."

"Babbling?"

"Yeah. I don't know, though. It all sounded pretty good, what you said. The dialogue and everything. It all sounded pretty much like what might have gone on just before he killed her. Did you get any visual images?"

"I'm not sure. It all happened so fast. There were images, but they're all a little blurred and run-together in my mind."

"See if you can remember any of them."

"OK."

It's crazy, he thinks. It's completely crazy. But what if she really *can* tune in to some mystical channel in which she is able to see and hear everything that happened in the last few minutes of a victim's life? From what Natale told him, others have claimed to be able to do just that. The Dutch clairvoyants. Peter Hurkos, and that other guy, the one in the Bronx that Natale suggested he see. Dykshoorn. Marinus Dykshoorn. Those guys were supposed to be able to go to a crime scene and relive with all five senses the last few minutes of a victim's life. They've helped solve cases for police departments all over the world. What if this chick has the very same powers?

"Dancing," says Babette.

"What?"

"I see them dancing. The victim and the killer."

"Dancing? Why would they be dancing? The guy was unknown to her. He came there to kill her. What would either of them have been doing dancing?"

"I don't know. I'm just telling you what I'm getting. I'm not saying it makes any sense."

"Well, it doesn't," says Max. "Dancing. God!"

"Look, Max. I tell you I see her wounded in the throat, you say I probably read that in the papers. I tell you I see a cut in the hand, you say there was only one wound, in the throat. I tell you I see anemones, you say I probably read that in the papers, too. I tell you I see them dancing, you say it doesn't make sense. Maybe you don't want my help after all."

"I'm sorry, Babette, it's just that I—"

"This isn't such a great treat for me, you know, getting all these sickening images and becoming dizzy and nauseous and screaming. I have better ways I could be spending my time, if you really want to—"

"Babette, I'm sorry, really I am. I don't mean to sound so suspicious of everything you tell me. I really want to be convinced that what you're telling me is coming from some psychic source, but so far I just can't frankly—"

"The phone."

"What?"

Babette's eyes are closed again.

"The phone," she says quietly. "I hear it ringing while the killer is with her."

Max waits for her to go on. She doesn't.

"At what point do you hear it ringing?" he says.

"When the killer first comes into her apartment. No. When he kills her. Especially when he kills her. It just goes on ringing. Ringing and ringing and ringing."

Max looks at her a long moment, then sighs and shakes his head.

"OK, Babette, that's pretty good stuff. Not many people know about the phone calls, and those that do wouldn't have told you. I'm prepared to believe you're not a phony after all."

"Thanks," says Babette without smiling. "Thanks a heap."

Across the street the man scans Linda's building with his binoculars. The light is on in Linda's apartment. A young woman with long blond hair is seated on Linda's bed, talking to somebody. A man, also blond. Could they have rented poor Linda's apartment already? The young woman's hair is lovely. Lovelier even than Linda's. And so long, too. How he'd love to run his hands through that long blond hair. Well, she was worth keeping an eye on. Maybe he'd do a little research on her. If she wasn't too involved with the blond fellow, maybe she'd be open to a date with a *real* man.

31

12:05 P.M.

He sees Pamela Marlin exit from the office building along with about a dozen of her co-workers. He counts her co-workers and gets eleven. That does not seem to be a healthy number for them. He wills another person out of the revolving doors. Better.

Pamela and two other women—one about twenty or twenty-one like her and another perhaps fifteen to twenty years older—stand a moment in front of the building. He edges closer to catch what they are saying.

"Well, as long as it's done by five tonight," says the older woman, unsmiling. "But if it's not, Pamela, then heads are going to roll, I can promise you that."

"Don't worry, Miss Winston," says Pamela quietly, "It'll be done by five. I promise."

"If I were you, young lady, I'd limit my lunch today to twenty minutes," says the older woman.

"It'll be done by five," says Pamela, "don't worry."

"If *I* don't worry," says the older woman, "who's going to?"

The older woman turns on her heel and strides off uptown.

"That bitch," says Pamela under her breath.

"I don't know why you even put up with her," says her companion, and they head downtown toward an abbreviated lunch.

"I know," says Pamela. "Actually, she's not that bad

116

of a person. She just thinks that sort of behavior is what they expect of her as a supervisor."

He follows at a discreet distance, counting sidewalk squares and being careful not to step on cracks, and lets them cross the street and enter the Chock Full O'Nuts and hang up their coats and mufflers. Then he enters, pretends to look about for a place to sit, and drifts over to them.

The two people whose counter stools they are standing behind are just finishing their coffee. One of them has his paper turned to a story about the killings.

"God," says Pamela, looking at the paper and shaking her head, "it's getting so you're afraid to go home at night."

"You're not kidding me," says her friend. "Not that that particularly affects *you,* though."

"I know," says Pamela with a rueful laugh. "I doubt whether I'm going to be home one night before midnight all this week, the way old Frieda is hounding me."

"If she's so damned worried about those precious deadlines of hers, why doesn't she pitch in and help you herself?"

"I know," says Pamela.

The man in front of Pamela pays his check and stands up. The woman next to him gives him some change, which he puts down on the counter for a tip.

"Excuse me," says Pamela's companion, "but are you through with that newspaper? I want to see if they've got anything new on the killings."

"Oh, sure, go ahead," says the man. "Take it. Although I'm not sure it's the best thing to read while you're eating."

Both girls laugh.

"Especially for *her,*" says Pamela's companion, pointing to Pamela. "She lives practically next door to the first one who was killed."

"That right?"

Several people turn around to look at Pamela.

"I'm not too worried, though," says Pamela, blushing at having become the center of attention. "I bought something for protection. Just let him try to get into my apartment. He'll get the surprise of his life."

Not anymore I won't, thinks the man in the dark overcoat. Thanks for the tip, Pammy.

32

There is no getting around it. Max is either going to have to start acting upon the information Babette seems to be getting by extrasensory means, or else he can no longer justify taking her to crime scenes or spending time on anything but straight old-fashioned investigative techniques.

Max punches the playback button on his cassette recorder.

". . . They're anemones," says Babette's voice on the tape, "your favorites . . . how did you know that? . . . I know a lot about you, Linda . . ."

OK. Assuming that what he's listening to really is Babette psychically parroting a dialogue between Linda Lowry and her killer, that part suggests that the killer had been studying her a long time without her knowledge. Following her, observing her.

". . . What do you want with me? . . . A date . . . A what? . . . A date. I want to date you . . . I'd *love* to dance, provided you put that thing away . . . Well, they certainly taught you very nicely at Arthur Murray . . ."

He stops the tape. A date, dancing, Arthur Murray—what the hell was *that* about? Part of the same scene with the killer, or perhaps a snippet of dialogue out of Babette's own dating past? He starts the machine again.

". . . You should have simply called me . . . you didn't have to force your way in here at knifepoint . . . I didn't think you'd agree to go out with me . . . I thought I had to do it this way . . ."

No, it was part of the same scene. So the killer forced his way in at knifepoint, then asked for a date and began to dance with her? The way they taught him at Arthur Murray? Possible then the killer really did take dancing lessons at Arthur Murray? Worth checking out? Perhaps . . .

". . . Bitch! Dirty stinking scheming bitch. . . . Please don't hurt me, I'll do anything, anything, please please please please please . . . get me a first-aid kit and take off your clothes . . ."

First-*aid* kit? Max stops the tape, punches the rewind button, lets it go back near the start of the recording, before the part about the anemones.

". . . Her wound, the one that she died of," says Babette's voice on the tape, "was it in the throat?"

"How did you know that?" Max hears his voice reply. "Was it in the papers?"

"Not that I know of," says Babette, then: "Also in her hand."

"What?"

"He cut her in the hand."

"I don't think so."

Max stops the machine again. The first-aid kit and the part about cutting her in the hand seem to go together, but not quite. "Get me a first-aid kit and take off your clothes."

She cut *him*. That's it, *she* cut *him*. She goes for his knife, maybe when they're dancing, and in the struggle of trying to get it away from her, he gets cut in the hand. Then he screams at her, she begs him not to hurt her, he demands a first-aid kit and tells her to take off her clothes. Somehow he gets his cut taken care of, and she either takes off her own clothes or else he takes them off her, and then at some point he strangles her and cuts her throat.

OK, so where does that get us? What have we learned, if anything? Well, assuming that we can trust the source, we've learned that the killer has a thing about dancing, that he may have taken lessons at Arthur Murray, and that he has a cut hand, for starters. Big deal. Big goddamn deal.

33

It is marvelous, the man thinks, how everything works out.

It always seemed to him in the early stages of research on a woman that ultimate decisions about when and how to make face-to-face contact for his actual first dates would be arbitrary and hard. And yet, by the time all his research had been completed and neatly catalogued in his little book, the details of contact always seemed to suggest themselves quite logically and there was scarcely ever a need to ponder them for long.

That had been the case with Linda, and Bev, and

Ginny, and now it had proven to be true of Pamela as well. He'd originally planned to have his first date with Pam in her apartment like the others, and so he was understandably distressed to overhear her say at the lunch counter that she'd bought something for protection and dared the man who'd killed Linda, Bev, and Ginny to show up there.

Not that he blamed her. If *he* were a young single gal and had heard the accounts of Linda's, Bev's, and Ginny's deaths without knowing the full story of what happened, he'd probably be scared and get something for protection too.

But when he learned that Pammy's terrible supervisor was making her work late at the office he began to see how it might be a sign that his date with her was meant to take place there and not in her apartment.

Naturally, if he were going to plan a date at her office it was going to be necessary to get a sense of the place. So the following day he bought three box lunches —sandwiches, coffee, side orders of fries and slaw— scrawled something indecipherable on each container, and took it all up to Pam's office at lunchtime.

The girl at the reception desk couldn't make out the names on the lunches, of course, and since most of the bosses were out, she finally allowed him to wander around the office and show the lunches to those who were eating in and ask them if they recognized the orders. The tour of the office enabled him to case the place, to get an idea of the layout, to see that the head man had a private room as plush and comfortable as anyone's apartment and that it would do very nicely for his date with Pam. In fact, he even thought he'd caught a glimpse of a phonograph in there!

So now everything was set. From what he managed to overhear on his latest lunch near Pam, Frieda was

making her work late again tonight—she'd be there at
least till 10:00 P.M. Everyone else would be gone by
6:30. Between 7:00 and 8:00 was the perfect time
for him to make his appearance.

34

The big smile on Marilyn Middleton's face had faded
the moment he'd said he was there not to sign up for
dance lessons but to ask her questions about a homicide.
That's all she needed today, answering questions about
a homicide. The way she felt, she would have been
far more interested in committing a couple of her own
rather than answering questions about one somebody
else had done.

Still the kid was young and fairly attractive, and if
he was also horny, then maybe this wouldn't turn out
to be a total waste at that.

"OK, sweetheart," says the chesty redhead, lighting
up a brown cigarillo and exhaling a cloud of smoke,
"how can I help you?"

"We're looking for a suspect in a homicide case
who we think was very fond of dancing. There's reason
to believe he took lessons at Arthur Murray."

"What's his name?"

"We don't know that. All we know is that he's a male
Caucasian, probably in his late thirties, with dark hair,
who is a real nut on dancing."

She lets her eyes run over Max's body, idly undress-

ing it as she goes. He seems to have a good one—lean
and firm, without any slack. A kid like this could
probably go all night without even getting winded.

"That description could fit maybe half the guys
who come in here," she says, letting her eyes drop to
his crotch, checking the size of his bundle. His bundle
looked encouraging. God bless tight pants.

"I know that. I just wondered if you might recall a
man of that general description who took dancing lessons here in the recent past. A guy who was shy with
ladies, something of a loner, who might have struck
you as an oddball. Somebody who might be capable
of some kind of sex-related violence."

"Again," she says, letting her gaze drift back to
his face, "that description could fit maybe half the guys
who come in here. What's your first name, sweetheart?"

"Max."

"Max, I've been teaching dance here for the past six
years, and at a few less classy places before that, although I won't tell you for how long. The men who
come to take ballroom dancing lessons are not, generally
speaking, your smooth, outgoing, poised young sophisti-
cates who want to learn the latest step to wow them
at the discos. They are, for the most part, exactly the
kind of guy you describe.

"I teach them as much as they're capable of learning,
I rub my bosom against them a little, I let them cop a
few innocent feels, and for the time I'm dancing with
them I try to make them feel like they're in the first-
class ballroom of the old *Queen Elizabeth*. And if any
one of them showed up one night to rape me in an
elevator or to slit my throat in a dark alleyway, I
wouldn't be the slightest bit surprised."

"You certainly seem to have a marvelous opinion of
your students."

"I have a marvelous opinion of *all* men, Max. And

I've been around just long enough to have had it con-
firmed and reconfirmed anytime my memory grows
dim."

"Swell. So then nobody in particular stands out as
being any weirder or scarier than the rest?"

She studies him thoughtfully, exhaling more clouds of
smoke from her cigarillo.

"I could probably think of three or four who might
be slightly better bets as sex murderers," she says after
awhile. "But it'll cost you."

"Yeah? What'll it cost me?"

"A steak, three to five very dry Tanqueray martinis,
straight up with a twist, and a few soothing words."

35

Velez lets them into the apartment, then slips away.
Max turns on the lights and shuts the door behind them.

"You OK, Babette?"

"Sure."

She looks around. Admires the antique hurricane
lamps, the New England bric-a-brac. Virginia Manteuffel didn't have bad taste. And Babette could have prevented her death. Maybe.

"You want to rest a bit beforehand, kid?"

"No," she says. "Let's just get it over with."

She walks to the sofa, lies down on it, stares up at
the ceiling a moment, then carefully closes her eyes.

Max turns on the tape recorder.

At first she gets nothing and is almost relieved. Then she realizes she hasn't quite gotten herself attuned yet. Just slide on into it, Babette. Just ease slowly into the space between the channels. That's it . . . that's it . . .

A sudden flash of nausea, but it's over before she can even react to it. Then an image, subliminally brief, of a clipboard. A clipboard like a lifeguard uses. She hears a snatch of dialogue. A question, an embarrassing one. Without stopping to censor herself, she echoes it aloud:

"First of all . . . are you a virgin?" says Babette. "No, I'm not."

Max's ears perk up. Babette does not wish to go on, but then she remembers that she could have warned the dead girl and maybe prevented her death. She continues:

"At what age did you lose your virginity? Nineteen. And are you presently involved in a . . ."

The dialogue is coming faster to her now, rushing together, folding inward on itself, collapsing inward, imploding, as if time and space were being compressed.

". . . About how many times a week now would you say you have sex, Oh I'd say about three times on the average, fine and do you usually have-an-orgasm-most-of-the-time-listen-is-there-much-more-of-this-becauseI reallyhaveto . . ."

Babette begins to choke and, choking, she hurls herself into a sitting position, eyes still closed.

"Babette," says Max, alarmed.

Babette is grappling with invisible hands around her throat which are choking her, yet through the choking rushes the runaway dialogue like an express train whose brakes first catch, then slip, then catch, then slip:

". . . how-many-times-a-week-ontheaveragedoyou-

masturbate-second-how-long-does-each-sessionlastthird
howlongdoesit-take-you-to-achieve—"

"Babette," says Max, "maybe you ought to—"

". . . look-I-really-don'twanttoansweranymore-ques-
tions-I-understand-that-question-anumberofwomenfind
particularly-embarrassing-I'm-afraid-I'm-going-to-have
toaskyoutoleave-I-understand-andIdon'tblameyou—"

Max tears Babette's hands away from their clawlike
grip on her throat. She throws herself on him, eyes
closed.

"Max! Don't stop me! Don't stop me yet, please!"

"Babette, calm down! Open your eyes, Babette!"

"Please don't stop me, Max, I see it! I see the killing!
I see him killing her!"

She wrenches herself free of Max and goes wheeling
around the room, eyes closed, trying to hold onto her
trance experience, trying to remain in both the past and
the present simultaneously, dragging Max after her with
superhuman force. Where the past and future come together, that's where she is now and she won't let go.

"Babette, can you hear me?"

"Don't stop me, Max, I'm with the killer, I'm *with*
him, I'm *inside* him, just stay with me and keep me from
falling down or running into things and I'm going to
lead you right to where he *is*."

"Babette, this is crazy. I can't let you do—"

"Yes, you can, come on, Max, *please*. I can do it, I
can, if you just help me . . ."

"OK, kid, I'll try to stay with you, but—"

Babette claws at the door, eyes still clamped shut.
Max, supporting her with one arm, opens the door with
the other and leads her out into the hallway. Neighbors'
heads poke out through partly opened doors and stare
at the crazy person and her friend. Max flashes them
nervous smiles and opts for taking her down the back
stairway instead of waiting for the elevator.

Out on the street, to Max's immense relief, Babette's movements are slower and less jerky, albeit less confident. Eyes still closed, with Max's strong arm to keep her from falling, Babette leads them east across 53rd Street toward Third Avenue, then down Third in a southerly direction.

Passersby look at them and then glance quickly away, not sure whether Babette is blind or crazed or possessed of something that might be contagious. The wind whips at her open coat, but Babette is oblivious to the cold.

At the corner of Third and 46th Street Babette pauses, like a hunting dog that has temporarily lost the scent, then leads them east on 46th. Fifty feet into the block she pauses again, as if confused, and starts across the street.

"Babette," Max whispers, "what's going on?"

"I'm losing him," she says. "I'm getting confused."

"Babette, I don't think you're following him anymore from the scene of the Manteuffel homicide. Do you know where you are now?"

"He's right around here somewhere," says Babette, as if looking for a pair of misplaced gloves, "but I just can't seem to put my hands on him."

"Babette, do you know where we are now? We're right across the street from Linda Lowry's apartment."

"I don't think that's what I'm . . . I think it's this way, Max."

Babette starts across the downtown side of 46th Street, then stops once more, turns around, and sniffs the psychic wind.

Upstairs, in the building just behind them, a man watches Babette's strange movements with growing fascination. He picks up a pair of binoculars and trains them on her as she turns first one way and then the other.

She looks familiar to him. Where has he seen . . . ? Yes. The other night. In Linda's apartment. The new tenants. But why are her eyes closed, and why is the blond guy holding her as if he thinks she'll fall? Something is not right about those two.

Still training the binoculars on them, he slides the phone over to where he's sitting and reaches for the Manhattan Directory. He looks up a number, then dials and waits. The number rings, then is answered.

"Executive House, good evening."

"Oh, uh, yes. I was calling about an apartment in your building that I heard was vacant? The one that poor Lowry woman was living in. Has it been rented yet, do you know?"

"No, sir, it hasn't. Were you interested in seeing it?"

The man replaces the receiver on its hook and puts both hands on his binoculars. So they *aren't* the new tenants. Then what were they doing in Linda's apartment? And, more importantly, what are they doing now in front of his building?

He appraises the girl carefully. She's sensational-looking. And that long blond hair. Why, she's better-looking than most of the women he's researching. Maybe better-looking than *all* of them. He would sure like to have a girl as beautiful as she is. Only one snag—the guy. If they're married, he'll have no part of her. But if they're not . . . ? Perhaps a little research on the girl would determine her suitability as a potential date.

He is just about to get his coat and prepare to follow them when he sees something metallic drop from the girl's coat. She and the guy proceed slowly on 46th Street. The metallic thing remains on the sidewalk.

36

As he approaches the locked glass door he sees that the
watchman is dozing. On the fourth ring the guy rouses
himself, looks at the door, starts to pretend he wasn't
asleep, says the hell with it and drops the pretense.

"Yeah, what is it?"

"Mercury Messenger. I have a delivery for Arista.
Sixteenth floor."

The nightman sighs and ushers him inside.

"Sign the book."

He signs the book simply Mercury, then follows the
nightman to the elevator.

"You might as well go up by yourself," says the
nightman.

"Thanks."

The elevator door opens, then closes behind him. He
presses sixteen, envisions how Pamela is going to look:
pale blond hair, washed-out blue eyes. A little sad, a
little vulnerable. Small breasts, nice behind. Little brown
mole on her right cheek up near the ear. Falling in love
again is already making him feel like he's walking on
air. When he and Pamela start dating seriously he'll
help her cope with Frieda the Tyrant so she'll never
have to work this late again.

The door opens. He alights, makes his way along the
hall. 1601. He turns the knob and enters.

"Oh!"

"Sorry to startle you, miss. Mercury Messenger. I have the type you ordered."

"You do? But we didn't . . . that is, *I* didn't . . . Well, let's have a look at it."

She reaches out for the flat square envelope in his hand. His hand remains at his side.

"Lonely up here this time of night. Aren't you afraid?"

Nervous giggle from Pamela.

"Well, sort of. But since Miss Winston . . ."

Changes her mind. Why talk to messengers anyway? She reaches out again for the envelope, a haughty expression on her face.

"May I have it?" she says.

He is surprised. He thought she'd be nicer, even to a messenger.

"Have it?" he says.

"Yes."

Pause. Savor her discomfort, greater than your own. Maybe Frieda is just what she deserves, the little bitch.

"Have what?" he says.

"The envelope, of course."

He pulls the door shut behind him.

"Not yet," he replies.

Giggles involuntarily. Thinks it's a game. Thinks you're kidding. *Hopes* you're kidding.

"Come *on* now," she says. "I don't have all night."

She represses her natural fear and approaches him, and reaches out for the envelope.

"I really must insist," she says.

Attempts to snatch it from under his arm. He resists. She's surprised, expected him to let it go.

"Come *o-on*," she says.

"All right, but first I have to ask you something."

"What?" she says.

"Do you have a phonograph?"

"A what?"

"A *phonograph*. Please do not say *what*."

"I don't know. What do you want with a phonograph?"

"I want to play a record. So we can dance."

"So we can *dance?* Are you crazy?"

He grabs her suddenly by the front of her blouse.

"No, I am not crazy. Kindly do not ask me such things if you know what's good for you."

Her eyes widen in fear. Her mouth drops open. He releases her, is suddenly contrite.

"I'm sorry, Pamela. I don't want to hurt you. But I will if I have to. If you don't cooperate with me. Do you understand?"

She's speechless.

"Do you understand me, Pamela? Nod your head if you understand."

Nods her head. Good.

"Now then. Do you have a phonograph or don't you?"

The girl stares at him, mute with terror. What does he want with a phonograph? Does he really only want to dance? Maybe so. Maybe if she dances with him, he'll be satisfied and leave. Or maybe Frieda . . .

"There's a phonograph in Mr. Frank's office," she says.

"Good girl. Come along, then, and trip the light fantastic with me."

She stands there immobilized.

"I said come along, Pamela."

She doesn't move. He takes out his knife and clicks it open. She looks like she's going to scream, but wisely chooses not to. She leads him out of the room and down a short hallway into the boss's office. Big antique desk. Thick carpet on the floor. Leather Chesterfield sofa.

Several expensive leather chairs. A little bar. A combination FM radio and stereo.

He takes out his record, puts it on the turntable, turns on the stereo, puts the needle into the first groove.

Did you say I've got a lot to learn?

Well, don't think I'm trying not to learn . . .

"What are you going to do to me?" she says.

"Have a date with you."

"A date?"

"Yes."

She just looks at him.

"Why?" she says.

"Why? Because I like you. Because I think you'll like me. Because I've been admiring you from afar for a long time and I know a great deal about you and I think we could have something good together."

"What is it you know about me?" she says.

"Oh, I know that if the man who's killed those women ever came to your apartment you'd spray him with Mace. And I know you don't have many dates. And I know how you satisfy yourself when you're alone—and I don't think there's anything wrong with it either— but now you won't have to do that anymore because you have *me*."

Her face has gotten very red. He holds out his hands.

"Shall we trip the light fantastic?" he says.

She bursts into tears.

"Please don't cry," he says.

• She continues to cry.

"Pamela, please don't cry," he says.

He tries to comfort her. It only makes her cry harder. He waits patiently for her to finish. She doesn't show any sign of finishing.

"I *said* don't cry," he repeats, but it doesn't seem to have any effect on her. He is getting impatient. He is getting, frankly, a little ticked. None of his *other* women responded to his offer to trip the light fantastic by crying.

"If you don't stop crying," he says, "then we can't dance."

No response.

"If we can't dance, then we will have to do something else. Something that you might not want to do right now."

No response.

"OK, Pamela, that's it. I've had it. Go and lie down."

Pamela doesn't move.

"I *said* go and lie down."

He holds the knife under her nose so she can see it through her tears. She stops crying and starts walking toward the leather couch. He looks at the leather couch and decides it won't do. The desk is bigger anyway.

"Not on the couch," he says. "On the desk."

He goes to the desk. He removes and neatly stacks the papers that were on the desk on the floor, aligning the edges of them with the molding at the floor line. He motions for her to lie down on the desk. She averts her eyes and climbs up on the desk and lies down on her stomach, sobbing softly.

"Good girl," he says.

"Please don't hurt me," she says in a tiny voice.

"Do as I say and you won't get hurt."

"I'll do whatever you say," she says and starts sobbing so heavily her body shakes.

"Stop crying," he says. "And stop shaking."

She tries to stop, both the crying and the shaking, but she can't. It is really ticking him off. The shaking even more than the crying.

"I said stop. Can't you stop?"

She is crying and shaking too hard to answer him. He has to stop that shaking. He looks around for something with which to stop the shaking. He sees the cord on the venetian blinds. He cuts off two lengths of it and brings them back to the desk.

He ties her wrists. Three coils each, three knots each. He ties the ends of the cords to the legs of the desk. He ties her ankles. Three coils each, three knots each. He ties the ends of the cords to the legs of the desk. She is still shaking, but not as badly. She has stopped crying.

He looks at her lying on the desk, wrists and ankles tightly bound, and finds himself beginning to get aroused. He slowly pulls the hem of her wool skirt up her legs, past the calves, past the knees, past mid-thighs, past the legbands of her pale pink panties, over the swell of her buttocks.

He pauses to take it all in. Then he slowly pulls the waistband of her panties down, over the swell of her now-bare buttocks, down, down, down below the crotch with the fuzzy blond hair.

Suddenly he hears a noise behind him. He whirls around. An older woman stands there, startled, face amazed. Of course. It's Frieda.

"Hello, Frieda."

"What's . . . what's the meaning of this? How did you get in here?"

He feels suddenly exhausted. Suppressing a yawn, he walks over to Frieda and shows her the knife. She doesn't look at it.

"I don't want to hurt you, Frieda—no, not even you —but I will if I have to."

"If you don't get out of here this instant, I'm going to scream."

"I wouldn't advise that, Frieda, I really wouldn't advise that at all."

He holds the knife under her nose. Frieda thinks it over. He might be bluffing, but he might not be.

"What do you want me to do?" she says, sotto voce.

"Do what I say and you won't get hurt," he says. "Come over here. Right next to the desk."

She approaches the desk. Uncertainly.

"Good girl, Frieda. Now then. I would like you to kiss Pamela's ass."

"What?"

"Kindly do not say *what*. You heard me. Kiss Pamela's ass. How many times have you made her kiss *yours*? Well, now it's time to turn the tables. Kiss it, Frieda. Left cheek first."

An involuntary snort of laughter betrays Pamela's mixed feelings over this new turn of events.

"You *can't* be serious," says Frieda.

"Try me."

He moves closer. He touches the tip of the blade to Frieda's neck. She shudders.

"Go on, Frieda. Left cheek first."

Frieda bends down, a millimeter at a time, virginal lips extended toward virginal buttock.

"Go on, Frieda. Do it."

A tentative kiss. A little peck.

"Good girl. Now do it like you mean it."

Another peck with the lips. A shudder of revulsion.

"Once more with feeling now. Go ahead. A great big smack, Frieda. A great big wet one. Go ahead."

Lips press against gluteal cheek, linger.

"Go ahead, that's right. Kiss it, Frieda. Kiss it a lot. Cover it with kisses."

Tentatively at first, then with mounting fervor, the older woman rains kisses on the young girl's buttocks.

"Good, Frieda, good! More! Don't stop!"

Hands come up to frame the target. More kisses on both cheeks.

"Very good. Very good, Frieda. Now for step two. Climb on top of her."

"What?"

"I *said* climb on top of her."

"I thought you said if I . . ."

"What I *said* was, if you do what I say you won't get hurt. You did the first part fine, but there's more. Now climb on top of her."

Frieda doesn't move.

"I won't do this."

"Suit yourself."

He scratches the tip of the blade against the skin of Frieda's neck. A thin red line, like a cotton thread, appears. Frieda climbs heavily up on the desk.

"Good girl, Frieda. Now lie down on top of Pamela."

She lies down on top of Pamela.

"Don't worry, Pamela," she whispers.

He goes to the drapes and cuts more lengths of cord. He comes back to the desk. He ties Frieda's left ankle to Pamela's left ankle, Frieda's right ankle to Pamela's right ankle, Frieda's wrists to Pamela's wrists.

"You won't get away with this, you know," says Frieda. "They'll catch you and they'll send you to the electric chair."

"Quiet, Frieda. Remember what I said. Do what I say and you won't get hurt."

Frieda is tied securely. Her gray wool skirt lies primly across her calves. He slowly pulls it up. Past calves to surprisingly firm thighs. Tops of stockings rolled in garters. He pulls the hem of Frieda's skirt up above her crotch. Baggy beige old-lady panties. He pulls them down.

A whisper: "No . . ."

Nice ass for an old lady, he thinks. Very nice. Touch it. Pretty firm. Surprisingly firm. Run finger down into crack. Some wetness there. Frieda, you old dog, you! Run finger back down Frieda's crack to Pamela's crack. A little wetness there too. Well well well . . .

37

Babette has been through every article of clothing she owns. She has searched every square inch of floor in her mother's apartment. She has looked between the cushions on the upholstered chairs and couches and everywhere else it is possible to look, and she has not found it.

It is by now obvious to Babette that the fireman's medallion which her father had given her and which she'd sworn to wear every day and night for the rest of her life was lost, gone forever, probably dropped in Virginia Manteuffel's apartment or somewhere outside it on the street, and it would never be recovered. She will, of course, have Max take her back to the Manteuffel apartment to search for it, but she already knows she will never see it again.

She feels heartsick. She knows it's irrational but she nonetheless feels that losing the medallion has in some way weakened the link between her and her father's protection.

38

After retrieving the fireman's medallion from the side-walk the man had followed the girl and her companion to an apartment house on East 82nd Street. The girl had gone inside alone. He'd then tailed her companion to—of all places—the 17th Precinct on 51st Street. Her boy-friend was a cop!

Further research disclosed that the girl's name was Babette Watson, that she was twenty years old and Catholic, that her boyfriend was a homicide cop named Max Segal, that he was Jewish, and that he was working on the Lowry, Rachlin, and Manteuffel cases. Well well well.

Since Babette was Catholic, this automatically made her eligible in his eyes as a prospective date—mixed marriage, as everybody knew, was a sin. Besides which, if he couldn't beat the time of some dumb Jew cop whom he'd been able to tail unobserved to Babette's house and then back to the 17th Precinct, then he might as well give up girls entirely!

39

"Two very dry Tanqueray martinis with a twist," says Max to the waitress.

"I'll have the same," says Marilyn Middleton.

The waitress looks to see if she is kidding. She is not kidding. Marilyn waves the waitress away.

"So," says Marilyn, puffing thoughtfully on her brown cigarillo, "you want me to give you three or four weirdos who I've taught to dance, do you?"

"That is what you promised to deliver," says Max.

"And, sweetheart, I *always* deliver what I promise," she replies. "OK, let's see. First of all, there was a little beauty by the name of Henry."

"Henry what?"

"I'll think of it, just give me time. Henry was a certified public accountant. Short, mild-mannered little guy. Bald. Had baby-soft hands. Always dressed very prissily, like any minute he expected there to be an inspection or something. I swear to you, he looked like he had hospital corners on his underwear. Henry . . . what the hell was his last name? Never mind, it'll come to me.

"Anyway, old Henry was the soul of politeness. It was always 'Miss Middleton this' and 'Miss Middleton that,' and all the while we were dancing he was copping feels and pretending they were accidental. Well, one night as we conclude his lesson, he asks me if we can have a drink. He being my last lesson of the day, and me being somewhat lonelier than usual that night, I say what the hell, let's do it.

"Well, first of all it turns out that where old Henry is inviting me to have a drink is, you guessed it, nowhere but Chez Henry. Now I've been around a little in my time, even tangled with a few CPA's, so I didn't see this as anything I couldn't handle.

"No sooner do we get settled with drinks than old Henry drops his hand on my knee and lets it sort of die there. Since *he* didn't make any mention of it, neither did *I,* and when he hadn't moved it for about ten minutes I stopped thinking about it. Which is exactly when the hand, with a mind of its own, begins creeping steadily upward. Henry, of course, never even acknowledges that he *has* a hand, much less that it's doing anything at all unusual.

"You know, Max, I like a good feel as much as the next gal, but I sure would have preferred it if he'd been aboveboard about the whole thing. If he'd said something like, 'Miss Middleton, I'd certainly like to run my hand up your leg and fool around inside your undies.'

"Anyway, some nights I'm less discriminating about playmates than others, and I figured a hand on the bird is worth two in my bush, so I let him have his way with me. Well, let me tell you, was *that* ever a mistake. No sooner do we really get down to it than shy polite little Henry becomes a tiny tyrant. 'Miss Middleton, lie *this* way,' and 'Miss Middleton, lie *that* way,' and 'Miss Middleton, don't make so much noise.' Aside from which old Henry's pecker never attained a more rigid consistency than al dente linguini. And to top it all off, when he sees me for his next lesson at the studio he acts like I'm some nasty old tart who'd seduced *him.*"

"So that little beauty is Henry," says Max, jotting down some notes. "Henry X."

"Henry . . . Fortenbaugh," she replies. "Yes, that's it, Fortenbaugh. Henry Fortenbaugh, CPA. Certified Prissy Asshole. Then the next little number I remember was a character named Volkening. He signs up for the basic course and right away it strikes the instructor who's assigned to him that he's a little off the wall. I agreed to take Volkening off her hands because I figured I can handle *anybody*.

"The guy develops an immediate crush on me. Then he asks me for a drink. The experience with Henry is still fresh in my mind, so I say, 'Thanks, but no thanks, sweetheart.' The minute I refuse him he starts getting very weird. Talking very ominously about how all the women who have rejected him have met with bad ends. Wonderful stuff like that. He alternates between acting very snide and superior and being very obsequious— very, you know, kissyassy.

"Then he starts following me home from the studio. Wonderful, huh? Just what I need. I talked to my boss about it and I got him to back me up on terminating Volkening's contract and refunding his fees for the unused lessons, when old Volkening just ups and disappears. Just totally never shows up again. After a while I forgot about him. I've never even *thought* about him till you asked me to find you some weirdos."

"What was Volkening's first name?"

"Uh . . . Steven. No. Stefan. That's it, Stefan."

"What did he look like?"

"Like you described. Dark hair, a *tiny* bit deranged-looking, I suppose. Not all that bad-looking, really. About average height, maybe a shade taller."

"About five-ten?"

"About that, yeah."

"Did he wear a dark overcoat?"

"It was spring. He just wore a topcoat—as I remember, I *think* it was dark."

"Well, he sounds like a better bet than old Henry."

"He does, doesn't he? But so does another guy I taught by the name of Fred Fredericks. About the same height and build, also had dark hair, and eyes that were a little on the weird side. Also wore dark clothing. Fred's thing was apologizing. He'd step on your toes just so he could apologize. He literally fell all over himself apologizing. And then he'd have flashes of anger over nothing at all that were really scary. I think he hated women. But that didn't stop him from copping feels, no sir. At least Fred completed the course, which is more than most of the weirdos do."

"Did Fred ask you for a drink?"

"Of *course* he asked me for a drink, sweetheart. What *else* are you going to do with a nice lady who's been letting you rub against her bosom and cop feels while pretending it's all part of the basic course?"

"And did you go?"

"Nope. Which didn't endear me to Fred anymore than it did to Volkening. Fred didn't follow me home from the studio, but I did start getting a lot of calls from a breather. I'm pretty sure it was Fred. I think I recognized his wheeze."

"Well, that sounds like at least two leads worth following up so far," says Max. "Don't tell me there are others?"

The waitress sets the four Tanqueray martinis down on the table. Marilyn picks one up, chugalugs it, and sighs with pleasure.

"You keep setting up martinis, sweetheart, and old Marilyn will keep coming up with weirdos. Want to hear about Waldo?"

"Who's Waldo?" says Max.

"Waldo Nardo. I remember the name because we used to kid about it at the studio. Nardo the Weirdo we called him."

"Did he fit the description, too?"

She nods, while downing her second martini. "Oh sure. Dark hair, dark eyes, dark clothing. Same height. Eyes a little on the wild side. Waldo was another shy one. Never had much small talk. Also very polite, with occasional flashes of anger. Also hated women, I think. And loved them, too, naturally."

"And Waldo asked you for a drink, too, of course," says Max.

"Of course."

"And did you go?"

"Nope," she says. "Not with him either. But I didn't come right out and say I wasn't interested. I sort of kept putting him off. Kept stringing him along, you know?"

"How come?"

"Partly because I didn't think he'd take the rejection very well, I suppose. And partly because you never know when you might want a little male companionship, no matter *how* off-the-wall it might be. I don't know, I guess I figured old Waldo might be kinky. And that, frankly, intrigued me."

"Is that so?" says Max.

"That's so," says Marilyn. "What about you, sweetheart? Are you kinky?"

Max laughs, and signals the waitress for another round of double martinis.

"I presume," he says, "that you have addresses, telephone numbers, and so forth for these guys."

"Oh, absolutely," she says.

"Which you will be more than happy to share with me," says Max.

"Oh, absolutely," she says.

"And it will cost me," says Max.

"Oh, absolutely," she says.

"What will it cost me?" says Max.

"Well, after we get through eating those steaks you promised we were getting," she says, leaning forward and lightly combing his hair with her fingers, "how's about we have me for dessert?"

40

POLICE DEPARTMENT
NEW YORK, N.Y. 10038

OFFICE OF THE CHIEF OF DETECTIVES
TO ALL COMMANDING OFFICERS:

Please acquaint all members of your
command with the following information
concerning the individual responsible
for five homicides between Dec. 17 and
Dec. 22 in Manhattan.

DESCRIPTION:
Perpetrator is described as follows:
Male, white, 25 to 45 years of age,
medium to tall in height, medium build,
dark hair, pale complexion, dark eyes.

He has been seen in black or dark brown
overcoat, dark trousers and shoes.

MODUS OPERANDI:
He has thusfar confined himself to
Homicide Zone 3 in the midtown Manhattan
area, on both East and West Sides.
He has chosen attractive, single Caucasian
females, living alone, aged mid-20s to mid-40s
as victims. In all cases contact was made at
night in early evening hours.

       In one case perpetrator approached his
victims in a deserted office building posing
as a messenger. In other three cases perpetrator made contact with his victims in their
apartments shortly after they returned from
work. In one of these cases perpetrator posed
as delivery boy from florist.

       All these crimes indicate premeditation.
Perpetrator is clever enough to gain entrance
to scene of crime without forcible entry. In
all cases victims were wholly or partially

undressed prior to being killed, though not
necessarily molested sexually. No underpants
have been found either on or near any of the
victims, giving rise to speculation perpetrator
is underwear fetishist.

     Causes of death have been: strangulation,
knife wounds in throat, blows on head with fireplace tool. Despite varying causes of death,
all five homicides appear to have been committed
by one perpetrator. There is great similarity
of m.o.'s, and all witnesses' descriptions of
perpetrator correspond, as do partial latent
prints found at crime scenes.

PSYCHOLOGY:
Psychologists disagree on perpetrator's
motivations but diagnose him as schizophrenic
and paranoid. He is probably timid and
a loner and inept at establishing inter-
personal relationships, particularly with
women.

EDUCATION:

Educational consultants who have studied
perpetrator's letter to columnist Monahan
estimate he is probably a high school
graduate.

CAUTION:

This man is armed and dangerous. He
may attack anyone who attempts to
apprehend or arrest him.

NOTIFICATION:

Any information relating to this case
should be telephoned to 3rd Homicide
at the 17 Pct.:

                    Telephone #: 826-3234
                    Patrick J. Noonan
                    Chief of Detectives

41

The prospect of taking on a woman who had close to twenty years on him really had had Max worried. He did not believe in faking rapture in bed and he was afraid that he might have to do so.

He did not have to do so. The slack part just under Marilyn Middleton's chin was, in fact, the only really slack part on her entire body, and her body was remarkable.

He lies now with his head upon her naked bosom, and she continues to comb his hair with her fingers. For the last four hours—one hour for each of the four suspects she has given him—they have been making very spirited, very flashy love. She has been not only passionate, which was not that big of a surprise, but incredibly sweet and tender as well. He had not expected that much sweetness in somebody so outwardly tough.

"You're really something," he says, moving up to her face and gently kissing her on the chin, the forehead, the cheeks, the lips.

"You're not exactly nothing yourself," she says.

"I'm sure this is going to sound horrible," he says, "but I had no idea it was going to be this wonderful."

"Oh, shut up," she says. "You got your four suspects, I got a piece of ass."

"I'd really like to see you again," he says.

"Oh, *Christ,*" she says, "will you just shut *up?*"

"I mean it," he says. "I don't want this to be a one-night stand."

"Well, don't get your hopes up, sweetheart," she says, "because that's all it was. Two people using each other in a time-honored way."

"Why do you want to cheapen it?" he says.

"Why do you want to dignify it?" she says and stops, loses temporary control over her voice, and gets it back again.

"Look," she says. "You're very sweet and everything like that, all right? But you're really not my type. If you had any grace at all you'd just slip into your clothes and creep on out of here."

Max pulls himself up on one elbow and regards her carefully for a moment, then gets the rest of the way up.

"OK," he says, "if that's the way you want it. Here. I'll write down my phone number. If you ever decide you might want to see me again, you can call me."

"Don't hold your breath, big boy," she says.

She waits till he is out the door and down the hall before she bursts into tears.

42

Max and Caruso roll up to the office building where Pamela Marlin and Frieda Watson were killed. The big plate-glass doors are already locked for the night. Caruso taps on the glass with his shield.

The guy inside is nodding off, wakes with a jolt, sees

Max and Caruso, curses silently, comes to the door. They both flash their shields through the glass. The guy starts fiddling with locks so fast he almost breaks them off.

"Sorry, officers, I didn't realize you were—"

"We're looking for a night watchman named Rodriguez," says Caruso. "That you?"

The watchman nods about twenty times.

"Understand you were on duty the night of the Marlin and Winston homicides, Rodriguez, that right?"

The watchman gets off another twenty nods. It's chilly in the lobby, but his forehead is already pimpled with sweat.

"The guy was a maniac, that guy," says the watchman. "Who knew he would do something as sick as that, huh?"

Caruso wearily takes out his notebook and his ballpoint pen and slowly begins to write.

"The Medical Examiner has estimated the times of deaths at between 8:30 and 9:30 P.M.," says Caruso. "You were on duty at that time, weren't you?"

The watchman fires off a few more fast nods.

"You told the officer who made out the initial report that you admitted an individual to the building at about 8:15 P.M. on the night in question, that he identified himself as being a messenger from Mercury Messenger Service, that he signed the book and then went up to the sixteenth floor in the elevator, unescorted. Is that correct?"

"I didn't know he was a maniac, that guy. I couldn't tell from the way he looked, you know what I mean? I mean he looked like a messenger to me. How was I gonna know he would do such a thing, huh? How was I gonna know?"

"Rodriguez. What I asked you just now. Was that substantially correct, to the best of your recollection?"

Rodriguez fires off a few more fast nods.

"Admtted. mssngr. to bldg. about 2015 hrs.," writes Caruso in his notebook. "Idntfd. slf. as mssngr. frm. Merc. Mssngr., sgnd. bk., wnt. up to 16th flr. in elev., unescrtd."

"You said this individual came back down in the elevator about 9:00 P.M., signed the book again and exited from the premises, is that correct?"

Rodriguez nods some more. The nodding is beginning to get to Max.

"What were you doing during the period of time that the individual was upstairs?" says Caruso.

"I was here. Right here at my post, watching the door."

"Wtchman. was at pst., wtchng. door while mssnger. upstrs.," writes Caruso slowly in his notebook.

"Rodriguez," says Max, "didn't you think it was a little bit odd that this messenger was upstairs delivering a package for three-quarters of an *hour?*"

The watchman throws his hands up in the air.

"I didn't know the guy was a maniac, you know what I mean? I mean I couldn't tell from the way he *looked.* He looked—"

"Like a messenger," says Max. "I know. But you mean to say it never occurred to you to go up in the elevator to see what was taking him so long?"

The watchman shakes his head vigorously.

"Why not?" says Caruso.

"Because my job is at my post. Down here at the desk. Watching the door."

"You're making sure that nothing happens to the door," says Max, "but you don't give a shit that a guy is upstairs raping and killing the tenants of the building who you're being paid to protect, is that it?"

"Hey, gimme a break, willya?" says the watchman. "How was I gonna know he was upstairs raping and killing? I thought he was waiting for a delivery to go back and maybe goin' to the john or something in the meantime, y'know?"

"Going to the john?" says Max. "For three-quarters of an hour?"

"Can you give us a description of this individual?" says Caruso.

"Yeah. Like I told the other officer, he had on a dark coat and pants, dark shoes, and he wasn't wearing a hat or anything on his head."

"Drk. ct. & pnts., drk. shs., wsn't. wrng. ht.," writes Caruso in his notebook.

"Was he tall, short, dark, fair, or what?" says Max.

"Dark," says the watchman. "Regular height. You know."

"No we don't," says Max. "You saw him, we didn't."

"Did he have any distinguishing marks on his face that you remember?" says Caruso. "Moles, birthmarks, scars, or anything of that nature?"

"I don't know," says the watchman. "He could've."

"Did he or didn't he?" says Max.

"I don't think so," says the watchman.

"No disting. mks. on fce.," writes Caruso.

"Do you remember the color of his hair and eyes?" says Caruso.

"They were just your regular color," says the watchman. "Nothing unusual."

"What the fuck does that mean, 'regular color'?" says Max.

"You know, nothing special. Dark," says the watchman.

"Brown?" says Max.

"Yeah, brown," says the watchman.

"Brown *hair* or brown *eyes?*" says Max.

"Both," says the watchman.

"Can you think of any other unusual or distinguishing characteristics you might have noticed?" says Caruso.

The watchman shakes his head.

Max and Caruso stand looking at the watchman a long moment, then shake their heads. Max reaches out and taps the badge on the watchman's coat.

"Rodriguez," says Max, "you're a credit to your badge."

43

When the phone first starts to ring he is so deeply asleep that he doesn't even know what it is that is making the sound. Swimming heavily upward through the leaden layers of consciousness, he breaks surface and opens his eyes and tries to position himself in the room and in his life.

What the ringing is coming from is the telephone. But what it was you were supposed to say into it when you picked it up was still not clear to him. He picks up the receiver anyway and makes a noise with his voice.

"Gnnnngh."

"Max?"

"Nnnnh."

"Is Max Segal there? It's sort of an emergency."

At the word *emergency* Max's natural cop reflexes bring him instantly to full wakefulness.

"This is Max. Who's this?"

The voice, that of a girl, begins to cry.

"Max, I'm sorry to be calling you so late. I didn't know who else to call. It's Babette."

"Babette. What's wrong?"

"I, uh, had a bad experience, with Freddy, and—"

"With Freddy, your stepfather?"

"—and I can't stay in that apartment anymore, I just can't, and I don't have anywhere to go, and I wondered if I could stay with you tonight until I find a place to—"

"Sure."

"What?"

"I said sure, of course you can. Come on over."

"Is that all right? Are you sure? It'll just be for tonight."

"Where are you now?"

"I don't know. In a payphone."

"Are there any cabs on the street?"

"I don't know. A few. But I don't have any money."

"Just jump in a cab and come on over. The address is 346 East 19th Street. Between First and Second. Ring the bell and I'll come out and pay the guy."

"Thank you, Max. I'm sorry to be calling you so late. I just didn't know who else to call."

"Don't be silly. Hurry up and get into a cab."

"OK."

He replaces the receiver on the phone and turns on the light and looks at his watch: 3:30. Good God.

He gets out of bed and goes into the bathroom and surveys his appearance in the medicine cabinet mirror. His hair looks terrible and he needs a shave. Well, who the fuck wouldn't have terrible hair and need a shave at three-fucking-thirty in the morning? Besides which, if she's as upset as she sounded on the phone she's not going to be checking out hair and shaves.

He pulls on a pair of jeans and boots and decides that the Police Academy sweatshirt he had worn to bed is

OK to remain in and he really doesn't need to shave. Then he ducks back in the bathroom and plugs in his electric razor and shaves anyway.

Is there the slightest chance in the world that she might be up for a little lovemaking? Nah, for God's sake, Max, don't be such a pig—the goddam girl is crying her eyes out over some scene she had with her goddam stepfather, and all you can think about is whether she might be up for a little lovemaking. The goddam girl also does not seem like the worldliest person in town, plus which she fucking *trusts* you enough to come and stay in your apartment all night, and all you can thing of is getting laid. Jesus!

On the other hand. On the other hand, she certainly seems to have a gigantic crush on him, and he's made it plain he's pretty interested in her, too, and they *have* spent a fair amount of time together over drinks and going around to crime scenes together, and here she is coming over to his apartment at three-thirty in the A.M. to sleep—where is it she's expecting to sleep if not with him? After all, she's not a kid, she's twenty years old—old enough to have it at least cross her *mind* that when a girl comes over to a guy's house to spend the night the thought of sex might just possibly come *up*, right?

Where Max has gotten to on this issue by the time the doorbell rings is that if he *doesn't* make at least *some* kind of a rudimentary pass at her she'll probably think he's a fag, and if he *does* make a pass at her then he's a pig.

He goes out and pays the cabbie and takes her into the apartment and triple-locks the door behind them. She's wearing a coat and, apart from the fact that she looks like she's been crying, she looks just luscious.

"Hi," he says, suddenly shy with her.

"Hi," she says, picking up his shyness and betraying her own.

"Nice place you have here," she says, looking around.

"Thanks. Uh, you want a drink?"

She nods and takes off her coat. She is wearing jeans, a blouse, and a sweater.

"Scotch and soda, right?" he says.

She smiles.

"Scotch and soda is fine," she says. "Max, thank you, I mean that. I'm so sorry to have called you so late and come over here so late and—"

"*Stop* it, for God's sake," says Max kiddingly, then sees from the look in her eyes that she thought he was really yelling at her and he makes a fake laugh noise to prove he wasn't serious. "If you say you're sorry one more time, I'm going to deck you," he adds.

He pours her a scotch and soda, then fixes a brandy stinger for himself. He hands her the drink and motions her onto the sofa next to the bar, but she remains standing. She takes a big gulp of her drink.

"So," he says, "tell me what happened."

She stares at her drink and shakes her head.

"I don't really think I want to," she says.

"OK," he says.

"I'm sorry. That was terrible of me, especially after how nice you've been. Please forgive me, Max, I really—"

"*Stop*," says Max, holding up his hand like a traffic cop. "Remember what I said—you apologize one more time and I promise I'm going to deck you."

She flashes him a smile.

"I'm sor—" she begins, then catches herself and smiles again. "I don't know why but I can't stop apologizing tonight."

"That's all right," says Max. "As long as you don't apologize for it."

"I'll tell you what happened."

"You don't have to if you don't want to."

"No, I want to. I mean I think I should."

"OK."

"Well. I had already gone to bed. I wasn't asleep yet, but I had turned off the light and I was just about to try and get to sleep, when Freddy comes in. He'd been out drinking and he'd really gotten smashed. I hate him when he's like that."

"Your mother wasn't with him?"

"No. He was alone. So anyway, he comes and knocks at my door and asks if I'm awake. I say I'm just dozing off. He asks if he can come in and talk. I say no, I'm just about half-asleep already, but he comes in anyway and just about crashes into my bed he's so smashed. I turn on the little light on my night table to see if he's all right, and he comes over and sits down on the bed. I tell him I don't want him in there, and he starts crying and asking me why I don't like him and telling me he loves me just like I was his very own daughter . . ."

She starts to cry.

"He, uh, made a pass at you, right?" says Max quietly.

She nods.

Sonofabitch, he thinks. And I was almost on the verge of making a big sloppy pass at her myself. Her terrible drunken pig of a stepfather makes a grab at her and she's so upset she calls up her trusty friend Max, because he's a cop and he'll protect her, and the minute she gets to his apartment he's ready to leap on her himself. Beautiful. Just fucking gorgeous.

"It was awful," she says. "He wouldn't let go of me. He put his head on my bosom and held it there and cried and kept trying to push down the top of my nightgown to . . ."

She cries some more, and Max goes over to her and

takes her drink away because she is about to spill it on
the couch and pats her on the back, berating himself
soundly because instead of thinking how terrible her
stepfather is to have done such a thing, all he can think
of is how much he would like to do the same thing himself. What an animal he is to think such a thing. What
a fucking animal.

"That's terrible, Babette," he says, patting her back.
"Just terrible. The man is an animal. The man is a
fucking animal. Uh, excuse me."

Babette eventually calms down and is silent. Max
continues idiotically patting her back, afraid that anything more intimate will be interpreted as a pass and
will send her screaming away into the night.

"How did it finally end?" says Max when the silence
has gone on a little longer than he can bear.

"I shoved him away from me and got out of bed,"
she says calmly, "and went to get my clothes."

"And what did *he* do?"

"Came after me. Tried to tear off my nightgown before I could get to the bathroom."

Her tone is calmer, almost resigned. Nothing seems as
though it's going to follow the last statement and, although he hates himself for it, Max is dying to know
what happened next.

"So," he says at last. *"Then* what happened? No, I'm
sorry, forget it. I'm sure you don't want to talk about it
anymore."

No point in being obvious, he decides. Besides, he
could picture what happened anyway. He swallows
dryly and downs about half of his drink.

"You poor kid" is about all he can think of to say.

"I'm never going back there," she says tonelessly. "I
never want to see him or my mother again as long as I
live."

"I don't blame you," he says.

"I never even want to hear their names again."

"I don't blame you."

"Even if I have to live at the YWCA."

"I don't blame you."

"Even if I have to sleep on a bench in the *park.*"

Although he'd been sure she'd run out of tears, she suddenly locates a fresh supply.

"I feel so alone," she says. "Oh, God, I feel so alone . . ."

He puts his arms around her in an avuncular embrace. She hugs him hard and sobs so violently he fears she will not be able to breathe. He continues idiotically patting her back as her tears soak through the front of his Police Academy sweatshirt. She is holding him so tightly it is almost painful.

Eventually she calms down again, but she doesn't let go of him. He gives her a reassuring little fatherly kiss on the forehead and she snuggles her face up against his neck and continues to hold onto him.

"I've never felt so alone in the world," she whispers.

Choosing not to interpret this as a reflection on him, Max kisses her again on the forehead.

"Don't feel so alone, Babette," he murmurs. "I'll take care of you."

She turns to look at him, her eyes still brimming with fresh reserves of tears. And then she lifts her lips to his and kisses him beautifully on the mouth. He melts, his bones turning to molten marzipan. She pulls slightly away from him. Her hands come up to cup his face and she kisses him again.

A shiver of emotion races through his body and, to his utter amazement, he hears the words "I love you" walk right out of his mouth.

"I love you, too," Babette whispers and hugs him so tightly he can't breathe.

This is insane, he tells himself. A girl I hardly know?

A crazy kid who has precognitive flashes and a horny stepfather who tears off her nightgown? What am I doing suddenly telling her I love her?

She kisses him a third time and he thinks that he is going to for the first time in his entire life faint with pleasure. He has kissed girls before. Hundreds of girls. He has never kissed one in his entire life who has made him feel even remotely like this.

44

BLACK CHRISTMAS
BY JOHNNY MONAHAN

At one end of the gloomy sitting room in the musty apartment at 275 W. 96th St. in Manhattan, an old lady sits in an overstuffed chair and weeps.

At the opposite end of the room, under a brave little Christmas tree trimmed with red and green lights and silvery tinsel and fake snow, lies a gaily wrapped package. The card on the package is addressed to Pamela, but Pamela Marlin will never read that card, never open that gaily wrapped package, never be able to share Christmas this year or any other year with the old lady in the overstuffed chair.

Pamela Marlin is dead. Her slim, blond, 21-year-old body was found along with that of a co-worker in the office where they worked by the cleaning woman. The bodies—half-naked, lashed to a desk with ropes—had been choked to death sometime during the night by an unknown assailant.

The old lady in the overstuffed chair has no more idea of who might have wanted to do such things to her youngest daughter than do the cops, and the cops have no idea at all.

"Pammy was such a good girl," the old woman says for maybe the dozenth time since you entered the apartment on W. 96th St. "Why would anybody do such a thing to her?"

You have no answer for the aging mother of Pamela Marlin, nor do you have answers for the mother of Frieda Winston, the co-worker whose body was found with Pamela's, nor for the mothers of Virginia Manteuffel or Beverly Rachlin or Linda Lowry either. They, too, as any child who reads the headlines or looks at television is well aware, lost their lives within the past few days, probably to the same man, and God only knows how many more will follow these unfortunate women to the city morgue in days to come.

The animal who slaugh-tered these women is still at large, lurking in the shadows and stalking his prey like a hyena. What motivates such a beast? What combination of lust and rage against your fellow beings does it take to make you into someone who forces women into intimate acts that should only be shared in the marriage bed and then deprives them of their lives? Can you build a hate that big all by yourself? Or do you need the help of a raw, brutalizing city where your spirit is raped so frequently and your dreams murdered so consistently that the very acts have become a commonplace?

"Whoever killed my Pammy," the old lady murmurs, "they're going to pay a terrible price."

They will indeed, you think. They will indeed.

The man walks slowly upstairs, automatically counting the steps, holding the newspaper open in front of him, his eyes milking each phrase in the column.

". . . What motivates such a beast? . . . What combination of lust and rage? . . . Can you build a hate that big all by yourself? . . ."

But it *wasn't* hate that made him do it. And it wasn't lust either. It was love. His love for women was so great that he needed to pursue a great many of them all at once. Too bad that meeting women in the normal ways didn't work for him. Only one way he knew of worked

—get to know the woman in question as well as it was possible to know anybody before talking to them, and then pick the time and place when you could be alone with her.

Well, that's what he was doing. No detective or espionage agent in the world could have built up better dossiers than he had on Linda Lowry, Beverly Rachlin, Pamela Marlin, or Virginia Manteuffel. The one on Virginia Manteuffel had been so good he could have answered all the questions he'd asked her for his pretend survey better than she could herself!

He unlocks the door to his apartment and steps inside. He takes the newspaper to his work table and carefully cuts out the column headed BLACK CHRISTMAS with a large pair of shears. He tapes it up on the wall, next to the short account of Virginia's death and the ones about Linda and Beverly.

He feels bad that Pamela's old mother was weeping in the newspaper story. He feels bad that Pamela won't be getting her Christmas present.

He pats his binoculars fondly and lets his gaze sweep the buildings across the street, letting it come to rest briefly on the windows where Linda Lowry used to live, and recalls the many pleasant and titillating evenings he'd spent with Linda in the first few weeks of his getting to know her.

He swings his binoculars up and to the right, coming to rest on a set of windows in a high-rise building in the next block, on 47th Street, a set of windows he has lately developed a particular fondness for. The windows of Sharon Hammond. No, she's not home from work yet. Probably stopped at the A&P. Nice girl, Sharon. Twenty-two years old. Legal secretary. Good tits. Good taste in lingerie. It would be a real pleasure someday to add her panties to his collection, one way or another.

He puts down his field glasses, goes to the bureau

and opens the bottom drawer, looks over the neatly folded pairs of panties. Funny, he'd always known he'd get panties from Linda, Beverly, Pamela, and Virginia, but he'd never figured on Frieda. Frieda's appearance at the office almost screwed things up, but he'd handled her nicely. What a bitch *she'd* been. He'd never have selected her for herself. He never could have felt any love for her, as he had for the others. In fact, if she hadn't made him so angry, perhaps Pamela would still be alive today. Yes, Frieda would have to take most of the blame for poor Pamela's death.

His gaze returns to the BLACK CHRISTMAS column. Something there that disturbs him. More than Pamela not getting her Christmas present. What was it?

". . . What motivates such a beast? . . ."

Beast? Was that what they thought of him? Would a beast be capable of the feelings of love that he'd had for Linda, Bev, Pam, and Ginny? Would a beast be capable of researching these gals as exhaustively and as cunningly as he had done? Would a beast be capable of the ingenious characterizations he'd created to trick women into letting him into their apartments—characterizations which, if they had been presented on the stage of any theater on the Great White Way, would have brought the audience and the critics to their feet with standing ovations and bravos?

". . . The animal who slaughtered these women is still at large, lurking in the shadows and stalking his prey like a hyena . . ."

Like a hyena. He wasn't sure that wasn't some sort of compliment, to be likened to a hyena. "Stalking his prey like a hyena." Well, that *was* what he was doing, in a sense. Like the assassin who stalked Charles de Gaulle in *The Day of the Jackal*. You couldn't find a better man than *that* to model yourself after, now could you?

Ah, the lights are on in Sharon's place now. He picks

up the binoculars, breathes on the lenses, wipes them clean, and trains them on the tall, pretty girl as she puts down a large bag of groceries and begins removing her coat. What means of skipping small talk and getting into her apartment would he use with Sharon Hammond? What means would the Jackal have used? What means will the Hyena use?

He counts the number of pictures he can see on Sharon's walls and wishes he could straighten them a bit. He furrows his brow in thought, decides he would like to see Sharon a little closer. He reaches for his little book, finds the section headed HAMMOND, SHARON, and dials her number. He watches as she takes a bottle of nail polish out of her bag, turns, and walks to the table near the window to pick up the telephone.

"Hello?" says Sharon Hammond.

Just as he's about to hang up, he hits upon the perfect means of gaining entrance to Sharon's apartment. He puts the receiver back in its cradle and laughs a high, girlish laugh. A maniacal laugh, like a hyena.

45

Max leads Babette to the couch and collapses onto it and they kiss some more. Slowly, slowly, they tumble off the couch onto the floor.

New groups of words are marching into formation in his mind and arranging themselves to walk out of his mouth again, dangerous and premature and inappropriate words having to do with such alien things as living together and getting married. Max clenches his teeth together and forbids them to come out.

"Max . . . ?"

"Yes, baby?"

"Where is your bedroom?"

"My bedroom?"

"Yes."

"Uh, downstairs. Right downstairs."

"I think we should go to bed, don't you?"

"Yes. Oh, yes. Oh, absolutely."

They get up off the floor and walk downstairs to the bedroom and Babette goes into the bathroom and closes the door. Well, how about *that,* thinks Max to himself. And here he had been berating himself for even *thinking* about the possibility of making a pass at her, yet she herself says to him, "I think we should go to bed, don't you?"

He pulls back the covers on the bed and plumps up the pillows and takes off his sweatshirt and his jeans. He starts to take off his jockey shorts as well, but is suddenly self-conscious. Better leave them on till she gets under the covers.

He gets into bed and pulls the covers up to his chin and waits. The toilet flushes. The water runs in the sink. The bathroom door opens. She stands in the doorway.

"Max?"

"Right here, baby."

"Where am I going to sleep?"

"What, baby?"

"Where am I going to sleep?"

"Uh, well . . . What? I mean what do you mean?"

"Well, if you're taking the bed, then I guess I'll take the couch upstairs. Do you have some extra sheets and blankets?"

"Wait a minute. Just a minute."

Max gets out of bed and realizes that the sight of him in just his undershorts is embarrassing her, because she has turned her head. He can't believe it. He absolutely cannot believe it.

"Babette?"

"Yes, Max?"

"Babette, I think I lost you around the last turn. Weren't you coming to bed with me and weren't we going to sleep together?"

"*Sleep* together?"

"Yes."

"What ever gave you *that* idea?"

"Babette, hang on a second. Didn't you just say to me upstairs, 'I think we should go to bed, don't you?' "

"Well, yes. I mean, look at the *time*. It's so *late*."

"But Babette, I don't understand. I mean we were kissing each other so beautifully up there. And I told you I loved you. And you even said you love *me* . . ."

"Yes . . . ?"

"You really don't want to sleep with me?"

"Max, why would I want to do *that?*"

"That's what people do who kiss a lot and tell each other they love each other, goddammit."

Babette shakes her head sadly.

"Not you, too," she says.

"What?"

"Why is it that every time I find a guy I like really a lot and start necking with him and tell him I love him, sooner or later he gets the wrong idea? Why *is* it?"

"Babette, listen to me. I'm not understanding this here, Babette . . ."

Babette starts walking upstairs.

"Babette, where are you going?"

He follows her up the stairs.

"Babette, you aren't leaving, are you?"

She gets her coat and starts putting it on.

"Babette, please don't leave."

She begins fastening the coat and walks to the door.

"Babette, you are not leaving. I forbid you to leave."

She looks up, startled.

"What?"

"I *forbid* you to leave this apartment."

She stares at him, wide-eyed.

I have gone too far, he thinks. She is going to hit me or throw something at me.

He didn't know why he was forbidding her to leave his apartment, except that he liked her and he knew she needed help. She wasn't a cock-tease either. She was only from a different century.

"What do you mean you forbid me to leave this apartment?" she says, but there is no backbone in it and no rancor; it is possibly only a sincere request for clarification.

"Just that," he says, brazening it out. "You will not go outside. You will remain here. You will take off your coat and you will go to sleep right here. And if you want to sleep on the couch in this room instead of downstairs with me, that is perfectly all right, but you are not going outside."

She thinks this over a moment, then sighs and takes off her coat.

"OK," she says, as if relieved to have finally found out the rules of the house.

"Now the sheets are in the linen closet here and there's a couple of extra blankets in there, too, and I'll help you make up the couch."

He bustles about, getting out the sheets and the blankets and making up a bed on the couch.

"I have an extra pillow downstairs if you want to come down and get it. Do you have something to sleep in?"

"No."

"Well, I have a sweatshirt you can wear on top, but I don't have anything you can wear on the bottom. I mean I don't have any pajamas or anything."

"That's all right."

"Well, come on downstairs then and get the sweatshirt and the pillow."

"All right."

She follows him downstairs. He gives her his other Police Academy sweatshirt and his extra pillow.

"OK," he says coolly, "goodnight."

"Goodnight," she says, but doesn't move.

He gets into bed and pulls up the covers.

"I'm sorry if I hurt your feelings, Max."

"OK, kid."

"Did I hurt your feelings?"

"No. Not too much."

"I'm sorry I said what I said. Especially after how nice you've been."

"Don't start with that again."

"I'm sor—OK. Max?"

"Yes, Babette?"

"I think part of the thing is that I don't feel it's right."

"You don't feel *what's* right?"

"Sleeping together. When a man and a woman aren't married. I guess that probably sounds really amazing in this day and age, but that's what I believe."

"OK, kid."

"I don't really consider myself a very good Catholic, but I guess I still believe some of the things I was taught, and that's one of them."

"OK, kid."

She seems to have run out of things to say, but she still makes no move to go.

"Max?"

"Yes?"

"It's not so wonderful being a virgin these days."

"I can imagine."

"But I have to do what I believe in. Don't I?"

"I . . . guess you do, Babette."

"Max?"

"Yes, baby?"

"What are you?"

"What *am* I? A nonvirgin, I guess. Is that what you mean?"

"No. I mean you're not a Catholic, are you?"

"No. Oh, no. I'm Jewish."

"Jewish?"

"Yes."

"Oh, boy. You're sure *not* a Catholic, are you?"

They both giggle.

"I don't think the Church is going to be too thrilled with me."

"How do you mean?"

"Falling in love with a Jew."

He reaches up and hugs her. She hugs him back hard, and kisses him, and then scampers upstairs.

46

In a book in the public library the man finds what he is looking for:

> *Hyena. A nocturnal carnivore feeding chiefly on dead and putrefying flesh. Strong though cowardly, the hyena is noted for its eerie howl. Hyenas whoop and laugh loudly over a fresh kill.*

He takes his knife out of his pocket and carefully cuts the page and its illustration out of the book with four almost perfectly straight cuts.

He tapes the cutting from the library book up on the wall next to the newspaper stories about the murders.

It's perfect. He is being talked about now by thousands of people who don't even know him. By *millions* of people. Within weeks everybody in the country, if not the entire world, will know about him and his handiwork. He might very well go down in history.

Well, he certainly deserved the acclaim. If and when he finally gave himself up, the world would learn how brilliant he had been, how much more he had researched and discovered about every woman he'd dated than he ever had to. He would tell all about it in his memoirs, which he'd write in jail and sell to a publisher for a lot of money. The advance would pay for his bail and for a fancy lawyer to get him acquitted.

He'd be a celebrity. The very people who were now clamoring for his capture would be falling all over themselves to see and hear him being interviewed on radio and in the papers and on TV talkshows like the "Tonight Show" by fellow celebrities like Johnny Carson and Ed McMahon. The people, yes, the people. Gobbling up every nasty morsel of sensationalism they could get their teeth into, turning his great romances into tawdry gossip, living vicariously through his exploits. Watchers, not doers. Spectators, not participants.

Well, now that he's becoming a public personage, there is one thing he has to do immediately.

47

A man who calls himself The Hyena has sent a letter to *Daily News* columnist Johnny Monahan in which he admits the slaying of five women in the Manhattan area.

The letter, written in response to a recent Monahan column, has been examined by police, who believe it may be genuine. Mailed from Manhattan and received yesterday at the *Daily News,* the letter said in part:

"It was not hate that made me do it but I do not suppose you would understand that Mr. Monahan. It began with love and love is the strongest feeling that even now [I] feel for Pammy, Ginny, Bev and Linda. Yes even for Frieda and greater love hath no man than that. . . ."

The five names presumably refer to the five victims of the recent sex-related slayings: Pamela Marlin, Virginia Manteuffel, Beverly Rachlin, Linda Lowry and Frieda Winston, all of Manhattan.

The letter continues: "Yes, Mr. Monahan *my* spirit was raped and *my* dreams were murdered also but my idealism and optimism and also my belief in the goodness of womankind never gets exhausted. Like Dyoganese [*sic*] with his lamp I search for one good woman but should they prove themselves betrayers as usual and as they have so far do no doubt that they shall feel my wrath even as the others.

"Yes, Mr. Monahan the animal who killed these five is still at large lurking in the shadows but only till he might one day end his quest for what he seeks."

The letter is signed "The Hyena," presumably in reference to a phrase in the Monahan column, and concludes:

"P.S. Mr. Monahan I read your column daily and appreciate your taking an interest in these brutal and unfortunate but believe me justified killings."

Columnist Monahan said he would be available to meet with the killer "any time, any place he names," should he wish to give himself up and seek psychiatric help.

48

Max hears Babette moving upstairs. Then the lights go out and he hears her getting into bed on the couch. He turns off the lights and lies there in the darkness.

It is very confusing, he thinks, and nothing works out the way you think it's going to. Upstairs is a young woman who professes to love him, whom it is even possible that he loves as well, to the extent that people who have spent so little time together and know each other so little can be said to love each other. And she clearly wants him at least *partly* as much as he wants her. And yet there they lie, her upstairs, him down. Separated by not more than twelve feet. Longing for each other.

He sighs. The house creaks. He lets his mind drift to the sex killer he has been pursuing. What kind of a maniac would do such things? What would Max himself do if the killer ever attacked Babette?

The house creaks again and Max jolts into a sitting position, automatically reaching down under the bed for his gun. He strains his ears in the silence, listening for inappropriate nighttime sounds, but hears nothing. Outside the trees groan in the wind. Max puts his gun back under the bed and sinks back down under the covers.

Funny. Pursuing the killer before, he didn't feel at all vulnerable. Now, with Babette to protect, he is conscious of vulnerability.

Another creaking noise. He listens, holds his breath. Footsteps. His hand moves quietly back under the bed to his holster. It's obviously Babette upstairs, unable to sleep. What is he so jumpy for?

Footsteps come slowly down the stairs.

"Babette?" he whispers.

No reply.

He silently unsnaps the holster. The stairs creak. He slips out of bed, gun in hand. This is ridiculous, he thinks. Why have you taken out your gun?

"Babette?" he whispers again.

"Max?"

He breathes a sigh of relief and reholsters the gun.

"What is it?" he says.

Babette creeps downstairs, feeling her way in the dark. He turns on a light. What she has chosen to sleep in is his Police Academy sweatshirt and her panties.

"Max, I'm frightened."

"What of?"

"I started falling asleep and I was sort of drifting . . ."

"Yes . . . ?"

"I thought I saw something, Max. Something terrible."

"What did you see?"

She starts to tremble.

"Come here, baby."

She comes over to the bed, sits down. Her panties are white cotton, like a little girl's.

"What did you see?" he says.

She shudders.

"Teeth. Fangs. Horrible fangs, like a wild animal's. Dripping blood."

She starts to tremble again. He puts his arms around her.

"Did you see anything else?" he says.

She doesn't reply.

"Babette?"

"Yes?"

"What else did you see?"

She buries her face suddenly in his neck and holds him tightly.

"What is it, Babette?"

"Never mind," she whispers.

She begins shuddering and her teeth chatter uncontrollably. He pulls her down under the covers and wraps his arms around her and makes a lot of comforting shooshing noises.

"I'm afraid to sleep up there alone, Max," she says.

"That's OK, baby."

"If I sleep down here with you tonight, do you promise we won't do anything?"

"I, uh, guess so," he says.

"Do you promise?"

"I guess so," he says.

"Let me hear you say, 'I promise.' "

"Oh, for God's sake, Babette."

"I'm serious, Max. You have to promise me we won't do anything, even if I want to. Because I might."

"You mean that?"

"Yes. I think I might want to. In fact, I do right now. But it would be wrong. It would be a mistake. I might even enjoy it at the time, but afterward I'd hate you and I'd hate myself and it would be terrible. So promise me we won't do anything, no matter what."

"I promise," he says.

She sighs and hugs him under the covers. Their bodies press together and he wonders whether he has just agreed to the most tantalizing experiment he has ever heard of or the absolute rock-bottom worst.

"Max?"

"Yes, baby?"

"Can I stay with you awhile? More than tonight, I mean?"

"Yes, baby."

Pause.

"Max?"

"Yes, baby?"

"What you said before when we were upstairs— about taking care of me? Did you mean that?"

"Yes, baby."

Pause.

"You've really got your work cut out for you, Max."

"What do you mean?"

Pause. Her teeth begin chattering again.

"The other part of the vision I had upstairs. That horrible thing with the fangs. He's going to kill me, Max. I saw it."

49

Going up in the elevator, she finds herself praying he won't be home. Praying nobody will be home so she can get in and get out with her clothes and stuff without having to confront either one of them.

The elevator stops. Babette walks quietly down the corridor to the door, fishes in her pocket for her key, unlocks the door, and enters the apartment. The door wasn't double-locked, but that doesn't mean anything. Freddy often leaves it that way when he goes out in a drunken stupor. It's a wonder their apartment hasn't been robbed by now.

She goes into her room, takes out a suitcase and begins to stuff it full of things she needs; clothes, makeup, her teddybear, her hair rollers, and so on. She hears a footfall in the hallway and spins around.

"Well well well. The prodigal daughter."

"Hi, Mom."

"And where, may I ask, have *you* been? If it's not too personal a question, that is?"

"Away."

"Away? Well, I *knew* you were away. That much even *I* could figure out for myself. Away *where?*"

"With friends. I hope you're not going to pretend that you were worried about me or that you had no idea why I left, because I presume you're still on speaking terms with Freddy."

"Freddy says that you and he had a spat."

"A *spat?* Is that what he told you?"

"Yes. Why?"

"Terrific. A spat."

Babette goes back to her packing.

"Which is not to say I was any less worried about you, Babette. Dear God, you run out of here without taking so much as a change of underwear and you're gone for I don't know how long, and not a *word* from you. Not a note, not a *phone* call even—I didn't know what had happened to you. I called the hospitals. I called the *police.* I asked them if there had been any accident victims who fit your description. I didn't know where to *turn.* Where were you?"

"I already told you. With friends."

"With *what* friends? I called Theresa, I called Bridget, I called Maryanne. None of them had heard a *word* from you. *What* friends?"

"Friends from school."

"What are their names?"

"One's named Maxine. They call her Max for short. It's Max's apartment."

"Max? I've never heard you speak about anyone named Max."

"You will."

"What's this Max person's last name? Where does she live?"

"Oh, no you don't. I'm not telling you any more than that. I'm not having you embarrass me in front of my friends. I've had enough of that already."

"You're moving in with this person?"

"Yes."

"For how long?"

"I don't know. Maybe forever."

"You can't do that. I forbid it."

Babette turns around.

"You forbid it? Let me tell you something, Mother. If you do anything to stop me, anything at all, I'm going to tell you what *really* happened between me and Freddy. And right after that I'm going to the police *myself,* except that when I do it's going to be to have Freddy arrested."

"What are you talking about, young lady?"

"Do you want to know? Do you really want to know, Mother? Because if you really want to know, I'll tell you."

Babette's mother stands facing her in silence. A vein is standing out on her forehead and a little tic in her

neck is going lickety-split, but Babette's mother makes
no reply.

Downstairs, across the street from Babette's building,
a man in a dark overcoat waits patiently for Babette
to reappear.

50

The letter from the killer has netted them little more
than a couple of inconclusive latent prints and confirmation of their suspicions that (1) he is a madman and
(2) he is going to strike again soon.

Johnny Monahan has informed the Chief of Detectives that he plans to answer the Hyena's letter in his
column. He has promised to let police psychiatrist Tony
Natale advise him on what to say.

Max and Caruso are headed across town, to a hotel
in the West 40s. A young Black junkie on the meth-
adone program has let it be known he saw a man in a
dark overcoat hanging around Beverly Rachlin's apartment house on a couple of occasions the week before
she was killed. The junkie's name is Walter Woodruff,
but he is known on the street as Slick.

Max and Caruso have already made two appoint-
ments to speak to Slick at the squad room and on a
corner in Hell's Kitchen, but Slick has failed to show
up both times. He has promised faithfully to meet them
this time at the Hotel Bellavista where he has a room.

Max spends five minutes looking for a parking place,

then says the hell with it and double-parks. Caruso pulls down the sun visor with the police I.D. on it and they go into the hotel lobby.

The hotel is a fleabag with pretensions. The carpet is worn through and shredded in places and the stained walls have very likely not seen a paintbrush in the last half-century, but the girl at the switchboard and the guy at the desk and the one who runs the elevator are all in uniform and seem, from their demeanor, to be pretending that the Hotel Bellavista just happens to be going through a lean period and will be back on its feet again in no time, kicking out the junkies and the pimps and the hookers and the minor underworld hit men and bringing back their regular clientele who were wintering in Dubrovnik.

Max and Caruso get into the elevator and are joined by two uniformed cops from the Manhattan North Precinct. One of them recognizes Caruso.

"Hey, Caruso, this where you live?"

"Yeah," says Caruso, "me and Max here have the honeymoon suite."

The uniformed men exit at the fifth floor. Max and Caruso get out at the seventh and make their way along the dimly lit corridors, checking room numbers on the doors which still have them. A Black person of indeterminate sex is just coming out of one of the rooms. Speaking to someone inside, he or she says: "I already *give* you one kiss, an' tha's all you're gettin'."

"Excuse me, honey," says Caruso to the single-kiss-giver, "is there a dude on this floor named Slick?"

The Black of indeterminate sex looks Caruso over from head to toe with great interest.

"Ah don' know nobody slick in *this* hotel, exceptin' me, mah man," it says flirtatiously.

Caruso flashes a weary smile. He and Max continue

down the corridor. Before a half-open door with the number 711 on the outside they pause and knock.

Inside a television set is blaring a rerun of "Barney Miller." There is no reply to their knocking. Max sticks his head inside the door and sees a young Black guy lying on a bed, watching the TV screen as if hypnotized. He and Caruso ease on into the room.

"Slick?" says Caruso over the TV.

"Yeah, bro'," says the guy on the bed without looking up.

"Detectives Caruso and Segal from Third Homicide," says Caruso loudly. "Glad we caught you in. You mind talking to us a few minutes?"

"Sure, bro', c'mon in."

The guy keeps his eyes glued to the TV.

"Mind if we sit down?" says Max above the dialogue on the TV.

"Sure, bro', make yourself comfortable."

"Would you mind turning down the volume on that thing so we can talk?" says Caruso.

"Sure, bro'," says Slick, moving to the set, turning the volume knob imperceptibly and then sinking back down on the mattress. There is no detectable difference in sound level.

"Could you turn down the volume a little more?" says Max. "It's hard to hear over it."

"Sure, bro'," says Slick, once more moving to the set, making a microscopic adjustment to the sound level, and sinking back down on the mattress.

"Is it OK if I turn this thing off altogether?" says Max, moving to the TV and turning it off.

"No problem, bro', no problem," says Slick.

Caruso sits down on the bed to Slick's left. Max takes a seat to the right of Slick and behind, where he can keep an eye on the door. The room is very small. The bed, the chair Max is sitting in, and a dresser next to the bed are the only pieces of furniture. A washstand is situated next to the door. Dirty shirts and underwear and socks lie on the floor. On top of the dresser in a metallic frame is a poorly executed pencil sketch of a Black man with an afro. The drawing looks like the police artists' sketches of suspects which are posted on the precinct bulletin board.

"We're sorry to have missed you those other two times," says Max pointedly.

"Oh, no problem, bro'," says Slick, entirely missing the sarcasm and making it sound as though he thought Max was apologizing.

"We hear you saw a white dude in a dark overcoat hanging around outside the building on West 37th Street where that white woman got killed," says Caruso, taking out his notebook and his ballpoint pen.

Slick nods.

"How many times did you see this guy?" says Caruso.

"Once or twice. I dunno."

"Was it once or was it twice?" says Max.

"Twice. Maybe three times."

"What was he doing there?" says Caruso, writing out his lengthy abbreviations in his notebook.

"Just mostly hanging around outside the building."

"How did you happen to notice him?" says Max.

"He looked wrong."

"How do you mean?" says Max.

"He didn't look like he *belonged*."

"How do you mean?" says Max.

Slick shrugs.

"Not too many white dudes hang out around there."

There is a knock at the door and a Black guy with a wide-brimmed white hat on peeks in the door. Slick waves him away and the guy ducks out of sight.

"When you saw this white dude hanging out around

this particular area, did you notice him doing anything unusual?" says Caruso.

Slick shrugs.

"I dunno."

"What don't you know?" says Max.

"What you call unusual?" says Slick.

"Did you notice him doing anything at all?" says Max.

Slick thinks this over.

"Well, the dude was, like I say, just mostly hangin' out. Sort of lookin' across the street every once and a while, y'know? And sometimes he'd kinda check his watch, like he was waitin' for somethin' to happen? And once and a while I seen him write somethin' down."

"Write something down?" says Caruso. "On what?"

"I dunno. In a little notebook. Like you got there, only smaller. And then another time I seen him take a pair of field glasses out of his coat and look through them."

"Where was he looking when he was looking through the field glasses?" says Caruso.

"Across the street. At that building you said."

"Where the Rachlin homicide took place?"

"I don' know her name, bro'. The one you said. And then another time it look to me like the dude rip off her garbage."

"He stole her *garbage?*" says Max.

"She come out and leave off her garbage at the curb —in a plastic *bag?* And after she go back in, the dude come along and pick it up and take it along with him."

"About how many days before the homicide did you see him do this?" says Caruso.

Slick shrugs.

"Was it two or three days?" says Caruso.

Slick shrugs.

"I dunno. Maybe."

"Were the two or three times you saw him hanging around out there during the same week?" says Max.

Slick shrugs.

"Could be," he says. "I wasn't paying no attention, bro'."

"What did you think he was stealing her garbage for?" says Max.

"I didn't know, bro'. I figured he had his reasons."

"Do you think you could come down to the precinct and look at some mug shots?" says Caruso.

Slick shrugs yet again.

"We'd appreciate it if you did," says Caruso pointedly.

"I don' know if it would do any good," says Slick.

"Why not?" says Max.

"Well," says Slick, "if it was a brother, then maybe I could tell somethin', but seeing as how it's a white dude, I don' know if I'd be able."

"Why not?" says Max.

"You mean because all white dudes look alike?" says Caruso.

Slick smiles a big smile.

51

They are lying in front of the fireplace in Max's apartment. The fire is crackling away and Babette's head is on Max's chest, and Max is stroking her head. For a long time they do not say anything at all. Then Babette kind of laughs.

"What's the joke?" says Max.

"I don't know. I was just thinking about us. About how we met and everything."

"What's so funny about it?"

"You don't think it's funny that we met at police headquarters with me trying to report psychic visions of murders? That one of the first things you did in our relationship was throw yourself across the hood of the cab I was in and try to arrest the driver? That two of our first dates were in apartments of murdered women, with me going into trances and babbling crazy things and screaming? You don't think that's funny?"

Max chuckles.

"I guess it's funny in a way," he says. "I guess it's not your usual cliché romantic beginning."

He places his hands on her cheeks and kisses her on the forehead.

"You don't think it's funny that I'm living with you and I don't even know a thing about you?" she says.

"What would you like to know about me?" he says.

"I don't know. Anything. Everything. *Something*. All I know about you is that you're Jewish and a cop."

"That's all?"

He looks hurt. She smiles, strokes his face.

"Not really all," she says. "I know how you are when you're with me. You're very gentle, and you're very sweet, and you're very strong. I know that much. But I wish I knew other things, too."

"Like what?"

"I don't know. Like what did you study in school? What was your childhood like? What are your parents like? What do they think about your being a detective?"

Max shifts position so that his head is lying on her chest. He exhales slowly.

"OK, let's see. Well, what I studied in school was law. Pre-law, actually. Which was not all that interesting to me, frankly, although my *grades* were good enough. I had good enough grades so that I could've gone through law school and become a lawyer and taken on clients, but it just wasn't that exciting a prospect to me, is all."

"Why not?"

"I don't know. It seemed too passive to me, in a way."

"What do you mean?"

"Well, look, this is going to sound corny, OK? But I want to do something to help people. To help humanity, OK? Big deal, right? And I'm sure that lawyers help people and all of that, but I finally decided that the way *I* wanted to help people was in a much more active, direct way. Not in a law office or a courtroom, but out on the street, where it was actively happening, you know? Using my mind, but also using my legs and my fists and even my gun, if it came to that. I don't know, maybe it's just a big macho trip and there's nothing noble about it at all. Maybe I just did it to prove I'm a tough guy, even though I'm Jewish. I don't know. Who knows?"

"How do your parents feel about your giving up law to become a cop?"

Max snorts with laughter.

"Are you kidding me? Jewish parents? They think I've flipped my cookies. Jewish parents don't *know* from cop sons. *Irish* parents know. *Italian* parents know. Not Jewish ones. Jewish parents know from lawyer sons, from doctor sons, from CPA sons. From artist sons, from teacher sons, from businessman sons. Jewish parents are funny. They have some strange prejudice against their sons getting their heads shot off or their guts blown out. They want their kids to be physically and financially comfortable, to get married, to raise a family, to give them grandchildren. All that stuff works better with lawyer sons than with cop sons."

Max thinks awhile about his parents.

"I'll tell you the truth, Babette. As crazy as they think I am for throwing a chance to be a comfortable middle-class lawyer out the window, to go into the streets and fight with meshuggenehs, I think they're sort of proud of me. They'd never admit it, but I think they're sort of proud of me."

"Where do they live, in Manhattan?"

"In the Bronx. In Riverdale, actually. I grew up in the Bronx. My dad runs a laundry there. He always wanted to be a lawyer himself, but he never got any further with it than I did. Only with him it was strictly a matter of money. He didn't have enough to go on to law school. So instead he went into the laundry business and earned enough to support his wife and family and to send his son to law school in his place. Only when the ungrateful son grew up, he quit school and became a cop."

"You're pretty hard on yourself, aren't you?" she says.

"I guess so. I wish I didn't feel I had let them down by not becoming a lawyer. I know I *didn't* let them down, I mean, but I wish I didn't *feel* I had, you know?"

"I know. I feel in a way that I let my parents down, too."

"How do you mean?"

"Well, as creepy as they are, I guess I feel I've been sort of a failure as a daughter. As a student in school. As a Catholic. I'm not exactly the worst scholar at NYU or the biggest sinner on the Atlantic seaboard, but I'll never make the dean's list. Or the Pope's list either, for that matter."

"You're pretty hard on yourself, too," says Max gently.

"Well, Jews don't have a corner on the guilt market, you know."

He laughs. They spend a while just hugging.

"Have you had a lot of affairs?" says Babette.

"Why?"

"No reason. I'd just like to know."

"Not that many."

"Good," she says.

"What does it matter?"

"It doesn't."

"Good," he says.

"How many, though?"

"Not that many."

"More than twenty?"

"Are you serious?"

"No," she says. "Yes. Was it more than twenty?"

"No. Much less than twenty."

"How much less?"

"I don't know."

"Less than fifteen?"

"Probably less than fifteen."

"Good. Less than ten?"

"Look, what is all this? What is this about?"

"I just want to know, that's all. Was it less than ten?"

"Probably about ten."

"Oh."

"Are you satisfied?"

"Yes."

"Good."

"Did you like them better than me?"

"Did I like *who* better than you—all ten of them?"

"Yes."

"I am not going to dignify that question with an answer. I can't believe you even asked me that."

"I just thought maybe you liked them better because they let you make love to them and I haven't."

"I see. So *that's* what this is about."

"Are you sure that's not the way you feel?"

"Yes."

"Yes, that's the way you feel, or Yes, you're sure that's *not* the way you feel?"

Max lifts his head off her chest and cranes his neck around to look at her.

"I can't believe we're having this discussion," he says. "What do I have to do to get out of this discussion?"

"I just worry that you might get tired of me because I'm not letting you make love to me and the others have."

"Well, don't worry about it. I'm not getting tired of you, OK? Jesus!"

"The really ironic thing is that my mother thinks I'm screwing my brains out."

"Why does she think that?"

"I don't know. Maybe because that's what she'd like to do herself. Who *wouldn't* want to with that moron of a husband she's got now."

"What was your real father like?"

Babette is silent for a while.

"My real father was wonderful. My real father was so wonderful it was ridiculous. I don't know what he ever saw in my mother. That's a terrible thing to say, but it's true. I think my real father's trouble was that he was too good. Too innocent, maybe. He died while trying to rescue somebody in a fire who not only wasn't *in* the fire, but who was the person who'd set the fire in the first place—some lunatic of a woman who got tired of her boyfriend and poured gasoline on him while he was asleep and then set him on fire."

"Good God."

"So she burned up her boyfriend and she burned up my father, and she didn't even go to jail because some psychiatrists said she wasn't *psychologically capable* of standing trial or of *understanding* the *consequences* of her act. She's in some sanitarium in Queens, I think."

"Your father was a fireman?"

She nods.

"Not only a fireman, but a truck man, and not only a truck man but a roof man. Do you know what any of that means?"

"Not really."

"There are two pieces of fire apparatus in most New York firehouses, the hook-and-ladder truck and the engine. All the men on the engine have to do is hook up hoses to the hydrant and throw water on the fire. I'm not saying that's a soft job, but my father and the other men on the truck had the real dirty work. The minute they get to a fire, before the engine men have even hooked up the hoses, the truck men have to make a search of the fire building, locate the source of the fire, rescue anybody in the building, and vent the roof. Do you know what that means?"

"Ventilating the roof?"

She nods.

"To let the burning gases escape. Otherwise you can't put out the fire. Venting the roof is the most dangerous job because all the heat and smoke and gases collect up there. The roof man's job is to somehow get to the roof and vent it. That's the job that my father volunteered for. He was a roof man for almost the whole time he was in the fire department, about fifteen years. It's a miracle he even lasted that long, I guess."

"He sounds like an amazing man."

"He was. He was a real hero."

She is quiet for a long time. Eventually Max gets up, douses the smoldering logs in the fireplace with water, and turns off the living room light.

Outside, a figure in a dark overcoat sees the lights go out, notes the time on his watch, and writes it very, very neatly in his little book.

52

Waiting for Sharon Hammond to return home, he surveys his souvenir collection: panties from Pamela Marlin, Frieda Winston, and Linda Lowry—Linda's splotched with blood, Pam's and Frieda's slit from the process of pulling them off without untying their ankles. Panties, brassieres, slips, and stockings from both Beverly Rachlin and Virginia Manteuffel. Oh, OK, maybe a *few* specks of blood on Beverly's.

Women's underwear had always fascinated him. As a child he had saved lingerie ads from newspapers and magazines. There was something about the clean-cut, attractive models in underwear ads that was so much more *wholesome* than the women in the girlie publications with their costumey unserious underwear and their lustful leers that frankly turned him off. Whereas the wholesome models in their wholesome panties and brassieres were just like the girl next door, or members of your own family.

The members of *his* family, his mother and older sister, often walked around in their underwear when he was little. Whenever he was home alone he used to sneak into his sister's bedroom and go through her underwear drawers, examining and counting bras and panties. If she was going to be gone for several hours, sometimes he would even get undressed and try some of it on.

One time—one terrible time—when his sister was

supposed to be at a slumber party, she returned unexpectedly with two of her teenaged friends and he had to hide in her closet, still wearing her panties. She wandered into the closet and jumped three feet into the air when she saw him. At first she was mad as hell, but then she started laughing and called her friends into the room and the three of them just stood there, laughing their guts out. Then they saw his boner and they practically fell on the floor. While her two friends held his arms, his sister pulled down the panties so they could see his little thing standing straight out in front of him. He was so humiliated he wanted to die. He was also very excited.

When he was a little older he often walked through the lingerie sections of department stores and tried to imagine that the mannikins wearing bras and panties were real women. Once a saleswoman asked him whether he needed any help. His face grew hot with shame. He told her he wanted to buy a pair of panties for his mother's birthday. The saleswoman brought out several pairs to show him but he was so flustered that he couldn't choose from among them. Finally the saleslady asked if he wanted her to pick out a pair that *she* would like to wear, and he said yes. She held up a pair of pink ones that you could practically see right through, and smiled at him in a way that made him realize she knew the panties were not for his mother but for him. It was terribly humiliating. It was very exciting.

For as long as he could remember he had always been stirred by the sight of a clothed woman's behind when he could make out her panty lines. The indentations in the flesh of her waist and upper thighs made by the elastic of the waistband and legbands of her panties enabled him to clearly visualize how she would look in various stages of undress. In the past few years he found himself following many women through the city, studying their panty lines and fantasizing sexual adventures with them, then coming home and improvising the dialogue on the little stage in his apartment. It was only in the past few months that he had decided to do something active and positive about meeting these women, and Linda Lowry was his first.

Poor Linda. He would always treasure her memory. He would always treasure her panties.

He takes Linda's panties out of the drawer and holds them against his face. Then, impulsively, he begins removing his clothes and folding them into neat piles. The moment he is naked he pulls on Linda's panties and gets an immediate erection. The sensation of slippery nylon against his flesh, the nylon that once encased Linda's precious private parts, is almost overpowering. He opens the bathroom door and looks at his reflection in the mirror. At the shininess of the fabric, at the delicate lacework around the legbands, at his penis pole tenting out the front of the garment where it wasn't double-reinforced like a man's underpants were.

He looks ludicrous, he thinks. The image of himself in Linda's panties is humiliating. And exciting.

The light in Sharon Hammond's apartment goes on. He turns off the light in his own apartment, goes to the window, and picks up his binoculars.

53

"I just want to know one reason," says the man in the dark overcoat with the gaily colored wool scarf around his neck that is considerably gayer than the expression on his face. "Won't you at least give me *one reason?*"

"Because," says Sharon Hammond, putting down two shopping bags filled with Christmas presents and taking off her coat.

" 'Because' is not a reason," says the man, taking off his own coat and moving toward the little wall-hung bar to fix himself a drink.

"I don't *need* a reason," says Sharon tiredly. "I just don't happen to feel like continuing our relationship is all, Phil, and that's that."

"But why *not?*"

"Because. Because it's not going anywhere, for one thing. And because I'm sick of relationships. I want something more than a relationship."

"But I already *told* you why I can't get married," says the man, downing his drink and pouring himself a second. "Do I have to go through the whole thing again?"

"Please don't," she says, pouring a drink for herself, "I know it all by heart. Anyway, I don't even *want* to marry you anymore. I did once, I admit that, but not anymore."

"Because of the drinking? I *told* you I'm cutting down."

"It's not because of the drinking."

"Then why? Why, right before Christmas?"

"Christmas is a marvelous time for breaking up. I know about a dozen girls who are breaking up with their boyfriends for Christmas."

"Don't talk nonsense."

"I'm not talking nonsense. You don't care that much about me anyway, Phil. You're just scared it'll be too late to get another date for New Year's Eve."

The man sits down heavily and glares at her.

"I'm not giving you up," he says finally.

"What?"

"You heard me," he says. "I am not giving you up. I'll keep coming by and calling you on the phone and sooner or later you'll just have to see me."

"That's what *you* think," she says and goes into the bathroom and closes the door. The man follows her to the door.

"OK, Sharon," he says in a strange tone of voice. "Go ahead and dump me, then. But if *I* can't have you, then *no* one can."

The toilet flushes. The bathroom door opens.

"What was that you said?"

"You heard me. If I can't have you, no one can. I'm going to kill you."

"That's not funny, Phil."

"It wasn't meant to be. If you persist in breaking up with me, I'm going to strangle you. It won't be the first time, you know."

"What in God's name are you saying?"

"Think about it. I'm in my late thirties. I have dark hair and dark eyes. I wear a dark overcoat. My eyes occasionally take on a vacant stare, just as they're doing now, if you'll notice. Sharon, I am the Hyena."

54

Max stops typing his report just long enough to pick up the ringing telephone on his desk.

"Third Homicide, Detective Segal."

"I'd like to, uh, talk to somebody about the killer who calls himself the Hyena?"

"Yes, ma'am. Do you think you spotted him?"

Max catches Caruso's eye, points to the phone, and rolls his eyes ceilingward. They are fielding an average of eighty calls a day now from people who think they've spotted the Hyena. Every schmuck in the city in his thirties who wears a dark overcoat is being looked at suspiciously, and every time he gets a slightly preoccupied look on his face, somebody thinks it's the famous vacant look they've heard about on TV and in the papers and they're dialing Homicide.

"I don't know what I think. I'm probably crazy to even be bothering you with this at all, but about ten minutes ago a man I've been going out with told me that he's the killer. He said if I break up with him he's going to kill *me*."

"Maybe he's kidding," says Max. "Some guys have a weird sense of humor."

"That's what *I* thought at first, that he was kidding. But that's not something you kid about, is it? Maybe I'm crazy, but I'm scared he's serious. He just left, and I'm really scared. Can you do anything?"

"Of course, of course. Give me your name and address. We'll come over in a while and talk to you."

"It's Sharon Hammond. The address is 226 East 47th Street, Apartment 12E."

"226 East 47th? That's right around the corner from—"

"Linda Lowry, right."

"We'll be right over."

Max hangs up and grabs his jacket.

"Woman lives right around the corner from Linda Lowry. Says her boyfriend confessed he's the Hyena and threatened to kill her. I want to go talk to her."

Caruso shakes his head.

"You got nothin' there," he says. "Some broad has a fight with her boyfriend, she's got her tits in an uproar."

"I *know* it's nothing," says Max, "but I still want to check it out. This is the first time anybody has actually admitted he's the killer."

"It may be the first time," says Caruso, getting up and putting on his jacket. "It sure as hell ain't gonna be the last."

55

"Who's there?"

"Police, Miss Hammond."

Sharon Hammond goes to the door, starts to unlock it, stops, looks through the peephole. Two men, neither

of them Phil. She quickly unlocks the door. The two
detectives flash their shields and come inside.

"Thank you for coming," she says. "Please sit down."

Max and Caruso sit down on the two least comfortable chairs in the living room. Caruso takes out his notebook and his ballpoint pen.

"OK, now," says Caruso, pen poised, "who is the individual who said he was the Hyena and threatened
your life, and what were the circumstances of this
threat?"

She looks at them a moment with great ambivalence
and then covers her face and cries softly.

"What is it, Miss Hammond?" says Max gently.

She shakes her head.

"What am I doing?" she says through her hands.

"Ma'am?"

"I'm reporting a man to the police as a killer. A man
I once thought I loved and wanted to marry. What kind
of a woman would do such a thing?"

Caruso looks to the heavens for commiseration and
puts his notebook away.

"Miss Hammond," says Max, "claiming to be a murderer and making threats on someone's life is not a
laughing matter. Anybody who does that *deserves* to be
reported to the police. He may not be the killer, but we
can't afford not to check it out."

She takes her hands away from her face and dabs at
her eyes with a handkerchief.

"I suppose you're right," she says.

"Now what is this joker's name?" says Max.

Caruso takes out his notebook again.

"Phil. Philip Varsi. You know, I just realized something."

"What's that?"

"If he wasn't serious about killing me *before,* he
might very well be now."

56

Babette sits in her philosophy class, taking a quiz. Her bluebook is open on her desk. The answer to the first question is not forthcoming. To stall for time, Babette has restated the question in the beginning of her answer but, having done that, she doesn't know what to put down next.

Her mind wanders. Her vision blurs. And before she knows it a vision of Max has formed in her head. Max without a shirt on. Max without any clothes on at all. Max in bed with . . . Babette? No. Max in bed with somebody else! Another woman. An older woman. A much older woman. Who?

Babette squeezes her eyelids together to make the other woman go away, but the woman persists. Suddenly the briefest flash of a name: Midtown or Miltown or . . . Middleton. Yes, Middleton. Max is in bed with somebody named Middleton. Just before the image fades the flesh of the-woman's face suddenly ages, dies, putrefies, turns black, and falls away from her skull, exposing a leering death's-head.

57

7:45 A.M. Time for Sharon Hammond to get out of bed and into the shower. Let's go, Sharon. Let's get this show on the road.

He picks up his field glasses and pans across to Sharon's building, idly counting windows with blinds drawn and windows with them open. The open ones win, twenty-nine to twenty-three. If the closed ones had won it might have been dangerous for anyone on an even-numbered floor.

Where is Sharon? She's usually so punctual you can set your watch by her.

Ah, there she is. Still in her nightie. Stretching those lovely arms. She suddenly walks to the window and looks out in his direction. He hits the deck.

Phew! Close call. He peeks back. She's turned away from the window, unconcerned. Maybe not such a close call. After all, he's a block away from her. She can't see his windows with the naked eye. Why would she be looking at his windows anyway, out of all the windows she could look at from her own? Why would *she* be researching *him?* Why would *anybody* be researching him, except the cops, and the cops didn't even know where to start, much less find him. Oh, no, he'd been too clever for that.

Sharon goes into the bathroom and closes the door. Twelve minutes, that's what it takes her to shower. Then she will open the door to let out the steam. That's the best part. She's usually naked then, or wearing a towel around her waist at most. Lovely tits Sharon has. He's seen them so many times he has a proprietary feeling about them.

He picks up his little notebook and checks something in code under Sharon's schedule, carefully erasing and relettering a sloppily printed word. Ah, yes. Cleaners this morning on the way to work, since she didn't do it yesterday. Unless she waits until tomorrow, in which case she won't have enough clothes for the weekend.

He swings the binoculars one building to the right. The apartment of Myrna Rice. Short, petite, close-cropped brown hair like a boy's. Myrna doesn't get up till Sharon leaves. Plenty of time.

Aha, Sharon is ready to come out of the shower. There she is, wearing a towel around her head, nothing more. Good old Sharon, right on schedule. What a pair of breasts. What a pair of legs. Sharon goes back into the bathroom to do her hair. He feels a surging, restless feeling.

He swings his binoculars up to the apartment of Ronnie Nolan, two floors up in Sharon's building. Blond, freckles, very wholesome. But Ronnie didn't adhere to a schedule as tight as Sharon's, and she wasn't up yet. Also, she didn't always leave her blinds open. Almost not worth the bother.

Sharon again. She emerges from the bathroom wearing her ratty old terrycloth robe, her hair up in rollers. Ugh. He hates how she looks in rollers. If he and Sharon ever hit it off well enough for him to consider moving in with her, he's going to insist she not walk around with her hair up in rollers.

Sharon walks into the bedroom to put on her underwear. Another best part coming up. Which bra and panties will she choose today—the yellow, the white, or the blue with the flowers perhaps?

She walks back into view. It's the blue ones with the flowers. Oh, Sharon, really. The white ones become you more. Look more wholesome. And the bra is much more flattering to your bustline.

When he had first spotted Sharon and started researching her she wasn't going with anybody. If she had, he'd never even have started up with her. He didn't much care for competition. Which was one reason why so many girls washed out in his research. He only liked the attractive ones, and not all of the attractive ones were unattached, although more than you would think.

Now this person Phil that she was going out with was almost no competition at all—a lush, a womanizer, by the current look of things, definitely on his way out. At least by the evidence of how much less frequently she was seeing him and how much less frequently he was being allowed to spend the night at her place, and by how little she was showing him any visible signs of affection. As soon as Phil began dating Sharon he had gone and checked him out. Followed him to a neighborhood liquor store, observed what he bought and how much—cheap bourbon, the man had no class—noted his name and address on the check he wrote for the liquor, the usual stuff.

Well, when Sharon breaks up with this creep Phil is when he will make his move.

58

Max unlocks the door to his apartment, steps inside and turns on the lights. He is surprised to see Babette sitting on the couch. Her eyes are open. She must have been sitting there in the dark.

"Hi, baby," he says, going over to kiss her.

She just looks at him.

"Hey, Babette, you all right?"

"Max?"

"Yes?"

"Do you know a woman named Middleton?"

He is a little startled, but recovers quickly.

"Yeah, sure. She's a dance instructor at Arthur Murray. Why?"

"How do you know her?"

"She's given us several suspects. Guys who've taken dance lessons at Arthur Murray who seemed a little weird. I went over there after I analyzed the tape I made of you in Linda Lowry's apartment."

"And have any of those suspects turned into anything?"

"Yeah, sort of. One in particular. A guy named Volkening. We've got a tail on him, as a matter of fact."

"Max?"

"Yes?"

"Did you have sex with her?"

"With Marilyn Middleton?" he says.

"Yes?"

"Why in God's name would you even *ask* me such a question?"

"Did you have sex with her?"

"Why are you asking that?"

"Did you or didn't you? I want to know."

"And I want to know why you're asking me that."

"You *did* have sex with her, didn't you?"

Max goes to put his arms around her, but she wriggles free of him.

"OK, what if I did? What does that have to do with you?"

"When was it? Was it since I've been living with you?"

"No, of course not," he says.

"When was it?"

"A while ago. I don't know."

"Was it since we've known each other?"

"Of course. You were the one who gave me the Arthur Murray lead, right?"

"Oh. That's right. Boy, that's really wonderful. I practically pushed you into her arms, didn't I?"

"Don't be silly. It just happened. But what does it matter? You and I hardly even *knew* each other then. We weren't even in love with each other then."

"*Some* of us were."

He tries to kiss her. She pulls away.

"Hey, Babette."

"Go away."

"Aw, c'mon."

"I was right," says Babette, "wasn't I?"

"About what?"

"About your liking the girls who let you make love to them better than you like me."

"Don't be ridiculous."

"It's true, though, isn't it?"

"Not at all."

"Why did you have sex with Marilyn Middleton?"

"I don't know. Because she asked me to, I guess."

"Do you have sex with everyone who asks you to?"

"Of course not."

"Then why did you have sex with *her?*"

"I don't know. Because she asked me to and because we were both drunk, for one thing."

"Was she good?"

"What do you mean?"

"You know what I mean. Was she good in bed?"

"I don't know. I suppose so."

"What did she do?"

"I don't remember."

"You don't *remember?* You had sex with her and you don't remember what she did? That doesn't speak very well of you, Max."

"Look, gimme a break, willya? She was fine. She did whatever you're supposed to do. She was responsive and appreciative and she was a good cuddler. To me that's being good in bed."

"That's all there is to being good in bed?"

"More or less."

"Then am *I* good in bed? Even though I haven't let you go, you know, all the way?"

"Yes, of course you are. You're responsive and appreciative and you're a good cuddler, aren't you?"

"And if I decided to let you go all the way, do you think I'd be as good in bed as Marilyn Middleton?"

"Of course you would."

Babette thinks this over.

"Do you think you're ever going to want to go to bed with Marilyn Middleton again?"

"I seriously doubt it."

"Do you seriously doubt it or are you sure?"

"I'm sure—OK?"

"You are? You're absolutely positive you don't ever want to go to bed with Marilyn Middleton again?"

"I'm absolutely positive."

"You mean all she was to you was a one-night stand?"

"Babette, give me a *break*. What do I have to do to make you stop this?"

"What do you have to do? I don't know. Maybe you have to hug me a lot."

He takes her in his arms and hugs her. She buries her nose in his neck. He kisses the top of her head and inhales the fragrance of her hair.

And neither of them thinks to inquire further about Marilyn Middleton and about how it was that her name happened to come up at all in Babette's trance and whether that meant somebody should warn her she was in danger.

59

8:45 A.M. Time for a rendezvous with Sharon.

He strolls into the Riteway Cleaners and gives one of the women behind the counter a suit to clean. Not a moment too soon, either, because in comes Sharon with her week's cleaning. The beige dress, the brown suit, the little blue outfit with the brass buttons, and, oh yes, that white blouse with the terrible print. Five pieces. No, maybe four. Count again. Yes, five. Five is a lucky number for today.

God, how he wished she wouldn't wear that white blouse. It did absolutely nothing for her bustline, and it was scooped too low besides. Made her look like she was some kind of B-girl. Well, he'd tell her about it one of these days. Maybe one day quite soon.

"Thursday evening OK, Miss Hammond?" says one of the women behind the counter.

"Is that the earliest you can have it?"

"I'm afraid so. We've been pretty jammed up."

"Oh, OK. Thursday then," says Sharon.

"About six?" says the woman.

"OK," says Sharon. "Oh, listen. Could you deliver it? I don't have time to pick it up. I have to meet somebody at seven sharp."

"Very well."

Hmmm. Thursday evening at six—what a perfect opportunity, he thinks. Is it too soon? Should he wait for confirmation that Phil is definitely out of the picture? He must be. Phil always comes to pick her up. The only chivalrous habit in all of Phil's repertoire.

Well, no need to make a decision right now. Plenty of time till Thursday. Plenty of time to think it over, weigh all the factors. If the timing isn't perfect, then forget it. But if the timing seems right, then strike!

60

OPEN LETTER TO THE HYENA
BY JOHNNY MONAHAN

It is not within me to judge a fellow human being. I know only too well the depths of my own depravity, the rottenness I have inflicted on my friends and loved ones and those who trusted me whose trust I constantly betray. Nothing human is alien to me, as the fellow says.

A man who writes what you have written is a man in pain. I cannot bear the pain of any fellow creature, no matter how grave the deeds to which he has confessed. I want to help you, if I can. If I can, and if you'll let me.

First of all, you are obviously an intelligent man—I do not say this to flatter you, it is apparent from your writing. Second, you are a romantic—it takes one to know one, the kids on my block used to say. Third, you are extremely sensitive and, fourth, you have been treated unfairly and you are furious about it.

You are not wrong to feel furious. You are not right to punish the objects of your fury in a manner you do not yourself approve. I gather from your letter that you do not approve of killing these women who betrayed you. I gather from this letter that you are punishing yourself even as you punish them.

Stop punishing yourself. Stop doing deeds of which you disapprove. Stop treating yourself as badly as those who have betrayed you treated you.

I want to help you, if you'll let me. You *need* help —professional help. I will see that you get it. I will meet with you anytime, anyplace you name, if you want to talk it over.

Hey, you know what? I kinda think you might have done the same for me.

Sincerely,
Johnny Monahan

It is amazing. It is hard to keep from crying. The famous Johnny Monahan offering—in print, in the actual *New York Daily News,* where everybody in the whole entire *world* can see it—to help *him,* to be *his friend.*

He sits down and spreads the newspaper out neatly in front of him on the couch so that its bottom edge is parallel with the edge of the cushion and reads it again. Yes, there it is, right in black and white: Johnny Monahan does not judge me. Johnny Monahan sees my pain. Johnny Monahan thinks I'm intelligent. *Intelligent.* Johnny Monahan sees that I'm a *romantic,*

that I'm *sensitive,* that I've been *unfairly treated*—
Johnny Monahan the famous columnist sees that,
not some stupid asshole on the subway. Johnny Monahan knows that I'm *furious.* Johnny Monahan says that
I'm not *wrong* to feel furious. Oho!

Then, of course, there is all that nonsense about not
punishing the objects of my fury in a manner that,
ummm, something about approving, about punishing
myself as badly, ummm . . . and some other nonsense.

And *then.* Then comes the best part of all—Johnny
Monahan wants to *meet* me. Johnny Monahan, the
famous columnist wants to meet *me!* Anytime, anyplace I name. What would the stupid assholes I audi-
tion for and bus dishes for and deliver things to, who
wouldn't even give me the time of day, say if they knew
that Johnny Monahan wanted to meet me anytime, anyplace I name? What would the women who think I'm
scum under their shoes say if they knew that I was
friends with Johnny Monahan? They would kiss my ass,
that's what they would do!

Well, where would be a good time and place to meet
him? Maybe he could come up to the apartment for a
drink. True, it wasn't such a fancy apartment, and
you did have to walk up a few flights of stairs to get
there, but Johnny didn't seem like the kind of man who
would mind that.

Well now, what would Johnny drink? Probably bourbon. Have to get some bourbon. The good stuff, not
rotgut. Maybe even Jack Daniels. You don't have
Johnny Monahan to your apartment every night of the
week, after all. Yes, Jack Daniels sounds just right.

Assuming I time his visit properly, I could even let
him look at Sharon Hammond. Hell—*I could take him
to meet Sharon Hammond in person.* Once she saw I
was a friend of Johnny's, she'd probably even go out
with me.

Oh-oh. What if Sharon Hammond liked Johnny *better* than me? What if Sharon and Johnny became, as he puts it, an *item?* After all, who is the famous one, me or Johnny? Well, so much for that idea. Better stick to giving him a peek at her through the field glasses and let it go at that. After all, as Johnny himself is the first to admit, he constantly betrays those who trust him, so why tempt fate?

Wait a minute. Hold on there. If he constantly betrays those who trust him, what's to stop him from bringing along the cops when he comes to meet me? What indeed? Well, forewarned is forearmed. He would just have to figure out a way to meet Johnny that would not allow the man to give in to his baser instincts. In the meantime, there was work to do on present projects . . .

61

5:45 P.M. Thursday. Contact time for Sharon Hammond, assuming contact is going to be made. Is contact going to be made? The factors have been weighed. The timing seems perfect. The decision is yes. After an eternity of waiting, tonight is the night he will reveal his love for Sharon.

He picks up the phone, dials, waits, counts the rings. If they answer on an even-numbered ring it will be a sign for him to go ahead as planned. They answer on the sixth ring.

"Ah, yes," he says in a British accent, "Miss Hammond asked me to ring you up. She'd requested her cleaning delivered at six tonight? Ah. Well, she was originally intending to meet me at seven, you see, but our plans have changed and there won't be time. She wonders if she might just pick it up tomorrow instead, after work. Splendid. Very good. Thank you so much."

He hangs up the phone, congratulating himself on his performance. He goes to his closet, counts the number of garments, and takes out two of his suits which are covered in a plastic bag marked RITEWAY CLEANERS. He opens the front door, a big smile on his face.

"Who's there?"

"Miss Hammond?"

"Yes?"

"Riteway Cleaners, ma'am."

She goes to the door, starts to unlock it, stops. What if it's him? Nonsense. It's the cleaners. She told them to deliver her cleaning at six, it's six now, and here they are. Honestly, Sharon, you're really carrying all this a bit too far.

Just to be on the safe side, though, she looks through the peephole. There, you see? It's a man from the cleaners with a plastic bag in his hand. He even looks vaguely familiar. The important thing, in any case, is that it isn't Phil.

She unlocks the door and lets him in.

He hands her the cleaning. She takes it and starts to pay him when she notices that there's been a mistake.

"Oh, dear," she says, "I'm afraid they've made a mistake."

"Pardon me?"

"They've sent the wrong garments. See? These are men's suits. This isn't my cleaning. And I'm so rushed tonight as it is—darn."

The man just looks at her. What's the matter with

him, didn't he understand her? Is he deaf or feeble-minded or what?

"I said this isn't my *cleaning*. They've made a *mistake*."

The man continues to look at her.

"This *isn't* your cleaning," he says, "but there isn't any mistake."

"What? What are you talking about? Look. See this? This is some man's *suits*. It's not *mine*. It's not what I— oh, never mind," she says and goes to the telephone. "I'll tell them myself. I don't have time to—"

He moves so swiftly and so silently that she doesn't even realize he's moved at all until she reaches out for the phone and his hand closes over it and his other hand severs the cord with a long, horrible-looking knife.

Dizziness overtakes her and she feels as though she's going to faint. Something dreadful has just started happening to her and she doesn't know if she wants to be conscious for it.

"I don't want to hurt you, Sharon," the man is saying quietly. "I promise I won't hurt you if you do exactly as I say."

It doesn't make sense. The one to fear is Phil. This isn't Phil. This is the man from the cleaners. No, it's not the man from the cleaners, it can't be—he didn't even bring my cleaning. Well, the *real* man from the cleaners is coming any second now. When he does, perhaps this one will be scared away. The trick is to stall for time.

"What do you want me to do?" she says.

"I want to get to know you better. I want to have a date with you. So you can get to know me as well as I know you."

"You want a what? A date?"

"A date. I want to date you."

She turns around and looks at him to see if he is

serious. He looks as serious as she has ever seen any-body look in her life. He is mad, she thinks. He is ab-solutely mad. You can see it in his eyes. This must be the real one. The one who calls himself the Hyena. Then Phil wasn't serious after all. Poor Phil—she'd gone and reported him to the police when the real killer, the real Hyena, was this man the whole time.

The man reaches into the plastic bag and takes out a square package wrapped in brown paper. What has he got in there? Whatever it is, she thinks, I deserve it. I deserve it for what I did to Phil.

"May I put this on the phonograph?"

If she hadn't gone and reported Phil to the police, then she wouldn't have stopped dating him, and if she hadn't stopped dating him, she wouldn't have agreed to go out with Raymond tonight, and she wouldn't be meeting him at seven, and she would have picked up her cleaning instead of having it delivered, and she wouldn't be standing here now with a crazed sex killer in her apartment. It was all her doing. It was all her fault. And she deserved whatever she got.

"I *said* may I put this on the phonograph?"

"I don't care. Do whatever you want. What does it matter anymore?"

She feels the dizziness again and is amazed that she is still on her feet.

The man takes a record out of the square package and hands it to her.

"Put this on the phonograph," he says.

"Please. Do it yourself. Do whatever you want to."

The man sees that she truly doesn't seem to care. He shrugs, locates the phonograph, turns it on, and puts the record on to play. Sharon leans against the wall for support. The music begins:

Did you say I've got a lot to learn?
Well, don't think I'm trying not to learn,

Since this is the perfect spot to learn,
Teach me tonight . . ."

"April Stevens," says the man pleasantly. "Do you remember her?"

"Please," she says, "no talking. Just do whatever you have to do. Let's get it over with."

"She looks a little like you in a way."

"What?"

"I *said* she looks a little like you in a way. April Stevens."

"Listen, I'm not really feeling too steady on my feet. I'm going to sit down, is that all right?"

"Oh, what a pity. I thought you might care to dance."

"What?"

"I *said* I thought you might care to dance. And please do not say *what.*"

"You want to *dance,* you say?"

"Yes."

"What for?"

"To get to know you. To establish a nice setting for our date. To trip the light fantastic. Just like you used to do with Phil and with Steven."

Staring at him, her eyelids droop and she slides to the floor. The man looks at her impassively a moment.

"Sharon?"

There is no reply. Sharon has fainted dead away.

This has never happened before. He doesn't know what to do. If they faint, you're supposed to slap their face. He slaps her face. She doesn't move. If they faint, you're supposed to give them smelling salts. He doesn't have any smelling salts. He wonders if she has some in the bathroom.

He wanders into the bathroom and looks in the medicine cabinet for smelling salts, but he doesn't see any. He counts the little bottles in the medicine cabinet. If there is an even number, it will be a sign to forget the smelling salts. There are eighteen little bottles. He goes back into the other room.

Sharon has still not moved. He bends down to look at her.

"Sharon?"

She is unconscious. He slaps her hard on the cheek. "Sharon! Talk to me, God damn you!"

He slaps her again viciously. Her head rolls with the slap. Is she still alive? He feels her pulse. It's still there. He doesn't know what to do. How can he finish this if she doesn't do something, doesn't either go along with it or else fight back? What is he supposed to do now?

He picks up his knife in one hand and grabs her by the front of the blouse in the other hand and puts the knife to her throat, but she isn't even aware of what he is doing.

He sticks the knife into the fabric of her blouse and cuts it, keeps cutting it until it's slit all the way down. He eases the tip of the knife in under her brassiere straps and cuts them loose. He puts the tip of the knife under her belt and cuts it. He sticks it into the fabric of her skirt, and slits it all the way down and peels her out of her clothing like a banana. He slits her slip and her pantyhose in the same fashion.

He delicately fits the tip of the knife inside the crotch of her panties and slices it open. There is her pussy. Her twat. Her cunt. Her va-*gi*-nah.

He touches the hairy part with the flat of his blade. He touches it experimentally with his finger. He puts his entire hand on it. It feels warm. It would be so easy to take advantage of her now. So easy, and so unfair. If you love someone—love them the way that he loves Sharon—then you respect them enough to wait. He will wait. Until Sharon herself decides that she is ready for sex. That way it will mean more.

He tugs the panties with the slit crotch off her hips, stands up, and stuffs them in his pocket so he can have something to remember her by till he sees her again.

He gets ready to leave. He puts away his knife and picks up his record and his plastic bag with the suits inside it and he is just about to go to the door when he hears her moan. He turns around.

"Sharon?"

She moans again and opens her eyes.

"Sharon, darling, you all right?"

She looks up at him, looks down at her clothes, which are slashed to pieces, and begins to scream.

"Sharon, darling, ssssshhh!"

She continues to scream.

"Sharon, darling, be quiet!"

She keeps on screaming. He lunges toward her and puts his hands around her throat and begins to squeeze.

62

Babette is watching the late show on TV, something about a man who's staying overnight in a haunted house on a bet. It's supposed to be a comedy. The telephone rings.

Not taking her eyes off the set, she picks up the phone.

"Hello?"

Silence at the other end.

"Hello?"

There is no answer, but somebody is definitely on the other end of the line.

"Who is this?"

Silence.

She hangs up the phone and goes back to the man in the haunted house.

63

Max is typing up yet another in an endless series of "fives"—the reports that every detective is required to type up, which summarize the results of daily jobs such as canvassing and tailing and interrogation. Max curses at his typing skill and at the ancient upright typewriter's apparent unwillingness to print the keys he's sure he's hitting.

The telephone rings. Larry Cassidy picks it up, speaks briefly, hangs up.

"Hey, Max," he says with unaccustomed seriousness, "bad news."

"What is it?" says Max, still fighting with his typewriter.

"The Hyena's scored another hit. I'm afraid he got your girlfriend."

Max's heart stops. No. Oh, please, no. Max swivels slowly in his chair.

"Sharon Hammond," says Larry sadly. "Isn't that the gal you and Caruso promised to take care of?"

"Yeah," says Max, giddy with relief and feeling instantly remorseful at having such a reaction to news of Sharon Hammond's death. "That's the one."

"OK, men," says the C.O., "let's get over there and see if he's left us anything to work with."

64

DETECTIVE BUREAU UNUSUAL OCCURRENCE REPORT · Misc. 300 (Rev. 8-68)

DET. LOD. (PCT.) 17	DATE & DAY of original report	TIME	PLACE OF OCCURRENCE and type of premises	CRIME/CONDITION (BRIEF & CONCISE)
	12-23-77	0845	227 E. 47 St.	Homicide

DETAILS:

1. At time and place of occurence a female tentatively identified as Sharon Hammond was found DOA, victim of a homicide.

2. Victims' clothing cut off with sharp instrument (Not recovered).

3. Premises sealed.

COMPLAINANT(S)

NAME POSNY (Hammond)
ADDRESS 227 E. 47 St., Manhattan
SEX F RACE W AGE 22 BF
DESCRIPTION/VALUE
PROPERTY TAKEN
INJURED: YES NO
HOSPITAL CONDITION

NAME
ADDRESS
SEX RACE AGE BF
DESCRIPTION/VALUE
PROPERTY TAKEN
INJURED: YES NO
HOSPITAL CONDITION

PERPETRATOR(S)

PERPETRATOR ARRESTED? YES NO

NAME
ADDRESS
BF

SEX RACE AGE HGT. WT.
DESCRIPTION (CLOTHING)

INJURIES:
WEAPON(S)
AUTO USED: YES NO
PLATE/MAKE
NO. OF ARRESTS
ARRESTING OFFICER CMD.

PERPETRATOR ARRESTED? YES NO

NAME
ADDRESS
BF

SEX RACE AGE HGT. WT.
DESCRIPTION (CLOTHING)

INJURIES:
WEAPON(S)
AUTO USED: YES NO
PLATE/MAKE
NO. OF ARRESTS
ARRESTING OFFICER CMD.

VISIT TO IDENTIFICATION UNIT
YES NO DATE

SPECIAL SQUADS NOTIFIED: Homicide

UF 61# 11212	PCT. 17	CASE #	DET. ASSGND. Det. Lawrence Cassidy, 3rd Hom. Shield # 232	ALARM # or arrest message info:

DATE OF THIS REPORT 12-23-77

RANK AND SIGNATURE OF COMMANDING OFFICER/IN COMMAND
Lt. P. J. O'Malley

ANY ADDITIONAL NAMES OR INFORMATION SHALL BE ADDED ON REVERSE — NOT ON ADDITIONAL PAGES

65

Jerry and Larry and Max and Caruso sit in the dirty green Plymouth outside Philip Varsi's apartment house.

"So Varsi's got a sheet on him, has he?" says Caruso.

"Yep," says Jerry. "He's been booked for assault, aggravated assault, and assault and battery. He's a tough piece of work and a really unpleasant character, but I don't think he's our man."

"But you don't object to pulling him in, I take it?" says Max.

"Nah, pull him in," says Jerry, "what do *I* care?"

A cab stops ahead of them and a large man in a dark overcoat gets out and slams the door.

"That's him," says Larry.

The four detectives get out of the car and close in on Varsi.

"Philip Varsi?" says Larry.

Varsi turns, sees the four men, and looks alarmed.

"What do you want?" he says.

"Police officers," says Larry. "We'd like you to come back to the precinct and have a little chat."

"About what?" says Varsi.

"About Sharon Hammond," says Jerry, giving him the toss and finding him clean.

"What about her?" says Varsi.

"You told her you were the Hyena," says Jerry, snapping the cuffs on him.

"You're out of your fucking mind," says Varsi.

"Detective Mahoney," says Larry grandly, "would you care to inform Mr. Varsi of his rights?"

"With pleasure, Detective Cassidy," says Jerry. "Mr. Varsi, you have the right to remain silent. You have—"

"You guys are out of your fucking minds," says Varsi. "Since when is it a crime to say something to somebody as a joke?"

"It's not," says Larry. "But when the joke consists of telling somebody you're a famous killer, and when the person you have told it to winds up killed, then we like to take the joker back to the squad and swap funny stories with him."

Varsi looks genuinely shaken.

"Sharon's been *killed?*" he says.

"That's right, funny guy," says Larry. "Now let's go back to the squad and you can tell us some real knee-slappers. I can hardly wait."

66

Ranged against the back wall of the Lieutenant's office are five glowering, suspicious-looking men with numbered cards around their necks.

The one with a card with a number 1 on it is 6'2", 32 years old, stocky, about 208 lbs., with dishwater-blond hair. His name is Ralph Scanlon. Number 2 is about 5'11", 31 years old, on the slender side, about 155 lbs., with curly brown hair. His name is Everett Arder. Number 3 is 6'0", 39 years old, moderately well built,

about 180 lbs., with straight brown hair. His name is
Bob Lubash. Number 4 is 5'10", 36 years old, also
athletically built, 160 lbs., with reddish brown hair. His
name is David Kennedy. Number 5 is 6'0", 37 years old,
also athletically built, about 200 lbs., with dark brown
hair. His name is Philip Varsi.

Varsi is a suspect in a homicide case. The others are
all homicide detectives.

Detective Cassidy takes two Polaroids of the lineup,
then goes outside and closes the door and addresses
himself to the six men waiting just outside: Detectives
Jerry Mahoney, Max Segal, Sal Caruso; Abraham Weinstock, the neighbor who caught a glimpse of the killer
outside Beverly Rachlin's apartment; Ramon Rodriguez,
the night watchman who allowed the killer to sign in
and go upstairs to kill Pamela Marlin and Frieda Winston; and Frank McMartin, the doorman who permitted
the killer to deliver flowers to and then murder Linda
Lowry.

"All right, gentlemen," says Cassidy, "I want you to
look through the one-way glass in this here door and
see if you recognize any of the men standing against the
back wall with numbers around their necks. If you do,
write down the man's number on the slip of paper that
Detective Mahoney has given you. I do not wish you to
discuss this matter with any of the other witnesses, nor
do I wish you to let any of the other witnesses see what
number you have written down on your slip of paper.
Everybody understand?"

Weinstock, Rodriguez, and McMartin nod.

"What if it isn't any of them?" says McMartin.

"Then don't write down *any* number on your slip of
paper," says Cassidy. "This is not a popularity contest,
gentlemen. This is not the 'Ted Mack Amateur Hour.'
If you do not recognize any of the lineup, then do not

write any number on your slip of paper. Any more questions?"

"Can they see us?" says Rodriguez.

"No, Rodriguez," says Cassidy. "The idea behind one-way glass is that you can only see through it one way. Any more questions? Good. Just step up to the window there and take a good look. Take all the time you need. Mr. Weinstock, you go first."

Weinstock steps up to the one-way window, takes his time, then steps aside. Cassidy points to Rodriguez, who steps up to the window, takes about the same length of time, then steps aside. Both Weinstock and Rodriguez write something on their slips of paper, Rodriguez trying unsuccessfully to sneak a fast peek at Weinstock's.

Cassidy points to McMartin. McMartin steps up to the window, shakes his head, then steps aside and writes something on his slip.

"All right, gentlemen," says Mahoney, "please give me your slips of paper. And thanks very much for coming in."

Weinstock, Rodriguez, and McMartin hand Mahoney their slips of paper, then file out of the squad room. Mahoney spreads the slips of paper out on a desk. Caruso, Cassidy, and Max gather around to see.

"Excellent," says Mahoney. "We have a unanimous decision: the killer is Detective Third Grade Everett Arder. Caruso, go read Detective Arder his rights and see if he wants to make a statement to the District Attorney."

67

Max and Babette are walking along Fifth Avenue just after dark on Christmas Eve. Miraculously, although the newspapers and TV weather reports had said there was no chance of it, it has begun to snow. Large, heavy white flakes begin falling splendidly to earth and not melting when they hit the ground. It will be a White Christmas after all.

Max and Babette walk happily, hand in hand, past frenzied last-minute shoppers, incredible motorized store window displays, skinny streetcorner Santas, clumps of zealous Salvation Army musicians playing very nearly in unison.

They swing across 49th Street to Rockefeller Plaza to take in the gigantic Christmas tree and the ice skaters on the rink just below, and then they head down 51st to Fifth Avenue again.

Babette has sworn up and down the avenue that she has absolutely no regrets about the fact that this is the first Christmas she is not spending with her crappy mother and her even crappier stepfather, and Max is trying his damnedest to make sure she doesn't change her mind. A few days ago he'd hidden presents for her in the closet, and this afternoon when she was out he sneaked in a tiny Christmas tree—the first one he'd ever had—decorated it with a Jewish guy's idea of how Christmas trees were decorated, which he hoped wouldn't cause her to burst out laughing when she saw it.

"Where we going, Max?"

"Little place I know on First Avenue and 48th. Terrific food, and very cozy, plus which they have this incredible piano bar with this guy who specializes in singing and playing these obscure Cole Porter and Noel Coward songs. I was there once or twice before around this time of year and, especially if there's snow on the ground, it's about the perfect New York Christmas atmosphere. After that we will go home, light a fire in the fireplace, drink hot-buttered rum, and snuggle."

She hugs him and her eyes grow teary.

"You're a marvelous man, Max Segal."

He returns her embrace, and neither of them notices the man in the dark overcoat with the vacant eyes who has been following them for several blocks, who now brushes past them for a closer look.

68

He pulls her head backward. Her long chestnut-colored hair falls into the sink. He soaks the hair in warm water, then rubs the lather into her scalp. She doesn't make a sound but her eyes are closed and he can tell that she is enjoying it as much as he is. Without any trouble at all he can sight right down her loosely tied dressing gown to see the stiff nipples on her breasts.

This job at the Monsieur Maurice hairdressing salon on 57th street is the only one he's gotten through Helping Hands that is the least bit pleasurable. It will probably only last a week, until the regular shampooer who is out sick returns. No matter. He is using the time beautifully. Having wordless and anonymous sensual experiences with scores of total strangers, touching them in absurdly familiar ways. It is hard to see how these women can continue their charade of remaining aloof from him when he can see the truth so plainly.

The women who have seemed the most aroused by the way he washed their hair deserve to see him again in a more private atmosphere. He will make sure they do. The hair colorist's address book lies open for him to memorize names and addresses of clients as he sweeps the floor between shampoos. In their own apartments they will be freer to respond to him in the way they so obviously want to.

The woman with the chestnut hair has a copy of the *Daily News* in her lap, opened to a story about the Hyena. What would she say if she knew that the Hyena himself was shampooing her hair?

The woman's last name is either Arvin or Armin, it's hard to see it clearly in the address book from where he stands. He can't make out the first name either. Maybe he ought to try to engage her in small talk, even though he isn't skilled in it. So they will already have spoken before they have their official date. Or maybe he should remain silent and not speak to her till he does his research. What is the wisest course? He will look for a sign. If the next woman who comes through the door from the dressing rooms has dark hair, he will try some small talk. If the next woman who comes through the door has light hair, he will remain silent.

He rinses the soap out, pulling the woman's hair a little more than he has to in the process, and lathers it up again. Somebody comes through the door. A woman with black hair. There is his sign.

He rubs the lather into her scalp and clears his throat.

"What's the latest on the Hyena?" he says.

"Pardon me?"

"I *said* what's the latest on the Hyena?"

"Oh," she says, "him. I don't know. They don't seem to have very many leads, though. I can't understand it."

"Perhaps he's just too clever for them."

"I don't know. I don't go out after dark, though, I can tell you that. And I don't let anyone into my apartment either, I don't care if they're the Pope."

"What would the Pope want to get into your apartment for?"

"What do you mean?"

"You said you wouldn't let anyone into your apartment, even if they're the Pope."

"Oh. Uh, yes."

She stops talking. That was stupid, he thinks. What the hell did I have to say that for? Just when I had some good small talk going, too. Now she thinks I'm crazy.

"Tell me," he says, "what do you think they ought to do to this guy if they *do* catch him, or if he gives himself up?"

"Tear him apart," she says. "Tear his arms and legs off. Any man who does what he has done doesn't deserve to even have a trial in court. They should just throw him to the parents of the women he's killed and let them tear him apart."

He envisions himself being torn apart by the woman with the chestnut hair. He finds the fantasy amusing. He will remind her of her words when he sees her next. In her apartment.

69

"Now that you've witnessed it yourself," says Natale, "are you a believer in psychic phenomena?"

"I don't know, doc," says Max. "At the time it's happening, sure. But looking back on it, I start having doubts."

Natale laughs. Max's reaction was just what he'd said it would be. He wonders if Max would let him meet his psychic friend. The fact that Max has so far gone out of his way to avoid using her name suggests he might be reluctant.

"Max, I'd sure like to meet this friend of yours. I could learn a helluva lot about parapsychology by observing her. What do you say?"

"I don't know, doc."

"You don't trust me, or what?"

"It's not that I don't trust you. Although, to be perfectly honest, I don't know yet that I can. It's more that I just have this very protective instinct toward her. And I don't know that I'm ready to introduce her to anybody yet."

"OK."

"On the other hand, I don't know that I'm not."

"OK."

Pause.

"Doc, do you think she's crazy?"

"I don't know, Max. I don't know enough about her

to even have an opinion yet. What do *you* think? Do you think she's crazy, Max?"

"I don't know. I mean, what about this trance stuff? She says it's like she's in the past and in the present at the same time. Or in the future and the present. She says that physicists today are screwing around with the idea that maybe the past, the present, and the future exist simultaneously."

"That *is* an idea physicists are screwing around with these days. You know, our whole concept of time is pretty fucked up. Physicists are beginning to think it's something very different than we were taught in school."

"How do you mean?"

"Well, what do you consider the past and what do you consider the future? Most people think of the past as yesterday, the present as today, and the future as tomorrow. That we move from the past, to the present, to the future."

"So?"

"So in fact, as I'm saying this sentence out loud, the part that I haven't said yet is really the future, the part that I've already said is the past, and the part that I'm saying right now—right *now*—is the present. But what was the exact point that the present occurred? And how long did it last? Maybe the future just passes directly into the past, and there isn't any present at all. Maybe the present is just an illusion."

"Maybe. But what does that have to do with how Ba—with how my friend could be in the past and the present at the same time? Like when she picks up past conversations. Or the *future* and the present? Like when she has these precognitive dreams about homicides that haven't even happened yet?"

"Max, listen."

"Yeah?"

"This idea that the past, the present, and the future exist simultaneously?"

"Yeah?"

"I realize that's a mind-buster. But only because we've been trained to think in linear modes, and that ain't a linear concept, OK? But if the past, the present, and the future *did* exist simultaneously, then maybe you could find a way to tune into one or the other. And see or hear something that—in linear terms—either hadn't happened yet or that happened already, you know?"

"Mmmmm."

Natale laughs.

"You're not buying any of this, are you?" he says.

"It's just that it sounds kind of screwy, is all," says Max.

"I know," says Natale. "Look. Do you know what a tachyon is?"

"No."

"A tachyon is a subatomic particle that travels faster than the speed of light, and gets where it's going, technically speaking, before it starts out. Screwy, huh?"

"Yeah."

"Well, that's pretty much an accepted concept in physics these days. Do you know what a black hole is?"

"Sort of."

"A black hole is a burnt-out star that keeps imploding and imploding until the magnetic field that surrounds it is so strong that it swallows up even light waves. That's pretty screwy, too, huh?"

"Yeah."

"Well, that's pretty much an accepted concept in astronomy these days. But you can find screwy things like that in all of the sciences. In biology, even. Do you know that there is a certain species of eel that has such a screwy sense of smell it can detect the presence of a *thimbleful* of rose scent diluted in a lake covering an area of *14,000 square miles?*"

"No kidding."

"And there's a type of moth that can detect the female of the species from one *molecule* of her essence thirty miles away. That's pretty screwy, too, isn't it?"

"Yeah. Doc . . . ?"

"The truth is, Max, that everything in the whole damned universe is pretty screwy. And psychic phenomena aren't really a whole lot screwier than stuff you find in respectable fields like physics, astronomy, and biology."

"Yeah. Doc?"

"What?"

"If I introduced you to Babette—that's her name, by the way, Babette—and you observed her do some of her stuff, *then* would you be able to tell me whether or not you think she's crazy?"

70

Babette is lying downstairs on Max's bed, reading. Upstairs the doorbell rings. She looks at the clock at the side of the bed: 11:30. Max is working the four-to-one shift tonight. Who could it be at this hour?

The doorbell rings again. She goes upstairs. She presses the intercom.

"Who is it?"

"Mrs. Segal?"

"Uh, yes?"

"It's Hector Gomez," says a voice with a faint Puerto Rican accent, "your neighbor in 4-C. I'm sorry to disturb you at this hour, but I've locked myself out of my apartment. Could you buzz me in?"

Hector Gomez? Come to think of it, she did recall seeing such a name on one of the mailboxes outside.

"OK, Mr. Gomez."

She buzzes the buzzer and hears the hall door open and close. Footsteps walk down the hallway and stop just outside the door to Max's apartment. There is something wrong about this.

There is a knock at the door.

"Mrs. Segal?"

"Yes?"

"It's Hector Gomez, Mrs. Segal. I wonder if I could talk to you a moment?"

"What about?"

"I wonder if you could open the door, please?"

"What is it you want?"

"Well, I appreciate your letting me in the hall door, but I'm still locked out of my apartment. I wonder if I could use your phone to call a locksmith?"

There is something very wrong about this. Babette goes to the peephole and looks through it. She sees nothing. She sees blackness. Why can't she see through the peephole? Then, suddenly, she knows why. The person on the other side of the door is covering it with his hand.

"Mr. Gomez?"

"Yes?"

"Just stay there. I'll call the locksmith for you."

Babette checks to make sure that all the locks on the door are locked, then goes swiftly to the phone. She dials Max's number at Homicide.

"Third Homicide, Detective Segal."

"Hello, this is Mrs. Segal. My neighbor, Mr. Gomez,

has locked himself out of his apartment and wonders if you could come and let him in?"

"Babette what is it?"

"The address is 346 East 19th Street. He would appreciate it if you could get here as fast as you can."

"Babette, are you in trouble? Is somebody there?"

"Yes, that's right. As fast as you can, please."

71

Max drops the phone back into the cradle, grabs his coat, and tears out of the squad room and down the hallway to the stairs.

"Hey, Segal, what is it?" shouts Caruso from the squad room, but Max is already down the stairs and out on the street, flagging down a cab, which screeches to a stop.

He hops in and flashes his shield in the cabbie's face.

"346 East 19th Street, as fast as you can get there—this is police business!"

"Since when are the cops using cabs?"

"As fast as you can get there, or I'm commandeering your fucking cab!"

The cabbie puts the car in gear and takes off. The cab races across 51st Street, turns left on Lexington, and is going about forty-five miles per hour when the signal at 48th and Lex begins to turn red. The cab screeches to a halt.

"Run it! Run the fucking signal!"

"I can't—I'll get a ticket!"

"You *can't* get a ticket, you asshole—I'm a *cop!*"

The cabbie starts up again and runs the light. The cab proceeds down Lex, weaving around slow-moving cars and continuing to run red lights. Outraged motorists blare their horns at him, but the cabbie keeps on going.

"Don't you guys have your own goddam cars anymore or what?" says the cabbie.

"This is an emergency. There wasn't time to get a police car, OK? Can't you drive any faster than this?"

The cabbie guns it harder and begins to chuckle.

"I feel like we're in the car chase in *The French Connection,*" says the cabbie. "You know, I've always dreamed of being able to do this."

A siren starts up behind them and lights begin flashing. A radio car begins bearing down on them. The cab slows down.

"Don't stop, goddammit!" says Max.

"I *have* to stop! They'll *shoot* me if I don't stop!"

The cab grinds to a halt. Max leaps out of the car, rushes over to the radio car, and jams his shield in the driver's face.

"On the *job,* you asshole!" Max screams at him, "On the *job,* you fucking creep!"

The radio car cop's mouth falls open, and Max jumps back in the cab.

"C'mon, move it!"

"Jesus," says the cabbie, "wait till I tell my kids about this."

The cab rips off a left turn on 23rd Street and continues to weave in and out of traffic and run red lights till it arrives at Max's apartment at 346 East 19th Street. Max is already out of the cab by the time it stops, gun drawn.

He unlocks the hall door and charges up to the door of his apartment. He unlocks the door and kicks it open, falling into a two-handed firing crouch.

"My God, don't shoot!"

Babette cowers against the far wall. Max spins around, checks all corners of the room. Babette runs to him, falls into his arms.

"Oh, God, Max, he's gone. He disappeared as soon as I called you. I'm sorry. I'm sorry I made you do this. But I think it was him, Max. I think it was the Hyena."

Footfalls in the hall outside the apartment door. Max spins around, revolver out ahead of him, and almost collides with a man.

"Jesus Christ, put that thing away, will you? All I want is my *fare!*"

72

Marilyn Middleton pours off the last martini in the pitcher and takes a healthy gulp from the glass. The ice makes her fillings ache but the booze has made her warm and woozy enough to not mind.

She is wearing only the trenchcoat she slipped on to take the trash to the incinerator in the hallway, with nothing underneath. It would be perfect, she thinks, if there were a man here with her now. She would pull him down on the bed and tear his clothes off, savagely ripping the material in the process. Then she would cover his flesh with such sweet kisses he would never mind she'd torn his clothes. Then she'd have him just lie back on the bed while she made love to him for about four hours.

Who did she know who could last that long. What about the Segal kid? He was such a kid, that kid. Not a bad lover, however. Where was that card he'd given her with his number?

She finds the card, goes to the phone, and dials. It rings three times. On the fourth ring it's picked up.

"Hello?" says an unfamiliar voice at the other end. A woman's voice. The damned Segal kid was married!

"Is Harry there?" says Marilyn.

"Harry? No, I'm afraid you've got the wrong number."

"Sorry, sweetheart," says Marilyn and hangs up the phone.

That bastard, she thinks. Why had he given her that number anyway? To humiliate her? "If you ever decide you want to see me again, call me." The bastard.

All men were bastards—when was she ever going to learn her lesson? When was she ever going to quit making herself vulnerable to them?

She goes to the window with her drink and opens the blinds to a wider angle and looks down at the street. Two hookers huddle in a doorway across the street to the left. A few doors to the right a man in a dark overcoat stands looking upward in her direction. He appears startled at her appearance. Is he a peeping tom?

She impulsively whips open her trenchcoat and gives the man a good look at her nakedness before letting the blinds fall closed all the way.

The man in the dark overcoat remains staring at the window with the closed blinds for several minutes. The sight of the woman's naked body has filled him to the bursting point. He does not know what possessed her to do what she did, but he doesn't care. He has been researching her for such a long time, he cannot wait much longer. His love is too tremendous.

73

The meeting is called for 1600 hours at the change of tours. Sitting in chairs and on top of desks in the Third Homicide squad room are all eight detectives from the eight-to-four tour, six of the eight from the four-to-one tour, two from the one-to-eight, and Tony Natale. Lieutenant O'Malley looks over some reports, then addresses the men:

"As you know, gentlemen, we are beginning to get a lot of flak from the public and from the media about our lack of progress on the Hyena homicides. The Mayor's office informs me that a group of local businessmen are concerned because tourists, which are this city's single biggest source of income, are beginning to avoid New York like the plague. I know how upset you gentlemen would be if this city lost its tourists."

Good-natured chuckles from the men.

"Now then," says Lieutenant O'Malley, "the Mayor is busting the Commissioner's chops about this case, the Commissioner is busting Chief Noonan's chops, Chief Noonan is busting *my* chops, and now, gentlemen, I am going to have to start busting *yours*.

"Now I know that some of you men have been working extra tours without pay on this thing, and I appreciate it. The Commissioner is going to be reassigning some men from Fourth Homicide to work with us in a day or so. In the meantime, what new developments can I report to Chief Noonan at my six o'clock meeting today? Cassidy, are you getting anywhere on Philip Varsi?"

"Lieutenant," says Larry, "I would personally be tickled to death for Philip Varsi to turn out to be the Hyena as he claimed, but I'm afraid he's going to disappoint us."

"What did you get on him, Cassidy?"

"Me and Mahoney probably know more about this joker now than we know about our wives, Lieutenant. The guy is quite a little charmer. He's been booked for assault, aggravated assault, assault and battery. Not only did he threaten Sharon Hammond's life when she refused to see him anymore, he also went out with a girl named Alice Drummond and on one occasion belted her in the mouth and broke three of her teeth."

"Unfortunately," says Jerry, "we can't put Varsi anywhere near any of the victims' apartments on the evenings any of the homicides took place. Also, the prints me and Cassidy got off Varsi and sent to the lab don't match the ones the Crime Scene Unit picked up at either Rachlin's or Lowry's apartment. And we didn't get any I.D.'s on him from the lineup we did in your office. Plus which, the composite they're making up on the perpetrator don't look nothing at all like our pal Varsi."

"Or anyone else, for that matter," says Larry.

Laughter.

"Well," says Larry, "I've never seen a composite that looked anything like the perp once they collared him."

"Scanlon," says the Lieutenant, "what did you get from Riteway on that call?"

"The individual who telephoned to cancel the delivery to Sharon Hammond called at approximately 1745 hours, Lieutenant. It was definitely a man. The woman who took the call thinks he might be English, but she isn't sure. She says she has an uncle who's English and he doesn't talk like that. She thinks the caller might have been faking the accent."

"OK," says the Lieutenant. "Now Duffy and Nostra tell me that all the victims had phonographs, including the location of the Marlin-Winston homicides, and that all the turntables were found on 78 rpm. Have you taken that anywhere, Duffy?"

"Lieutenant," says Duffy, "Nostra and I have been canvassing record stores that still sell 78s, but it's a blind alley. We've only found evidence of two recent purchases—one by an old lady in Yorkville who bought an album by Hugo Winterhalter, and one by an elderly gentleman in Staten Island who bought an album by Benny Goodman."

"Caruso," says the Lieutenant, "what have you and Segal got?"

"Well, Lieutenant," says Caruso, "a neighbor of Beverly Rachlin told us he thinks he heard the individual who entered her apartment the night of the homicide tell her he was a police officer. He says he thinks the individual showed her some kind of police I.D."

"A shield?"

"He couldn't tell. I figured there may be a chance the perp is a cop, so I've notified Internal Affairs and they've come up with a few names we're in the process of checking out. The most interesting one so far is a patrolman named Micelli in the two-eight."

"What do you think, Caruso?"

"Lieutenant?"

"Do you think the killer is a cop?"

"I don't know, Lieutenant. I've seen some pretty weird individuals in the P.D. Yeah, I think the guy could be a cop."

"What about Segal?"

"I think it could be Segal, sir," says Caruso with a wink. "He's weird enough."

Laughter.

"Segal," says the Lieutenant, "what've you got?"

"Lieutenant, I've been checking out a tip that the killer is a nut on dancing, that he took dancing lessons at a studio like Arthur Murray. I've checked with Arthur Murray and some of the other studios, and I'm running down four men who took lessons who fit the killer's general description who struck some of the instructors as being kind of weird and ambivalent about women."

"Where did you get the tip that the killer is a nut on dancing?" says the Lieutenant.

Max looks at the Lieutenant and seems suddenly uncomfortable.

"Sir?"

"I said where did you get the tip that the killer is a nut on dancing?"

"From . . . from this young lady I know."

"And on what does she base her information?"

"On . . . something she heard."

The Lieutenant frowns. Several detectives turn to look at Max, wondering why he looks so uncomfortable.

"What's with Max?" says Larry sotto voce to Caruso.

Caruso shrugs his shoulders.

"I *told* you he was weird," says Caruso, but this time he is not winking.

74

Max walks into the Lieutenant's office and closes the door behind him.

"Lieutenant, can I talk to you a minute?"

"Yes, Segal?"

"I'm not anxious to have this circulated around the squad, but I'm going with a girl who's . . . a girl who's got some very interesting information about the Hyena, and—"

"What kind of information?"

"Psychic information. She has these psychic visions about the crimes before they happen, and the visions seem to check out. Then she's given me further information on them after they've happened, stuff she couldn't have known about, and most of that checks out, too."

"How?"

"Well, things that weren't in the papers or on TV that she knows about anyway. Like the fact that the killer brought Linda Lowry anemones. We purposely didn't give that out, right? And like the fact that while the killer was in the Lowry apartment, Linda received a phone call from Arnold Kupperman. Stuff like that."

"So you think she's psychic," says the Lieutenant.

"I don't know what I think," says Max, "but most of what she's told me checks out. One of the things she told me, for example, is that the killer is a big nut on dancing and that he took lessons at Arthur Murray. I'm following up four leads I got from interviewing an

Arthur Murray dance instructor, and they look pretty promising."

"Well, follow up on everything, Segal. We can't afford *not* to. Even the crazy stuff sometimes pays off."

"I know that," says Max. "But here's the thing I think you ought to know. I have reason to believe that the killer is watching me and my girlfriend. I have reason to believe that he made a definite attempt to get into my apartment the other night to grab her."

"What makes you think that?" says the Lieutenant.

"Because a man claiming to be a neighbor of mine named Hector Gomez tried to get her to let him into my apartment. It wasn't Gomez, because I *checked* Gomez and he wasn't even in town till this morning."

"So some guy who wasn't Gomez was trying to get into your apartment," says the Lieutenant. "I don't see why you think it was the guy we're after."

"My girlfriend seems to feel that's who it was," says Max. "I didn't want to even mention it till now, but it's really got me worried."

The Lieutenant sighs.

"What do you want me to do about it, Segal?"

"I don't know. I thought maybe you could assign a couple of men to stake out my apartment or to tail her when she goes out."

"Segal, I'm short-handed as it is. I've got men assigned to me from other Homicide squads, I've got men working overtime without pay, I've got more pressure on me from Noonan and the Commissioner and the Mayor himself than I've ever had on me in the thirty years I've been on the job. You don't really expect me to assign any of my men, besides you, to watch your girlfriend, do you?"

"I guess not, Lieutenant."

Well, he thinks, at least I tried. And what more I can do to protect her I simply do not know, because I cannot bring her along on the job and I cannot quit the job and stay home full-time and protect her myself. But if she handles herself as well as she did when whoever it was tried to get into the apartment, then maybe she'll be OK.

75

"This is one of the ESP experiments that we do here," says Dr. Kronenfeld, leading Max, Babette, and Tony Natale down the narrow basement corridor at the Maimonides Medical Center in Brooklyn. "We first of all place the person who is to be the receiver in this room in *ganzfeld*. Do you know what *ganzfeld* is?"

"Uh, isn't that a kind of partial sensory deprivation?" says Natale.

"Right. We place these little cups—actually they're halves of Ping-Pong balls—over the eyes of the person who's to be the receiver, with cotton around the edges to prevent any leakage of light. Then we place these headphones over his ears. The headphones emit white noise to screen out any random sounds. Do you all know what white noise is?"

"White noise sounds like the name of a rock group," says Max.

Everybody chuckles politely. Max decides it is a mistake to make jokes when people are explaining serious scientific stuff to you.

"White noise, of course," says Dr. Kronenfeld, "is

sound that contains the full spectrum of frequencies of audible sound, just as white light is light that contains the full spectrum of frequencies of visible light."

"Mmmmm," says Max.

"Now the reason for screening out most of the normal sensory input from the eyes and ears is to enable the receiver to be a bit more sensitive to information that might be coming through to him by *extra*sensory means. We place the person who is to be the receiver in this room in *ganzfeld*. The room is fully soundproofed and lightproofed. We place electrodes on the surface of his scalp to monitor for alpha. You know, of course, what alpha is?"

Babette and Max look at each other and shrug.

"Alpha is one of the four brain-wave frequencies," says Natale. "It's the one where most ESP happens."

"Right," says Dr. Kronenfeld. "So as soon as the receiver is producing a lot of alpha, the sender, who is in another soundproofed and lightproofed room down the corridor, is shown a slide. A collage of various unrelated elements. The sender concentrates on the slide— tries to 'send' the images to the receiver in the other room. The receiver tells what images he sees, and we record these and see how close he came to what the sender sent. Would you like to try the experiment?"

"Sure," says Max.

"I guess so," says Babette.

"Good," says Dr. Kronenfeld. "Who would like to be the sender and who the receiver?"

"Well," says Max, "Babette is the psychic, so I guess she should be the receiver."

"I have a better idea," says Natale. "Why doesn't Babette send and *Max* receive?"

"What's the point of that?" says Max.

"To let you see if you have any psychic powers," says Natale. "We already know about Babette."

"OK," says Max. "Why not?"

Dr. Kronenfeld takes Max into the receiver's room, seats him in a comfortable chair, attaches electrodes to his scalp, earphones to his ears, halves of Ping-Pong balls to his eyes. The white noise in the headphones sounds like breakers at the beach, a restful sound. Dr. Kronenfeld tells Max to start describing any images he gets when the white noise lessens and he hears a beep.

The white noise is wonderful. Max contemplates buying a cassette of it and running it at Homicide. He relaxes into the cushions of the chair. He feels himself drifting off. After a while he hears the beep. He tries to put into words the images that flicker past his consciousness.

". . . Round, something round . . ." says Max. "I'm looking down on it . . . I see a figure . . . a figure of a man in silhouette . . . also a ladder. And . . . a big red seven, like the Seagram's logo . . . and . . . a big round shape, like a porthole. And . . . the figure in silhouette is a man . . . I see a swimming pool, a round swimming pool, with several smaller round shapes inside of it . . . I see . . . well, that's about all that I see . . ."

Dr. Kronenfeld eventually returns, removes the headphones, the electrodes, and the Ping-Pong balls, and leads Max into an adjoining room.

"This is the room that your friend was in when we showed her the slide," says Dr. Kronenfeld. "We are now going to show you a series of slides, and you will tell us which of them you think she was trying to send you."

Dr. Kronenfeld dims the lights, turns on the slide projector, and shows the first slide. It is a collage of New England buildings, including something that looks like a church, and a cross, and a rocky shoreline, and a portrait of Teddy Kennedy.

"That's not it," says Max.

"You're sure?" says Kronenfeld.

"Pretty sure," says Max.

Kronenfeld flips to the next slide. It's a picture of a gigantic eye, with various mystical symbols surrounding it, including a five-pointed star, an ankh, a cross, a six-pointed star, and a ceremonial sword and dagger.

"Nope," says Max, "that's not it either."

"You're sure?" says Kronenfeld.

"I'm sure," says Max.

Kronenfeld flips to the next slide. It's a picture of a sailing boat with overlaid images of the sun and moon and a compass. The round shapes momentarily confuse him, but then he's sure.

"That's not it either," says Max.

"You are sure?" says Kronenfeld.

"Yep," says Max, "I'm sure."

Kronenfeld flips to the next slide. It's a picture of the dance floor of an underground café. The dance floor is round, and the tables that surround it are round too. In the middle of the dance floor are two flamenco dancers in silhouette. The view of the dance floor is from above. There is a superimposed image of a glass of what appears to be liquor.

"That's the one," says Max.

"You are sure?" says Kronenfeld.

"Absolutely," says Max. "Look at it. The dance floor is a large round shape, like the round swimming pool and the round porthole I saw. And those tables are like the several smaller round shapes inside of it. And those two figures in silhouette . . . well, I saw *one* figure in silhouette, but that's close. And the point of view is looking down from above, like I said. And . . . let's see, what else did I say I saw?"

"A ladder, and a big seven like a Seagram's logo."

"Yeah. Well, I don't guess there's anything like that in this slide. Although that glass does look like it's filled with liquor. You think the Seagram's Seven I saw could have been the glass of booze?"

"It's possible," says Kronenfeld mildly. "Your brain was being activated in a way that it's activated during REM sleep, during dreaming. And dreams frequently give us those kinds of symbols."

Kronenfeld turns up the lights and opens the door. Babette and Natale come in.

"Well," says Kronenfeld, "that was very interesting."

"Was I right?" says Max. "Was that the slide that Babette was sending me?"

"Oh, yes," says Kronenfeld, smiling. "Absolutely."

"I'll be damned," says Max, slightly giddy at his unanticipated success. "I'll be goddamned. Hey, does this mean I'm a psychic?"

"It means," says Kronenfeld, "that you had a very high score on the experiment—not only on the correct identification of the slide, but in the high correlation between what you described and what was actually in the collage."

"But does that mean I'm psychic, doc?" says Max.

"Everyone is psychic, Max," says Natale. "The problem is they let their own bullshit get in the way of it."

76

"All we know about the killer," says Tony Natale, finishing off his can of beer, "is that he's killed six women. That is what we know. All the rest is speculation. It's true that all six women happen to live in Manhattan and were killed in Manhattan, that all six women were single and attractive and lived alone. You could say that therefore he is only going to go after attractive single women living alone in Manhattan, that anyone who's ugly, married, and living in Queens is safe. But if you did, you'd be stupid."

"You think," says Max, "that he could strike anywhere in the city, then?"

"I think he could strike anywhere in the *world*. He could get on a plane the same as you or me, right? If you looked at the first three killings and you thought you could figure out a pattern from them, then you'd have to say, well, this guy only kills young women, in their apartments, around six or seven in the evening, and whoever that doesn't apply to, you're in the clear. But—"

"But then he goes to an office building and—"

"Exactly. But then he goes to an office building later in the evening than he's been striking and he knocks off a young woman and a middle-aged one. And for the first time he ties his victims up with ropes. So go know."

"In other words," says Max, "there's not necessarily a pattern to his actions."

"Oh, there's a pattern all right," says Natale. "We just haven't found it yet. There's *always* a pattern with these things. Guys like this don't kill spontaneously. They have a certain ritual that makes sense to them alone. Certain ways they select their victims, certain ways they approach them, certain things they say to them, certain ritualized things they have to do in order for the whole thing to come out right in their plans.

"It's all worked out in advance, almost like a ballet. A few days before the actual hit they make contact of some kind with the victim—stop them on the street and ask them the time or ask directions to someplace nearby or something like that. It's all part of this elaborate fantasy they're living out, all part of the pleasure they get out of it. Then, when they get to the final act, the killing, that's their orgasm."

"You think he's ever had a real orgasm with a woman?" says Max.

"I doubt it. This guy feels terrible ambivalence toward women. Terrible anger. Terrible hurt. And a terrible need to be close to them, too. He's got to be pathologically shy with women, but driven, really *driven* to make contact with them.

"Some woman or women hurt him badly a long time ago. A mother, an aunt, a girlfriend. And now he's acting out his rage. To *him* his behavior makes perfect sense. To *him* these homicides are entirely justifiable. He's operating on a whole different plane of reality than we are. A whole different system of logic and morality. If we can figure out where he's coming from, what his point of view is, what is motivating him, then maybe we got a prayer of catching him. Otherwise, forget it. Otherwise, I don't want to even *think* about how many women he's going to hit before this is over."

77

"Who's there?"
   "Miss Middleton?"
   "Yes?"
   "Is your bathtub overflowing?"
   "Is my *bathtub* overflowing?"

"Yes."

"No. Why?"

"Well, because Mrs. Spellman, your neighbor just below you, called me to fix a leak in her bathroom ceiling and the water is just gushing out of her ceiling there. We figured maybe you left the water running in your tub and forgot about it, and it started overflowing."

"Well, I didn't. My bathtub is empty."

"Well, then, maybe a pipe burst. Can I come in and check it out?"

"Who did you say you were?"

"The plumber. Kohler Plumbing. You want to call downstairs and check with Mrs. Spellman?"

She looks through the peephole and sees a moustachioed blond man in green coveralls carrying a big toolbox.

"No, I don't guess so. What do you have to check out?" she says.

"Just take a look at the pipes under your sink and in the tub. It won't take more than a minute."

"Well, all right. If you're sure it won't take any longer than that."

"It won't."

"Well, all right, then."

Marilyn Middleton unlocks her door and lets the plumber inside, locking the door again after him.

"The bathroom is around to the right there."

"OK, thanks, Miss Middleton."

The plumber goes into the bathroom, putters around for a minute or two, then comes back out again, shaking his head.

"I don't understand it," he says. "There doesn't seem to be anything wrong in there."

"Well, then, maybe it's in Mrs. Spellman's ceiling, sweetheart. In the pipes in her ceiling."

"I guess you're right—OK, Miss Middleton, thanks anyway."

He starts toward the door, then turns back.

"Oh, yes, there was just one more thing," he says.

"Yes?"

"Do you happen to have a phonograph?"

"What?"

Smiling, the plumber pulls off what she now realizes is a blond wig and a blond moustache, and reveals a sinkingly familiar face.

"You know, Marilyn," says the man, "I've loved you since the first time we danced together at Arthur Murray. And I love you a hundred times more deeply than that boor Max Segal."

78

"Max?"

"Yeah, baby?"

"You busy?"

"Why?"

"You want to try that exercise with me? The one that Tony Natale showed us?"

"Not right now, baby."

"Why not?"

"I'm kind of tired. Caruso and I have been out all day chasing wild geese."

"Oh, come on. It's not tiring. You can even do it lying down. Please?"

Sigh.

"OK. How does it go?"

"OK, first we turn off the lights, lie down, and close our eyes—"

"Hey, that sounds like a nice exercise."

"C'mon, be serious, will you?"

"Sorry."

"Well, let's just do that much first, OK?"

"OK."

Babette turns off the lights. She and Max lie down on the floor and close their eyes.

"Now," says Babette, "we both imagine we're in an elevator, going down and down. We see the numbers go down slowly from 10 to 1."

"Yeah . . ."

"Then the elevator doors open and we enter this comfortable dark room with a big TV set in it with this huge screen. We turn on the set and then we describe out loud any images we get on the screen."

"Yeah . . ."

"That's it. That's all the receiver does. Tries to envision what the sender is sending. Just like when we were at Maimonides. You be the receiver."

"Why me?"

"Because. You did so well at Maimonides. I want to see you do it without the Ping-Pong balls and the headphones."

"OK. Have you got something you want to send me?"

"Yes."

"Then why not put a stamp on it and drop it in the mailbox?"

"Come on, Max."

"Sorry. OK. Here I go into the elevator."

"Sssshhh. No talking till you turn on the TV set and begin seeing something on the screen."

"OK."

They both lie still, breathing regularly. Babette goes through the elevator exercise herself to try to attune herself to Max's channel. When she goes into her comfortable dark room and turns on her sender set, she envisions a little house on the screen, a house that she'd like to live in with Max if they get married. A white frame house with green shutters and a white picket fence, and roses growing along the fence near the gate.

"OK," she whispers. "You see anything yet?"

"Mmmm. No, not really. I don't think this set gets very good reception. Maybe if it were on the cable . . ."

"Come on, Max."

"Sorry. Well, let's see. I see a kind of red thing. . ."

"Yes . . ."

"A red thing with . . . with things sticking out of it."

"What kind of red thing?"

"It's . . . it has kind of pins sticking out of it, I think . . ."

"Yes . . ."

"I think it's a red pincushion. Am I close?"

"Go on . . ."

"Am I close or not?"

"Just go on, OK? You're not doing badly at all."

"That means I'm doing lousy."

"No you're not. You're doing fine. Just keep going. Tell me what else you see."

"OK. Well, let's see now. I see . . . I see a bunch of bars. Like a jail cell. Vertical bars. And . . . they're white. A white jailhouse. How am I doing?"

"Uh, is that all you see?"

"Yeah. Why? You seem disappointed. Didn't I get it at all?"

"Well, yes, as a matter of fact you came very close, Max . . ."

"I did? You were thinking of a red pincushion and a white jailhouse?"

"No, not exactly. One of the things I was thinking of, though, was rosebushes. And that's red with things sticking out of it—thorns."

"Hey, how *about* that? That's not so bad, is it?"

"No, it's not."

"Then why do you sound so disappointed?"

"Well, because the rest of what I was thinking of was a white frame house with a white picket fence, like one that we might live in some day if we ever got married. And what you saw it as was a *jail*house."

Babette sounds like she's on the brink of tears.

"Aww, Babette . . ."

"That must be what you think of marriage."

"Aww, Babette. C'mon now. Hey, don't you think that those vertical white bars I was seeing could have been the white picket fence?"

"I guess so," she says. "I guess you're right. Actually, that was a pretty good try, Max. You're really very psychic, you know that?"

"Maybe."

"What do you mean *maybe?*"

"Maybe I did get things that were similar to what you were sending me. And then again, maybe it was a coincidence. But what good is it, really, if what you're sending is red roses and white frame houses with white picket fences and what I'm receiving is red pincushions and white jailhouses?"

"Tony Natale said people get screwed up more with the interpretations—what he called the reference points —than with receiving the actual images. I guess you have to work a little on your reference points, huh?"

"I guess."

"Max?"

"Yeah, baby?"

"Tomorrow, when you're on a night tour, close your

eyes at midnight for about sixty seconds and I'll send you something, OK?"

"OK."

"You promise you won't forget?"

"I promise."

"Good. And if I decide to send you another thing about marriage or living together and you come up with jailhouses again, I'm going to kill you."

79

Max and Caruso walk into the all-night diner across from the morgue. It is a place that the homicide cops hang out in a lot, and the help is very respectful. The diner specializes in Greek food, and the cops always look over the huge menu quite thoroughly, although nobody can remember a homicide cop ever ordering anything there but burgers and french fries and coffee.

Max and Caruso take a table against the back wall and slump down in their chairs. It has been another frustrating and fruitless night of running down promising-sounding leads that turn out to be not so promising. Of simple cases of not finding somebody at home because the person no longer lived there or never did or of the address not even existing. Of not-so-simple cases of somebody giving very damaging information about an acquaintance and then changing his story.

Tonight they had gone to interview a waitress they'd spoken to on the phone about a coworker she said had vacant-looking eyes, wore a dark overcoat, acted pathologically shy with women, and was mysteriously late to his dishwashing job on the nights of the Lowry, Rachlin, and Manteuffel homicides. But when they finally spoke to her in person she said she had been mistaken, that the dishwasher had been detained each of the three nights at the Animal Medical Center, waiting to have his schnauzer treated. They went to interview the dishwasher anyway, and he had treatment receipts from the Animal Medical Center for all three dates.

Another woman had told them on the phone that a neighbor of hers—also vacant-eyed, dark-overcoated, pathologically shy with women—had made indecent remarks to her in the building's self-service elevator and then mumbled something about her being his next victim. But when they spoke to her in person she told a much different story. All he'd done, she said, was drunkenly ask her to come to his apartment for a drink. He had said nothing about any next victims, she said.

There were two possibilities. Either she'd been telling the truth the first time and then gotten scared, or else she'd merely been trying to get the guy in trouble the first time and then thought better of it. In any case, the guy was neither at home nor at a couple of bars she thought he frequented. It was worth following up, but it was no longer a very hot lead.

"I keep thinking we're barking up the wrong tree in some real stupid way," says Caruso wearily.

"Like how?" says Max.

"I don't know. Like assuming the killer is a guy when he's a transvestite broad. Or like assuming it's one guy when it's really two."

"Two?" says Max. "What about the prints? Crime Scene says the prints in most of the apartments look similar."

"Prints like that don't mean shit. I wouldn't give you

a nickel for any set of prints they've lifted so far in this case."

A chubby, frizzy-haired waitress approaches, smiling.

"Hi, Max. Hi, Sal," she says.

"Hi, sweetheart," says Caruso.

"Hi, Liz," says Max.

"Two special burgers medium-well, two orders of fries and two black coffees?" she says.

"Just a minute, hon," says Caruso.

The two detectives quickly scan the names of the Greek dishes on both sides of the menu, as they always do, perhaps expecting that the words they've looked at so many times will suddenly take on new significance and dictate a change of order.

"I guess just the burger medium-well and the, uh, fries for me, hon," says Caruso. "And coffee, black."

"Yeah," says Max, wistfully bidding the exotic-sounding Greek dishes yet another goodbye. "Same for me, I guess."

The waitress, who had written up their orders in advance, chuckles fondly as she walks away. These men might be tough cops and wear heavy pistols under their jackets, but they still knew less than she did about their own eating habits.

"If it was more than one guy," says Max, "then why would the letter that the killer sent to Monahan say he'd done them all?"

Caruso shrugs.

"Who knows? The guy could be bragging. The letter might not even be from the killer at all. It could be from somebody who just wishes he had the *guts* to do sex homicides."

"Tony Natale says he thinks the letter really is from the killer," says Max.

Caruso snorts in disgust.

"Tony Natale," he says. "I was a homicide cop when

Tony Natale was a uniformed cop on foot patrol. *Before* he went to school and learned how to shrink heads."

"So what?"

"So what? So how come he knows so much about people's heads?"

"He studied it, that's how."

"He studied it in *books*. I studied it in the fucking *street*. What do you think's more valuable—a theory that some guy read in a *book* or something that he learned first-hand from experience in the *street?*"

"Tony Natale's been on the street, too, for God's sake."

Caruso gives Max a fishy look.

"What's with you? You got a crush on Tony Natale or what?"

"A *crush* on him. What the fuck you talking about, Caruso?"

"The way you talk about him—Tony Natale this, Tony Natale that—I swear to God, sometimes you sound like a goddam fairy."

"You're out of your fucking mind."

"I'll tell you very frankly, Segal, I do have my doubts about you sometimes. I really do. Sometimes you act pretty strange. How come you're not married, by the way?"

"How come I'm not *married?* Who the fuck are you, my *mother?* I'm not married because I haven't found anybody yet I'd like to *marry,* that's why I'm not married."

"You have a girlfriend?"

"I . . . Yes, I have a girlfriend, if it's any of your business."

"I thought I saw you hesitate before answering. How come you hesitated before answering, Segal? Don't you know if she's your girlfriend? Or don't you know if she's a girl?"

Max gets very red in the face. He starts to say something, then stops.

"You're way out of line, Caruso," is all he finally decides to say.

"Yeah? Maybe so. Maybe not. Tell me something, Segal. This girlfriend of yours—are you playing hide-the-salami with her?"

"What?" Max cannot believe his ears.

"You heard me. Are you slipping your wienie in your girlfriend's pants?"

Max starts breathing hard, again starts to say something, again controls himself.

"Caruso," he says in a very controlled voice, "if you want to have a fight about this, I'll be glad to meet you anytime, anyplace you say. You've got about eighty pounds on me, but I think I could probably drive your nose up into your brain before you could even land a punch. However, you are *not* going to get me busted out of this job for swinging on you in the cop diner, where you've got about twenty witnesses who'll say I started it, OK?"

Caruso seems tickled at Max's reaction.

"OK, calm down, Segal. Don't wet your pants."

"Don't tell me to fucking calm down, Caruso. I want to know what the fuck business it is of yours whether or not I'm sleeping with my girlfriend. I want to know what the fuck business it is of yours whether I'm even a heterosexual, for that matter. Which I *am,* in case it's any of your business. Which it's *not.*"

"OK," says Caruso, drawing himself up to his full seated height. "You want to know what business it is of mine? I'll *tell* you what business it is of mine. Whether you or I like it or not, buddy-boy, we happen to be partners. My fucking *life* depends on my knowing exactly what I can expect you to do under every fucking crazyass condition that could even come up. You got me? I don't want no fucking surprises when the chips are down, buddy-boy, because that might just cost me my ass. And I happen to be very *fond* of my ass. So if I got to put the screws to you a little, and if I got to needle you a little, and if I got to rag you to see what you do when you're hot under the collar and not thinking straight, then that's what I'm fucking well going to do, buddy-boy."

The waitress comes up with the burgers and fries and coffees and wishes she hadn't.

"Just because you supposedly pulled two old farts out of a fire and are supposed to be some kind of hot little hero don't indicate shit to me about what you'll do anywhere but in a fire with two old farts, and maybe not even that. And just because you're one of the Chosen People don't indicate shit to me about how special you are or about whether you'd lay your life on the line for a salmon-snapper or whether you'd maybe try a little harder for a fellow Jewboy either."

The waitress puts down the dishes and runs.

Max looks at Caruso and waits for him to finish.

"When are you going to cut all this 'Jewboy' shit?" says Max quietly.

"When?" says Caruso. "I'll tell you when. When it stops *bothering* you, buddy-boy, that's when."

80

All around them are well-dressed people having an expensive good time dancing and dining, and all around them are fabulous views of Manhattan in every direction, with the lights of the city so far below that it would seem to them that they were in an airliner if they were only looking, which they are not.

What they are doing is gazing into each other's eyes from a distance of about four inches. They are beautiful and young and they are very much in love.

"I can't believe we're here," she says. "I can't believe you actually took me here."

It is New Year's Eve, and where he has taken her is the Rainbow Room, at the top of the RCA Building, which is a throwback to an era they are totally free to be nostalgic about because it was before they were born.

How Max is going to pay for this evening on the salary of a detective third-grade is not altogether clear to him, but neither is anything else tonight, drinking champagne and gazing into the eyes of this silly girl with the impossibly beautiful face and figure and the head disconcertingly tuned to past and future events and the religion dedicated to relegating him to the status of God-killer.

"First of all, I have to tell you that I'm drunk," he says, grinning idiotically at her. "Next I have to tell you that I'm insane about you."

"Does the one depend on the other?" she says, grinning just as idiotically.

"No, I'm sure it doesn't. But I just wanted to tell you, while I'm still able to talk, that I'm childishly grateful that a raving maniac of a sex murderer brought us together and that a horny lunatic of a stepfather forced you to move in with me."

She touches his face.

"First I have to tell you that I'm drunk, too," she says. "And that I'm insane about you, too. Next I have to tell you that I'm so happy tonight that I could be murdered tomorrow by the Hyena and I would die happy to have been able to spend even this little time with you."

Max puts his hand over her mouth.

"No talking shop," says Max. "Not at these prices."

She giggles.

"Do you think the people at the other tables are having conversations as drunken and as corny as we are?" she says.

"I don't know," says Max, lurching unsteadily to his feet, "why don't I go and find out?"

"Come back here, you idiot," she laughs, grabbing him by the sleeve.

He settles tipsily back into his chair.

"Thank you for preventing me from making a total ass of myself. Do you know I think I would actually have gone around the room and asked people if they were having conversations as drunken and as corny as we were?"

"I know you would have," she says. "That's why I stopped you."

"Having said that," he continues, "what would you say to our *both* making total asses of ourselves in front of these seemingly sedate and sober people by attempting to dance in our totally inebriated condition?"

She looks dubiously at the dance floor, crowded with seemingly sober and sedate dancers.

"I think," she says, "that I would have to say: at these prices we *owe* it to ourselves."

They get up and begin to dance.

"Max," she whispers.

"Yes?"

"You're wearing your gun?"

"Mmmhmm."

"How come?"

"I always wear my gun."

"But why?"

"I have to. Detectives must carry their guns at all times, even off-duty."

"Why? You're not working now."

"Yes I am. Technically speaking, I'm always working. I'm a police officer, honey. I have to be ready at any moment to protect myself. And you. And anybody else who might need my help."

"Max, I can't dance with you with a loaded gun between us. Can't you check it in the checkroom or something?"

"No."

"Why not?"

"They don't check guns in this checkroom. Didn't you see the sign when we came in? It said, 'Sorry, no furs, no guns.' "

"Max, I'm serious."

"So am I."

They dance in silence for a while, her cheek against his neck. After a while he feels wetness there.

"Babette?"

"Yes?"

"You aren't crying, are you?"

No answer.

"Babette?"

"Yes?"

"Why are you crying?"

"Because."

"Because what?"

"Because dancing with a man who is wearing a loaded thirty-eight-caliber revolver is not romantic. It reminds me of death. And I don't want to be reminded about death right now."

"Babette, you were the one who brought up the subject of death not two minutes ago."

"I did?"

"Yes. Don't you remember? You said you were so happy tonight you could be murdered tomorrow by the Hyena and you'd die happy to have spent even this little time with me."

"That was different."

"It was? How was it different?"

"It was *my* death I was talking about."

"Uh . . . I don't think I understand."

"The prospect of my *own* death doesn't bother me that much. The prospect of yours I can't even bear to think about. And whenever I see that gun of yours, or when I just feel it through your jacket, that's *all* I can think about."

"Babette?"

"Yes?"

"Let's not have this discussion, OK?"

"OK."

"I'm not going to die and neither are you. Not till we're both very old, very decrepit people, OK?"

"OK."

"I absolutely guarantee that, OK?"

"OK. Max?"

"Yes?"

"Can I have that in writing?"

81

If she lives. If she lives, they will have a wonderful wedding, she and Max, she thinks, letting her attention stray from Professor Arlen and his boring lecture.

Babette envisions herself in a long white bridal gown just like the one that her bride doll wore, with a veil and a long train for her bridesmaids to carry and everything else. Who will she have as bridesmaids? Well, Maryanne, maybe, and maybe Theresa, and maybe Cathy, but maybe not. Maybe they won't think it's right for her to be marrying either a cop or a Jew. Maybe she won't *have* any bridesmaids.

Is Max going to insist upon having a rabbi at the ceremony as well as a priest? Will the priest allow a rabbi to be present? What if Max insists that the rabbi be the only one there, that no priest be there at all? What will she do then? Will she be forced to agree and burn forever in hell?

"How hot are the fires of hell?" Father Ryan used to say to them in the second or third grade. Dramatically striking a match and holding it close to the hand of a student in the first row, pulling it away. "You see how much that hurt? Now imagine a raging fire ten thousand times as hot as that match, burning over every square inch of your body, forever. Do you know how long forever is? You do not. The human mind has no conception of forever. Imagine an enormous iron ball the size of the earth. Imagine that once every hundred years a bird comes down to sharpen its beak on that iron ball. Now, when that bird wears that iron ball down to nothing, that will be just the *beginning* of forever."

How many times had Father Ryan made that speech to them? Hundreds of times, maybe thousands. Then, a few years later, came the rap about sex. Don't wear patent-leather shoes because they will reflect your underpants. Don't wear red because only prostitutes wear red. Don't wear "extreme clothing styles" or you will turn any boy into a slavering rapist. If you are having a boy over to dinner, don't use a white tablecloth because the white will remind him of bedsheets and turn him into a monster.

All boys are monsters—they don't have any self-control, and anything is likely to turn them into a Jekyll-and-Hyde nightmare. You must be on guard every second. You mustn't kiss anybody if you derive any pleasure from it. Save yourself for the good Catholic boy you marry, when it will become all right for you to derive pleasure from him. But there *are* no good Catholic boys, or any other kind, because all boys are only interested in One Thing.

You kissed a Jewish boy on the lips? Do five Our Fathers and ten Hail Marys. You lay with him in the same bed without having carnal knowledge of him? Do five hundred Our Fathers and a thousand Hail Marys. You want to marry him and live with him the rest of your life? You will surely burn forever in the fires of hell. How hot are the fires of hell? How long is forever?

"Miss Watson, perhaps *you* can tell us?"

"Imagine an enormous iron ball the size of the earth," says Babette automatically. Professor Arlen and Babette's entire philosophy class erupt into laughter. Babette is terribly embarrassed.

"An iron ball the size of the earth?" says Professor Arlen.

"I'm sorry," says Babette, "I'm afraid I wasn't paying attention, Professor Arlen."

"While the rest of us were having Christmas dinners and going to New Year's Eve parties," says Professor Arlen, "Miss Watson, it appears, was going bowling."

More laughter. Let them laugh, what do I care? she thinks. Either I'll be marrying Max and having babies with him and then burn forever in the fires of hell as punishment, or else I'm going to be killed by the Hyena. So who cares if these idiots laugh at me or not? I've got lots worse to worry about.

82

They are lying in each other's arms. Max looks at his watch and groans.

"What is it?" she says.

"Three forty-five. I lost track of the time. I have to go, Babette."

"To work? I thought you were off today."

"I volunteered an extra tour on the four-to-one. I told you. Remember?"

"Max, don't go."

"I have to, baby. I said I would."

"Max, don't go. Really don't. I can't explain why."

"Hey, come on."

"No, really. I just had a terrible feeling. Don't go. Something dreadful is going to happen if you do."

"Oh, come on, Babette, don't do this to me, baby.

I have to go. Nothing is going to happen, OK? Just do what I told you. Stay inside, don't go out for any reason, don't let anybody in. There are bars on all the windows now, so nobody can come in unless you *let* them in, and there's no reason to let anybody in but me. If anything scares you, call me. You've got the number."

"Max . . ."

"Yes?"

"Don't say I didn't warn you."

"Hey, c'mon. What kind of thing is that to say?"

"I mean it. If something happens tonight while you're gone, don't say I didn't warn you."

"Jesus Christ, Babette, ease up on me, will you? I can't just refuse to work tonight because you've got a premonition that something might happen. I admit you have some strange abilities from time to time, but you're not the goddam Oracle of Delphi."

"What's that supposed to mean?"

"That just because you have a premonition of something bad doesn't mean the whole N.Y.P.D. has to close up shop tonight."

"Not the whole N.Y.P.D. Just you."

"Well, I can't do it, OK? I'm due on the job in ten minutes, and with any luck I'll only be a few minutes late."

He takes her in his arms. She's so warm she feels like she has a fever. He kisses her forehead, her cheeks, her chin, her lips, her neck.

"I'm sorry I talked that way to you, baby. I love you."

"I love you too, Max. I'm sorry I carried on like that. I'm sure nothing dreadful will happen to either of us tonight. I'm sure that it's just that I miss you so much when you're gone and I thought you were off today."

They hug each other.

"Remember what I said now. Don't let anybody in for any reason. *Anybody*. Promise?"

"I promise."

"Hey. You want to come with me?"

"No. I'll be OK."

"OK. Go to sleep early. I'll be back before you know it."

"OK."

"See you later, baby."

"See you later, Max. Take extra care of yourself, will you?"

"I will. So long, kid."

He walks upstairs, unlocks all three locks, opens the door, exits, and triple-locks the door from the outside.

Maybe he should have taken her along tonight. No, that was absurd. She'd be safe in the apartment, far safer than on the street with him. And as for his *own* safety, well, he'd always been perfectly able to take care of himself till now, and he wasn't about to lose that ability tonight.

83

"In a Protestant hospital," says the uniformed officer named Strongin, "when they run into trouble in the delivery room, they save the mother. In a Catholic hospital, they save the baby."

"In a Jewish hospital," says Caruso, "they save the doctor."

Everybody laughs, including Max. Max and Caruso and two Vice Squad detectives named Brockman and Navasky are hanging out in the emergency receiving area at Bellevue, waiting for word on a hooker who was found beaten into unconsciousness. If she pulls through, the case goes to Vice. If not, it goes to Homicide. Which means that Max and Caruso, who are catching tonight, will have to spend several hours doing paperwork that will take them away from the Hyena homicides.

"Hey," says Brockman, "when are you guys going to hang a collar on this Hyena character? I'm sick of having Homicide hog all the headlines."

"We're not pulling him in till Yom Kippur," says Caruso. "See, we got this pool in the squad on what day he's going to be collared, and me and Max here drew Yom Kippur as our day."

"You already know who the perp is, eh?" says Strongin.

"Hey," says Caruso, "is a bear Catholic? Does the Pope shit in the woods? Of *course* we already know who he is. Too bad we have to wait another nine months to bring him in. Is it nine months to Yom Kippur, Max?"

Max nods.

"Yeah, nine months," says Caruso. "But we figure the guy won't knock off more than eighty broads in the meantime. We figure it's worth it to win the pool."

"What's the prize?" says Brockman.

"Two weeks' vacation in the Vice Squad," says Caruso.

Laughter.

"I hear you got a pretty hot little lead you're running down," says Navasky.

"Oh, yeah?" says Max. "What did you hear?"

"I heard you had Internal Affairs put a wire on a cop in the two-eight named Micelli."

Max and Caruso are momentarily stunned. The investigation of Micelli was a fairly closely guarded secret. How this guy Navasky in Vice ever heard about it was a little spooky.

"Your information is just a tiny bit off," says Max. "First of all, the guy's name is Marcelli, not Micelli. Second, he's not in the two-eight, he's in the two-two. Third, he was cleared about a week ago. Outside of that, you've got it perfectly."

Not bad, Max congratulates himself. Although, if these guys knew about the wire then probably every cop in the two-eight including Micelli knew about it, too.

"The other thing we heard," says Brockman, "is about a guy named Volkening."

Jesus H. Christ, who was passing out all this information? Not that it mattered who knew about Volkening, really.

"What did you hear about Volkening?" says Caruso.

"That you guys have a tail on him because some chick fingered him as a peeping tom last summer."

Max and Caruso exchange looks. They decide to give the vice cops a break. After all, it wasn't going to get back to Volkening. And besides, it might make them forget about Micelli.

"This guy Volkening," says Caruso, "we got from a dance instructor at Arthur Murray. What was her name again, Max?"

"Middleton. Marilyn Middleton," says Max.

"Marilyn Middleton," says Caruso. "Very tough broad. Anyway, we did a little checking on Volkening. His general description fit what's been reported on the killer. His neighbors said he was a loner, that he kept to himself pretty much, that he was out a lot at odd hours. One of them, a cute blond broad named Annie

Rush, told us she came out of the shower one evening last August to find the clown Volkening peering in at her from the fire escape. She called the 17th Precinct, but when they pulled him in, the guy was very apologetic, very pathetic. So she dropped the charges and they cut him loose."

"The 17th has him on the sheet, though," says Max, "with a full set of prints. When I checked them against the partial latents from the crime scenes, I thought there might be a match."

"There isn't any match," says Caruso. "How can you say there's a match?"

"Well, it's impossible to say there is or there isn't," says Max, "but you can't rule it out. Anyway, Volkening is an out-of-work actor, and he's working part-time as a busboy in an Eyetralian joint on West 45th. In fact, we were planning on going over there now to relieve two guys who've been staking out the restaurant when we caught *this* case."

"Even though we can't pull him in till Yom Kippur," says Caruso.

"Even though we can't pull him in till Yom Kippur," says Max.

A nurse comes out of the emergency room and approaches the group of cops.

"She's going to live," says the nurse. "She's paralyzed from the neck down, but she's going to live."

Caruso turns to the two Vice Squad cops.

"She's all yours, boys," he says, smiling.

84

Max and Caruso sit in an unmarked car on 45th Street just east of Sixth Avenue, across the street from the Italian restaurant where Volkening is currently working. All that Jerry and Larry had in the way of news when they were relieved was that Volkening had been wearing the dark overcoat when he came on tonight and that he was due off work around 11:00 P.M.

It is now 10:30, and Max is bored.

"Why don't we just pick him up and take him back to the squad for interrogation?" says Max.

"I don't know," says Caruso. "If he doesn't do anything interesting tonight, maybe we will."

"What are we hoping he'll do?"

"I don't know," says Caruso. "But I'll know it when I see it."

"I think we're wasting our time," says Max.

"Relax, kid," says Caruso. "Detective work isn't all car chases and shootouts like you see on TV. Mostly it's pushing papers across a desk, and freezing your ass for hours in a car on stakeout, just like we're doing now."

"There must be a better way."

"I'm sure there is. And when you get to be Chief of Detectives, you can tell us all about it. In the meantime, we do it this way."

At 11:08 Volkening leaves the restaurant, heading toward Sixth Avenue. Max gives him about a third of a block, then kicks over the motor. Volkening heads up-town on Sixth to 48th Street, where he turns and enters a bar with a green neon sign outside that says THE LOSERS. Very apt, thinks Max.

"You know, I'll bet there's a bar with that name in just about every city in this country," says Max.

"What name?"

"The Losers. I wonder what the attraction is for a name like that?"

"What do you mean?"

"I mean, why would anybody want to even go to a place called The Losers, much less *own* one?"

"Search me," says Caruso.

At 11:35 Volkening leaves the bar, his overcoat un-buttoned and flapping in the wind, and turns south on Sixth Avenue. Max curses softly under his breath. Sixth Avenue is one-way, going north.

"I'm going to tail him on foot," says Caruso, getting out of the car. "Pick me up at 43rd and Sixth."

Max nods and pulls out into traffic, circles the block, and cruises south on Fifth. At 11:45 Caruso gets back in the car at 43rd and Sixth.

"What's the matter, you lose him?" says Max.

Caruso shakes his head.

"Of course not. He went into a porno bookstore on 42nd and Seventh. Park the car. I feel like catching up on my reading."

Max parks the car at 43rd and Seventh. They stroll into the "adult" bookstore and try to blend in with the crowd of furtive men leafing through those maga-zines and books that aren't sealed in cellophane, trying to pretend that they've got better things to do with their time and aren't the least bit turned on by what they are looking at.

The store is one of the larger ones in the Times Square area, and the management has thoughtfully divided the pictorial material into special-interest sections identified by huge, hand-lettered signs: S&M, BONDAGE, DISCIPLINE, RUBBERWARE, WATERSPORTS, and so forth.

Volkening is checking out magazines in the BONDAGE department, which Max finds interesting, considering that Pamela Marlin and Frieda Winston were found bound together with rope.

Caruso ambles over to WATERSPORTS, perhaps believing he will find illustrative matter on deep-sea fishing or scuba diving rather than hijinx in urination.

Max drifts over to a section marked SPANKING and is amazed to find the range of subdivisions of an apparently popular pastime: there is spanking of submissive women by dominant men, spanking of submissive men by dominant women, spanking of young women by older women, of older women by young women, of younger men by older men, of older men by younger men, of younger men by older women, and so on. There is nude spanking; spanking executed in tricky underwear; teen spanking; spanking wherein the spanker wields a hairbrush, a paddle, or only an open hand; spanking wherein the spankee is secured with ropes; spanking wherein the spankee is dressed in transvestite attire.

Max wonders on what basis decisions are made to place a magazine with both spanking and transvestite elements or both spanking and bondage elements in one category and not the other and whether the management ever gets into heated philosophical debates about what belongs where.

"All right, gentlemen," says the man on the raised platform at the front of the store, "either put the magazines back on the rack or bring them up to the register. This isn't no library."

Max sees Volkening put the magazine he was looking

at back in the rack and head toward the door. Max catches Caruso's eye. Caruso indicates with a slight movement of his head that Max should follow the guy.

As soon as Volkening is outside Max walks swiftly to the door. Out on the street Max spots Volkening heading west on 42nd Street. He lets him get about a half-block ahead, then tails him from the opposite side of the street. Caruso has by now left the store and gone for the car.

At 42nd and Broadway Volkening goes into a bar for another drink. Max checks out the street life as he waits—the odd combination of hookers, muggers, tourists, theatergoers, crazies, vendors, beggars, bums, and pimps relentlessly swirling around the area—and wonders how the dignified and straitlaced *New York Times* feels about lending its name to such a stew.

Volkening leaves the bar at 42nd and Broadway about ten minutes later, strolls westward, and stops outside a store selling banjos, saxophones, electric guitars, snare drums, fake police badges, magnetic dog toys, holsters, pocket calculators, miniature TV sets, wireless telephones, walkie-talkies, joy buzzers, dribble glasses, whoopee cushions, vicious hunting knives, machetes, pennants, T-shirts, plastic dog turds, Statuettes of Liberty, and other souvenirs of New York.

Max crosses the street and affects fascination with the window display of a store specializing in men's suits made from iridescent fabrics. Volkening, he notes, has melded into a group of obvious out-of-towners outside the souvenir store. One girl in particular in the group catches Max's eye, a fresh-faced blond of about seventeen. Max can't tell whether or not she is with anyone, but Volkening seems to have spotted her as well.

The blond girl goes into the store, followed by a less-spectacular-looking girl with less dazzling blond hair, followed by Volkening. Max waits outside the iridescent clothing store. The girls emerge a short time later with purchases in plastic shopping bags with handles that won't snap together as they're supposed to. Volkening falls in behind them as they proceed farther west on 42nd Street.

Max figures they are headed toward the YMCA a few blocks down, on 34th and Ninth, not far from the Port Authority Bus Terminal. They obviously saved their pennies to come to New York on their Christmas vacation, figuring they could get away cheap at the Y, doubtlessly oblivious to the fact that merely strolling down the street in this neighborhood with their degree of sophistication is an activity only slightly less risky than skydiving.

Max follows Volkening about twenty yards back and catches sight of Caruso in the car, cruising about even with the girls and watching Volkening in the rearview mirror.

At a record store farther down the block the girls stop to talk. Then the less attractive one goes on into the store and the other one heads farther west on 42nd Street alone. God, thinks Max, it's like throwing steak to sharks. Volkening is tailing the girl about ten yards back now, Max about fifteen yards behind him, and Caruso about fifteen yards behind *him*. It is, Max decides, a parade. A New York parade.

The blond girl turns south on Ninth Avenue. Volkening starts closing in on her. Max picks up his pace. It is not clear to Max what Volkening is planning, but whatever it is there is almost no chance that it is legal.

Max walks faster. What is Volkening planning to do —snatch her purse, proposition her, expose himself, rape her—what? Volkening catches up with the girl, falls into stride beside her and says something. The girl answers him and keeps on walking. Volkening says something else. The girl ignores him and begins walking faster. Volkening grabs her.

"Freeze, Volkening! Police!" yells Max, unholstering his .38 and breaking into a dead run.

Volkening spins around, sees Max bearing down on him with gun in hand, and takes off down Ninth Avenue.

"You OK, miss?" Max blurts as he passes the girl.

She just stands there, mouth hanging open, not quite sure how she managed in a matter of seconds to become involved in a scene featuring cops and crooks and pistols.

Max races down the street after Volkening, amazed at his inability to close the distance between them. Caruso guns the car past them, hits the brakes, skids to a halt ahead of Volkening, and bounces the car up onto the sidewalk, cutting him off. Max sprints the last few yards and makes a lunge for Volkening, who whirls around, reverses field, and makes a break in the opposite direction. Max jams his gun back in his holster and grabs Volkening's arms, but Volkening wriggles out of his grasp and Max is left holding onto the overcoat with nobody inside it.

Max grabs for his gun again.

"Halt! Halt or I'll shoot!" shouts Max.

Volkening doesn't halt. Max shoots a warning shot over Volkening's head as he again passes the stupefied girl. Caruso, who had gotten out of the car to assist Max on the collar, now jumps back in again. He throws the car in reverse, laying a strip of rubber down on the pavement, whips the wheel around and tears off up Ninth Avenue after Volkening, directly against traffic.

Max is hotfooting it up the avenue as Caruso narrowly misses a cab and two passenger cars and once more bounces the unmarked police car up onto the curb in Volkening's path.

"Halt, Volkening, or I'll blow your fucking head off!" shouts Max, firing another shot over his head, fully aware that Volkening knows he is bluffing—with even these few pedestrians on the street there is not even the remotest chance that Max is going to be lobbing any shells low enough to hit anybody.

Caruso is just getting out of the car again, gun unholstered, as Max makes a flying leap, tackles Volkening around the knees, and brings him down hard on the sidewalk.

"Oh, you cocksucker," Max pants as he feels the pain of contact with concrete shoot through his right knee-cap, and only catches a glimpse of Volkening's knife in the nick of time.

Caruso kicks Volkening's knife arm and stomps on his hand. Volkening yelps with surprised pain and the knife goes clattering across the cement.

And then it is over, with Max cursing under his breath and snapping the cuffs on Volkening's wrists and with Caruso giving him the toss for further weapons.

"You have the right to remain silent," says Max, breathing hard, trying to remember the exact words of the *Miranda* warning, "You have the right to counsel. If you choose not to remain silent, anything you say can and will be used against you in, in—Caruso, what the fuck are the words?"

"That's close enough, hotshot," says Caruso.

85

VICTIM'S BOYFRIEND WILL TELL ALL—FOR A PRICE

Arnold Kupperman, 33, boyfriend of Linda Lowry, the first victim of the killer self-styled the Hyena, has reportedly offered the exclusive rights to the story of his love affair with the attractive 23-year-old junior stockbroker to the *Daily News* and the *N.Y. Post* for $50,000. Both the *News* and the *Post* have turned down Kupperman's offer.

Mr. and Mrs. Peter Lowry, parents of the victim, were angered at news of Kupperman's offer.

"I think he is the worst kind of opportunist," Mrs. Edna Lowry, the victim's mother, was quoted as saying. "To do this to the memory of a daughter whose body is not even cold in the grave is unspeakable. I wonder what kind of man could do such a thing."

"I am shocked and appalled," said Peter Lowry, 56, the victim's father, "that anyone would offer to do such a thing. I personally doubt whether he even knew my daughter, much less took her out. She wouldn't have given this guy the time of day."

86

Volkening is in the small interrogation room at Third Homicide, his stomped hand cuffed to the green metal chair with the worn vinyl upholstery that he's seated in. Max, Caruso, Jerry, Larry, Scanlon, and two reassigned detectives from another Homicide zone are in the room, but Max and Caruso are doing the actual interrogation. Caruso is taking notes in his notebook.

"Volkening," says Max, rubbing his aching knee, "have you been informed of your rights?"

Volkening looks at Max with a curious frown.

"Of *course*. You were the one who informed me of them."

"Great," says Max, glancing at a printed card with the *Miranda* warnings on it. "You know, then, that you have the right to remain silent, that anything you say can and will be used against you in a court of law, that you have the right to talk to a lawyer and have him present with you while you're being questioned and that, if you cannot afford to hire a lawyer, one will be appointed to represent you before any questioning, if you wish one—you know all that, right?"

"Of course," says Volkening, trying to rub the numbness out of his stomped hand.

"Great. And you understand each of these rights I've explained to you and you still wish to talk to us now?"

"Of course."

"Great. Volkening, you're being booked for assault,

assault and battery, possession of a deadly weapon, resisting arrest, and assaulting a police officer. You know all that already, right?"

"Of course."

"Great. Volkening, have you ever met the young woman you assaulted tonight prior to the assault?"

"I'm not sure. I don't think so. I don't know."

"You don't know?"

"No."

"What was your motive in assaulting her?"

Volkening spreads his palms skyward, as well as he can while being handcuffed to the chair.

"I have no idea," he says.

"You have no idea."

"No."

"You do remember it, though? I mean you do remember the incident which we are interrogating you about?"

"Of course."

"But you have no idea what you intended to do with this young woman once you assaulted her?"

"No."

"How could that be?"

"I don't know. I guess I must have been pretty drunk at the time."

"I see."

"Volkening," says Caruso, "do you remember assaulting Detective Segal?"

"Of course."

"And what was your motive in doing that?"

"I have no idea."

"You have no idea."

"No."

"I see," says Caruso. "You're in a hell of a lot of trouble, you know that, don't you?"

"This is the worst thing I've ever done in my life,"

says Volkening. "I don't know what made me do it. I don't know what came over me. I know it won't do any good, but I'd like to apologize to Detective Segal for assaulting him."

"You'd like to *apologize* to me?" says Max incredulously.

"Yes."

"He'd like to apologize," says Max to Caruso.

"I heard him," says Caruso. "I was in the room when he said it."

"Volkening," says Max, "is there anything else you'd like to apologize for while you're at it?"

"You mean for assaulting the girl?" he says. "Of course. I'd like to apologize to her, too, if she's here."

"Great," says Max. "And is there anything *else* you'd like to apologize for, as long as you're in the mood?"

"Like what?" says Volkening.

"I don't know," says Max. "I don't know what you've done that ought to be apologized for. Only you know that."

"Oh," says Volkening. He thinks this over for a while. "No, I don't think there's anything else I'd like to apologize for."

"You mean this is the only time you've ever been in trouble with the law?" says Max.

"That's right," says Volkening.

"You've never been in any kind of trouble involving women and the law prior to tonight?" says Max.

"That's right," says Volkening.

"You're absolutely sure of that?" says Max.

"That's right," says Volkening.

"You've never been arrested for, say, being a peeping tom?" says Max.

Volkening laughs.

"Oh, that," he says. "I forgot about that."

"You forgot about it?" says Caruso.

"Yes," says Volkening.

"But you *do* remember assaulting the girl and assaulting Detective Segal tonight—you *do* remember that?" says Caruso.

"Of course."

"Volkening," says Max, "do you remember a young woman named Linda Lowry?"

"Linda Lowry?" says Volkening.

"Yes," says Max.

"Of course," says Volkening.

"What do you remember about her?" says Caruso.

"I remember that she was killed," says Volkening.

"Do you remember who killed her?" says Max.

"Do I remember who killed her?" says Volkening.

"Yes," says Max.

"What do you mean?" says Volkening.

"I mean do you remember who killed her?" says Max.

"How would I remember who killed her?" says Volkening.

"I don't know," says Max. "I just thought you might remember."

"Do you remember a young woman named Beverly Rachlin?" says Caruso.

"I remember she was killed, too," says Volkening.

"Do you remember who killed her?" says Caruso.

"How would I remember who killed her?" says Volkening.

"Do you remember a young woman named Virginia Manteuffel?" says Max.

"Are you going to keep asking me if I remember who killed these various women, one after the other, is that what you're going to do?" says Volkening.

"Could be," says Caruso. "Why? Are we keeping you? Do you have a previous engagement we're keeping you from?"

"Oh, no," says Volkening. "I just wanted to know, that's all."

"Good," says Caruso. "I'm relieved that we're not keeping you."

"Volkening," says Max, "do you remember a girl named Pamela Marlin?"

"I remember she was another one of the women who were killed," says Volkening.

"Do you remember who killed her?" says Max.

"I'm not sure," says Volkening.

"You're not sure?" says Max.

"No," says Volkening.

"You're not sure who killed her, or you're not sure if you *remember* who killed her?" says Max.

"I'm not sure if I remember who killed her," says Volkening.

"Do you think you might have been sure and then forgotten?" says Max.

"I'm not sure," says Volkening. "I might have."

"Do you think that when she was killed you might have been the one who did it?"

Volkening looks down at his numb stomped hand which is cuffed to the arm of the green metal chair.

"I'm not sure," he says quietly. "I just really am not too sure right now. I've been under a lot of tension lately, you know."

87

Babette is downstairs in bed. She is so nervous she is practically jumping out of her skin. Perhaps she will watch television for a while to calm herself.

She turns on the set. It's an old horror movie. Not tonight. She changes the channel. Another old movie. It looks creepy, too. She tries a third channel. A woman in a nightgown is walking through a dark old house, carrying a candle. She tries a fourth channel. A commercial. A man is painting the ceiling of his den dressed in a tuxedo. She turns off the set and the bedside light and pulls the covers up over her head.

She tries to relax, to get in tune with the apartment, with her surroundings, to become one with them. She thinks she hears something. A soft scratching sound against the windowpane. A sound like that of claws.

She shudders. Stop it. Just your imagination. She holds her breath and listens. Nothing. See? Just your imagination.

She tries an exercise in yoga breathing, but halfway into it the phone rings and she jumps about a foot into the air.

She picks up the phone, suddenly knowing what she is going to hear.

"Hello?"

"Miss Watson, please."

"Yes, this is Miss Watson. Who is this?"

"Miss Watson, this is Officer Samuels of the 17th Precinct. I'm afraid I have some bad news for you."

Oh God, don't let it be what I think.

"Yes?"

"Miss Watson, Detective Segal has . . ."

"Yes? Yes? What?"

"I'm afraid there's been an accident. Detective Segal was on his way out of the station house to get a late bite to eat, and he . . . well, a taxicab ran a red light and hit him."

She screams. It's an awful sound, a primal, animal sound.

"Miss Watson?"

"Is he . . . ?"

"He's still alive, Miss Watson. He's going into surgery now. He asked me to call you."

"Where is he?"

"Bellevue. He asked if you would come and—"

"Yes, yes, of course I will. But how bad is it? Do you think he'll . . . ?"

"I don't know, Miss Watson. All we can do is wait and see what happens in surgery. Do you know how to get to Bellevue?"

"Yes. Is that where you're calling from?"

"Yes."

"OK. Tell Max I'm on my way."

Sobbing, she gets out of bed, throws on jeans and a blouse over her underwear, then a sweater, and shoes. She begins to pray. Oh God, don't let him die. Please don't let him die. I love him so much and we're so good together—please don't take him away from me. Oh, I knew this would happen. I tried to warn him, but he wouldn't listen. Oh, why didn't I insist? Why didn't I throw a temper tantrum, shriek at him, do anything, just to keep him at home tonight and prevent this awful thing.

She races upstairs, throws on her coat, unlocks the locks on the door, opens it, exits, slams it, relocks it. For what is she relocking it? What does it matter now? Never mind. She runs through the hall and opens the door to the outside and races down to First Avenue to get a cab and almost collides with a man who is walking toward her.

"Excuse me," she gasps.

"No problem, Miss Watson."

A strangely familiar voice. She looks up and sees that the man is smiling at her. It is not a pleasant smile. She tries to brush past him. He clamps his hand onto her arm.

"What are you *doing?*" she says, and then, all at once, and much too late, it comes to her.

"You're the man who just telephoned me, aren't you?" she says.

88

The Lieutenant enters the interrogation room, takes off his coat, and exchanges greetings with Max, Caruso, Larry, Jerry, and the others. When they called him at home he was already in bed, exhausted from doing three tours back-to-back.

"Mr. Volkening," he says, "I'm Lieutenant O'Malley, the Commanding Officer of Third Homicide."

"Glad to meet you, Lieutenant," says Volkening, extending his free hand.

The Lieutenant shakes his hand.

"Mr. Volkening, have you been informed of your rights?"

"Yes, I have, Lieutenant."

"So you're aware that you have the right to remain silent, that you have the right to be represented by counsel, that anything you say can and will be used against you in the courtroom, and all the rest of it?"

"Of course."

"Good. Mr. Volkening, the boys tell me that you have some recollections about the Pamela Marlin homicide, is that correct?"

"I don't know. I just really don't know right now, sir. I think so."

"What do you think it would take to refresh your memory?"

"It's hard to say, Lieutenant."

"But you do think you might have been there when Pamela Marlin was killed, do you?"

"I think so, yes."

"Do you think you might have been there when Frieda Winston was killed, too?"

"I think so."

"Do you remember who it was who did the killings?"

"I'm not sure."

"Do you think it might have been you?"

"I'm not sure. I think so. It's a little hazy right now in my mind."

"But you do think there's a chance that you remember doing the two killings, do you?"

"Off the top of my head, I would probably say yes."

"Good," says the Lieutenant, exchanging fast glances with the rest of the detectives in the room. "Very, very good. As you may know, Mr. Volkening, we've been working quite hard on these particular homicides, and—"

"The two you mentioned, you mean? Pamela Marlin and Frieda Winston?"

"Uh, yes. And the others."

"What others?"

"The . . . Linda Lowry case, the Virginia Manteuffel case, the Beverly Rachlin case and the, uh, Sharon Hammond case . . ."

"Oh yes, of course. I forgot about those."

"Do you remember anything about those cases too, Mr. Volkening?"

"Let me see now. Hmmmm. Possibly so, possibly so."

"Good. Do you remember being present at those homicides as well?"

"Possibly so, possibly so."

"Do you remember whether it was you who did the killings?"

"Possibly so. I would have to really sit down and think about it."

"But you do think there's a pretty good possibility that it was you who did them?"

"Oh my, yes," says Volkening, smiling. "A very good possibility, I would say."

"Excellent," says the Lieutenant, "excellent."

The Lieutenant turns to Caruso.

"Sal, what A.D.A. is catching tonight?" he says.

"Feinman," says Caruso.

"Mr. Volkening," says the Lieutenant, "if I were to call up Assistant District Attorney Feinman and have him come up here now, do you think you might be able to give him a statement?"

"I don't know," says Volkening. "Will it take long?"

"Not very long," says the Lieutenant. "Why? Do you have something else you have to do now?"

"Oh, no, not really," says Volkening. "It's just that it's kind of late, that's all."

"Well, it won't take very long, if you want to do it

now, so we can get that part of it out of the way and
not have to do it tomorrow."

"I think I'd prefer to do it tomorrow," says Volkening, "if it's all the same to you."

"Are you sure you wouldn't like to get it out of the
way right now?" says the Lieutenant.

"I'm pretty sure, thanks," says Volkening. "I'll really
be a lot fresher in the morning."

"OK," says the Lieutenant. "But you will give Mr.
Feinman a statement in the morning, then?"

"Oh, of course," says Volkening. "I *said* I would,
didn't I?"

"Very good," says the Lieutenant.

"Can I go now?" says Volkening.

"Go? Go where?" says the Lieutenant.

"Home," says Volkening.

"Well," says the Lieutenant, "I'm afraid not, Mr.
Volkening. We'd like you to stay tonight with us."

"Oh," says Volkening. "Well, all right. I could be
back here bright and early, though, if you let me go
now."

"I'm afraid I can't allow that," says the Lieutenant.
"I'm afraid we're going to have to keep you here."

"Oh," says Volkening. "Well, all right. If you insist."

"I insist," says the Lieutenant.

89

"You're the man who just telephoned me, aren't you?" she says.

He laughs a horrid laugh.

"That's right, Babette."

The same one who pretended to be Max's neighbor. The same one who murdered Linda Lowry and Beverly Rachlin and Virginia Manteuffel and Pamela Marlin and Frieda Winston and Sharon Hammond. The Hyena.

She has been expecting this. She has known it was coming toward her for a very long time. It is going to be terrible, but at least the waiting is over. The unfathomable dread is gone, and in its place is a very real here-and-now something she can understand. Whatever is going to happen is going to happen. Perhaps, in some weird way, it's happened already. At least the part about Max was a lie.

"What you said about Max," she says. "That wasn't true, was it? About Max being in an accident?"

"No," says the man, "it wasn't."

"Thank God," says Babette.

"Don't thank God so fast," says the man.

He shows her what he has in his hand. A flat square envelope and a switchblade knife.

"Please don't make me hurt you, Babette," says the man in a reasonable tone. "I love you too much to hurt you. But if you force me to, I will."

She looks wildly around. There is nobody else on the

street. If she yelled for help, who would hear her? If she ran, where could she run to? Besides, he looked like he could outrun her. And then there was the knife. It looked hopeless.

"What do you want me to do?" says Babette.

"Take me back inside. Take me into Max's apartment."

If I take him back inside, she thinks, will he kill me and leave, or will he set a trap for Max, with me as bait? She is not anxious to die. She is willing to, should it be necessary. But to die for nothing, to die for no purpose, to die without even saving Max in the process makes no sense. And if she doesn't take the killer back into the apartment he will probably kill her right there on the street.

"OK," she says, "I'll take you back inside."

With the man following closely behind her, she walks slowly back to the building, unlocks the lobby door, walks through the hallway, unlocks the door to Max's apartment, and lets them inside.

"If you promise to be a good girl," he says, "I will put the knife away."

"I promise," says Babette.

The man folds his knife and puts it away.

Babette gets a flash of something—distant dialogue, music—and has to steady herself against the wall.

"What do you want with me, a date, a what, a date, I want to date you," says Babette involuntarily.

The man looks shaken.

"What did you say?" he says.

". . . May I put this on the phonograph, get out, I'll count to ten and if you're not out of here by then . . ." There is another flash of music. She wobbles on her feet.

"What are you doing?" says the man, horrified. "How can you be . . . ?"

"*. . . Did you say I've got a lot to learn . . .*" she sings tonelessly. "*Well, don't think I'm trying not to learn . . .*"

She is unable to stop herself. It is as if she has lost control of what comes out of her mouth.

"*. . . Since this is the perfect spot to learn . . .*"

"Stop it! Stop it!" The man is becoming panicky.

She feels more about to come out. She tries closing her mouth. The words slip past anyway.

"*. . . Teach me tonight . . .*"

The man whips out his knife, clicks out the blade, and comes at her.

"Do you know what that song is?" he hisses.

"No."

"Then how do you know the words?"

"I don't."

"Then how could you have been singing it? And what was all that about wanting a date and putting something on the phonograph?"

"I don't know. It just . . . came to me."

"What do you mean it just *came* to you?"

"It just did. That happens to me sometimes."

"Tell me how you knew that song. Tell me why you said those things about dates and phonographs."

"I already told you. Because it came to me. Because I heard it."

"*Tell me the truth!*"

He grabs her around the neck with the hand that isn't holding the knife. She closes her eyes.

Hail - Mary - full - of - grace - the - Lord - is - with - Thee - blessed - art - Thou - among - women - and - blessed - is - the fruit-of-Thy-womb-Jesus—

90

Gunnar Schmidt, manager of the building at 121 Christopher Street in the West Village, is fed up.

It's not enough he has to serve as a combination janitor and nursemaid to a bunch of tenants who are constantly abusing the facilities in their apartments, clogging up toilet drains with used Tampaxes and worse, clogging up their sink and tub drains with hair, and making their sinks back up by allowing grease and rotting food to flow right down without stopping it, but they don't even seem to care about the most rudimentary forms of cleanliness and sanitary procedures.

The hallways are constantly littered with garbage, the incinerator is overloaded with the most incredible things—empty aerosol cans on which are printed warnings not to incinerate them, flammable paint removers, old articles of clothing, rubber galoshes—it's just amazing what they think to throw down that chute. It's a wonder the whole place doesn't always stink to high heaven, the way it does today.

Wherever the smell is coming from, this is just about the last straw. He's going to start throwing people out of the building in wholesale lots. If the animals he's got for tenants can't keep their building from stinking to high heaven, then he's going to get Health Department permission to have them evicted as health hazards.

He walks down the hall, trying to locate the source of the current smell. He stops before Apartment 2F, where the smell seems to be the strongest. He knocks on the door. No answer. He knocks again, louder.

"Miss Middleton, are you in there? It's Mr. Schmidt."

Still no answer, Schmidt takes out his passkey, slips it into the lock, and opens the door. The smell is so overpowering he has to hold his breath. He walks into the apartment, gasps, and nearly faints dead away at what he sees.

91

"Tell me the truth! How did you know that song? How did you know those things about dates and phonographs? Have you been following me? Have you been researching me? Is that it?"

She tries to nod her head.

He relaxes his grip on her throat and pulls himself together.

"Is that how you knew all that, Babette?" he asks in a normal tone of voice.

"Yes," she gasps.

She puts her hand up to her throat and feels the imprints of his fingers there. She cannot believe she is still alive.

Babette staggers over to the couch and sinks down on the cushions. She was wrong about being willing to die. She is not at all willing.

"Tell me," he says pleasantly, "how long have you been researching me?"

"I don't know," she says. "A few weeks."

He smiles and shakes his head.

"Boy, that's pretty funny. You know, I've been researching you, too. Did you know that?"

"I didn't know that," she says.

He chuckles and shakes his head again.

"Well," he says, "I must admit you're pretty good. I don't see how you got those things, I really don't. Unless you were there. You weren't there, were you? When I had my dates with Linda and the others?"

"No," she says, "I wasn't."

"Well, then, I don't see how you did it. Unless you had recording devices and the places were bugged. I don't suppose you'd tell me how you did it, would you? As one professional to another? Would you?"

Babette shakes her head.

"Aww. Well, I can't say I blame you," he says. "I don't know if I'd give away *my* secrets either. Well, I have enormous respect for you. From my research I didn't know you were capable of that kind of brilliance —of researching me that well without my even being aware of it, even while I was researching *you*. By the way, what was the point of your research?"

"What?"

"I *said* what was the point of your research? Was it to help Max? To help him catch me? Or were you doing it on your own behalf?"

Silence.

"Come to think of it, if you were doing it for Max or for the cops, you probably would have turned me in as soon as you knew who I was. Isn't that right, Babette?"

No answer. He chuckles softly.

"I can see why you're not answering. Maybe you *started* researching me for Max and the cops, but then you became intrigued enough to not turn me in, to keep researching me for your own purposes."

He chuckles again, suggestively.

"Tell me, my little lady, what might those purposes of yours have been, eh? Might they have anything to do with—how shall I put it?—with dating?"

No reply.

"That's the sort of thing that *I* would have done, you know that? We are somewhat alike, you and I. At least in that area anyway. Maybe not in other areas. Maybe not in areas like . . . sex."

He watches her face for clues.

"Isn't that true, Babette? We're not alike in the area of sex. I live alone. I don't have any regular sex partner like you do. I don't have sexual relations as often as you do. I don't *fornicate* every day and night like you do."

Babette says something so quietly he can't hear her.

"What's that?" he says. "What's that you say?"

"I don't fornicate."

"You don't? I don't understand. Maybe you don't know the meaning of the word. Maybe they didn't teach you that word. Maybe that word has fallen out of fashion these days. To fornicate means to have illicit sex. To have relations with somebody you're not married to. You're not married to Max, are you?"

No reply.

"You *are* having sex with him, aren't you? Aren't you, Babette?"

She doesn't answer.

"Answer me, Babette. It's not *polite* to not answer when somebody addresses you. Aren't you having sex with Max?"

Silence.

"Aren't you? *Answer* me, goddam you!"

"No!" she screams, and starts to cry, because it has

just occurred to her that now she and Max will never ever make love, that they waited and didn't do it when they both wanted to so desperately because she wanted it to be the right moment, she wanted to wait till they were maybe married or something, and now it was too late. They were fools to wait. What could it have mattered to God or to Jesus or to the Pope or to her father or to anybody else if she and her sweetheart had made love or not, because now she was going to be slaughtered by a madman and she was going to die a virgin, unless of course this filthy pig raped her first.

"No?" he says, frowning. "You're *not* having sex with Max? How could that be? That doesn't seem very likely. Although, now that I think of it, I never found anything in your garbage to indicate otherwise. No wrappers from birth-control pills or boxes from diaphragm jelly or anything else. I never wondered about it before, but now . . ."

Was there nothing she could do? Was there no way to escape or to kill him before he killed her? If there was, then why had none of the others escaped or killed him? What *had* they done? Had they been passive? Cooperative? Defiant? Cunning? One of them *had* tricked him, if the dialogue she babbled into Max's tape recorder had actually been spoken at the scene of the crime. Yes, Linda Lowry. The dialogue sounded like she had pretended to go along with it, pretended to be going along with the date part of it, danced with him and so on, and then done something to enrage him. Went for his knife, it sounded like. A lot of good *that* did her. No, there had to be something better than that.

"Babette, the more I think of it, the more I think you may be telling the truth. I am prepared to believe that you and Max are not having sex. Which makes you a lot more interesting to me as a woman. As a potential mate. We're even more alike than I thought, you know that?"

Perhaps I should encourage him. Tell him how alike we are. Let him think I really have been following him around the city with tape recorders and bugging devices and sifting through his garbage because I was seriously thinking of leaving Max for him. No, somebody else tried pretending to be interested in him sexually. Not Linda Lowry either, although her dialogue sounded like she might have had the same idea. Who was it? Never mind. That's not the answer either.

"All right, Babette," he says. "I've made a decision. I have an idea I think you're going to like."

The only idea *I'd* like, she thinks, is if you'd commit suicide.

"Do you want to hear my idea, Babette?"

She nods.

"I am going to give you a chance to prove yourself. To see if you are worthy of becoming my woman. There will be a number of tests you will have to pass, of course, but from what I've seen so far, I think that you just might be able to do it. Do you think you could measure up?"

"What kind of tests would I have to pass?" she says.

"Tests of courage. Tests of character. Tests of moral purity. And, most important of all, tests of loyalty. Do you think you can pass them?"

She nods.

"If you can convince me of your loyalty, then you will become very, very valuable to me. But if you think you might be able to use these tests as a way to escape from me, I must warn you: I will not tolerate disloyalty. I will not tolerate treachery. I will not tolerate traitors. Do you know what we do with traitors, Babette?"

She nods.

Max and Caruso are the last to leave the interrogation room. There are three reporters in the squad room talking to Jerry and Larry, who turn around expectantly as Max and Caruso enter.

"Who's that?" says one of the reporters to Jerry.

"That's Detectives Segal and Caruso, the guys that collared Volkening."

The three reporters descend on Max and Caruso.

"Detective Segal," says a short, balding man with a chunky build, "my name's Donnegan. *Daily News.* Could I speak to you a moment?"

"Not right now," says Max, rubbing his aching knee.

"Detective Cassidy says you were the ones who collared the Hyena."

"How did you know it was him?" says a taller man with pale skin and freckles.

"We didn't," says Max. "Look, I really don't have time to talk to you guys now, so—"

"Detective Cassidy says he and his partner and you and Detective Caruso had been staking—"

"Please, guys," says Max, pushing past them, "not right now, OK?"

The three reporters turn back to Larry.

"Not very friendly, is he?" says Donnegan.

"We've all had a hard day," says Larry.

"Well now," says the man, "Max is working a four-to-one tour tonight, so that means he should be here about one-twenty or so. We might as well make ourselves comfortable."

He takes off his coat and folds it neatly and puts it carefully down on a chair, then does the same with hers.

So she was right. He *is* going to wait for Max. She looks at the clock above the kitchen sink. A few minutes before midnight. Hardly more than an hour before Max gets here. How can she warn Max that he is walking into a trap?

"Is there a phonograph here?" says the man.

"Over there," she says, pointing.

He opens the flat square package he was carrying and takes out a recording. He places it carefully on the turntable, turns on the machine, and puts the needle in place. He lines up the album cover with the edge of the table. The record begins. With a jolt she realizes she is hearing in person for the first time the song she has previously heard only in her trances, the song that he has probably played for every one of his victims before he killed them:

Did you say I've got a lot to learn?
Well, don't think I'm trying not to learn . . .

"April Stevens," says the man. "Do you remember her?"

"Uh, not really, no."

"No? Isn't that the song you started singing earlier?"

"Oh. Yes. What I meant was that I don't remember her from when she was popular. I remember her only from . . . researching you."

"Ah. You know, she looks a little like you, in a way."

"Oh."

"Shall we trip the light fantastic?"

"Uh . . . what?"

"I *said* shall we trip the light fantastic?"

The man begins swaying in time to the music. He holds out his hands to her. She holds back the nausea which has once more started rising in her throat, stands up, and moves into dance position with him. They begin to dance. He is not really all that bad, she thinks.

"You dance very well," he says.

"Thank you, so do you," she says, and then, before she can stop herself, out comes: "I-ought-to-I-didn't-go-to-Arthur-Murray-for-a-whole-season-for-nothing-you-know."

The man stops dancing and glares at her with sudden fury.

"I'm sorry," she whispers, "it just came out without—"

He gives her a hard open-handed slap which throws her off balance and almost sends her to the floor.

"Don't you *dare* do that to me again," he hisses. "Don't you *dare*."

"I couldn't help it," she says.

"You expect me to believe that? You really expect me to believe that? You think I don't know what you're saying to me when you do that? That you've heard me say those things to other women when you were researching me? That I repeat myself? That I don't have the gift of gab, that I don't have any small talk, that I keep saying the same things to women in the same situation because I don't happen to have the talent of making useless, trivial, stupid, insignificant conversation and so I say the same things over and over again."

"Please," she says, "I really wasn't making fun of you, you have to believe me."

"You like to humiliate me, don't you?" he says. "It gives you pleasure to make me feel humiliated, doesn't it?"

"No," she says, "please don't say that, I swear I—"

"You think you're better than me because you can make small talk, because you're beautiful, because you never had to work like a dog for every cent the way I did, because nobody ever laughed at you and made you feel like an animal because nobody had bothered to teach you the socially accepted ways of doing things and saying things. Well, let's see how you like being without all those things. Let's see how you like being the very thing you mock in me. Let's take away that pretty little façade of yours and see what's underneath it. Take off your clothes."

"What?"

"I *said* take off your *clothes*. Kindly do not ask me to repeat what you have heard already. Take off your clothes."

She stares at him, unmoving.

"Didn't you hear me? I said take off your clothes. Take them off. If you don't take them off, I'll have to do it for you. And you won't like how I do it either."

Please, God, she thinks, tell me what to do now. Please give me a sign of what to do.

"You want me to do it *for* you? Is that what you want? Fine. Whatever you like."

He reaches into his pocket and takes out the switchblade and clicks it open.

Please, God. Please let me know what I should do. I didn't sleep with the man I love, even though we both wanted to and it would have hurt nobody, just because of You, just because I didn't want to offend You. That must be worth something, mustn't it? That must be worth something to You, mustn't it? Can't You show me a sign that You have been pleased with my actions? Can't You help me now when I need You the most?

"First your sweater," says the man, grabbing the front of her sweater, inserting the top of the knife blade into the material at the neck, and slitting it down to the bottom.

"Please don't do this," she says, reaching out and touching the arm that wields the knife. "Please don't."

"Are you going to do it yourself?" he says.

She nods her head.

"Then go ahead."

She starts unbuttoning her blouse, as the tears start running down her face. I'm not doing this, she thinks. This is not me who is doing this. This is somebody else who I don't know who is doing this, and it doesn't matter because that person has nothing to do with me.

When she has finished unbuttoning her blouse he holds out his hand and she takes it off and gives it to him. He drops it on the floor.

"Now your dungarees," he says.

She unzips her jeans and steps out of them and leaves them on the floor and tries not to think about the irony of how until now only one man in the world besides her doctor has ever seen her like this, in her bra and underpants, and that's Max, the man she loves, the man she thought she was going to marry, and how not even Max has seen her totally naked and how this pig is going to, and that is as far ahead as she is willing to let herself think.

"And now the brassiere."

She reaches behind her and starts to undo the catch and stops, eyes closed, trying to will herself out of the scene entirely.

"I *said* take off your brassiere."

She visualizes herself in a descending elevator with the floors going from 10 to 1, entering the darkened room with the TV set, turning it on, and visualizing on the screen the only thing she can think of to send Max as a visual symbol of warning: a snarling hyena with long fangs about to puncture her neck. Assuming that Max is capable of receiving such an image, and assuming that Max is able to correctly interpret it, and assuming that Max will even remember that it is midnight and think to turn on his own psychic receiver at all.

It is a lot to assume. But at this point it is about all that she can think of to do.

94

The 17th Precinct, and Third Homicide's offices on the second floor in particular, is quickly being engulfed by media people. Thick power cables run from klieg lights and television cameras down the stairs to generator trucks out in the street. Reporters and still photographers from the three metropolitan dailies, the wire services, the news magazines, and the neighborhood papers, stringers from the out-of-town papers and foreign periodicals, and people from the TV and radio networks and all the local channels and stations are running around interviewing and photographing everybody in sight, including the switchboard operator. The telephones do not stop ringing.

In the midst of this chaos the overworked and exhausted detectives maintain a weary good humor as they interrupt their paperwork to answer the same questions. The main thing is that the Hyena has been caught, and sanity is returning to the city and to the Police Department. The pressure from the Mayor, the Commissioner, and the general public has been replaced by adulation and congratulation. The Special Task Force is being dismantled, and soon everybody will be done with the paperwork and the interviews and they'll all go home and get some sleep.

Detective Scanlon answers one of the six ringing telephones in the squad room, turns suddenly grim, jots something down on a notepad, and puts down the phone.

"Lieutenant," says Scanlon, "we got another 10-83."

The Lieutenant fends off four TV reporters and turns to Scanlon, the horrid unasked question on his face.

"I don't know, Lieutenant," says Scanlon. "The deceased is a female Caucasian. She's nude, and the killer really carved her up. She's been dead for several days, judging by the smell. Pray it's our boy Volkening who did it before we collared him."

95

"Are you going to take off your brassiere or aren't you?" says the man, stepping toward her menacingly.

Babette once more reaches behind her and starts to undo the catch on her bra and once more stops, the tears running freely down her cheeks and onto her chest.

"I'm not taking anymore off," she says.

"Good girl," says the man.

She looks at him uncomprehendingly.

"You passed your first test," he says. "No woman I'd want would have taken off all her clothes for any man, unless she was married to him. Even if refusing would endanger her life."

Babette hugs herself and shivers.

"Are you cold?" says the man. "You must be. Poor Babette. I don't want you catching cold on me now."

He walks swiftly to their two coats and pulls his out from under hers without messing up the neat folds, comes back to her, and wraps his coat around her shoulders.

"I'm sorry I put you through that," he says. "That wasn't very nice of me. I apologize."

Babette goes over to the sofa and collapses on it, face down.

"I said I apologize," says the man. "Do you accept my apology?"

Babette remains lying face down on the sofa, unmoving.

"Come on, Babette," he says, "don't give me the silent treatment. I *said* I was sorry."

The man looks at her awhile longer, then sinks down beside her on the sofa and puts his arms around her. Neither of them moves for some time, and then the man begins to cry.

"I don't know what's wrong with me," he whispers, as much to himself as to her. "I don't know what makes me do such things. It's not hate, but I don't suppose you'd understand that. It begins with love. It always begins with love. Love is still the strongest feeling that I feel for *you,* Babette."

He strokes her hair.

"You know," he says, "you haven't really failed any important tests yet. You could still pass them and become my woman. We'd be some team, you and me. The two of us against the rest of them. With you at my side I could take on the world. What do you say, Babette?"

No reply.

"Babette? Please talk to me. I want you to talk to me."

He tries to turn her face toward him, but she resists.

"Babette, if you don't answer me, you're going to regret it."

Babette does not reply.

"All right, Babette. I had hoped to be able to conduct these tests on a warm, friendly basis, but you don't seem to want to do it that way. We are ready for your next test. A very important test, Babette. Your first test of loyalty. Your first opportunity to demonstrate to me who it is you are loyal to, me or Max."

The man begins to pace around the room, his hands clasped behind his back, an earnest expression on his face.

"Max gets off work tonight at one. It takes him about

twenty minutes to get back here, unless he goes to get a snack with one of the other detectives, in which case it takes him a little over an hour. Whatever the case, when Max opens the door, the lights will be out. I'll shut off all the power from the circuit-breaker box on the kitchen wall there. You'll be restrained only physically from going to his aid—I'll tie your wrists and ankles, but you'll be free to speak or shout or warn him verbally, if that is what you decide to do. However . . ."

The man turns to face Babette, who is still showing no evidence that she is even listening.

"However," says the man, "should you decide to warn him, I shall have no choice but to do away with both of you. Should you remain *silent,* however, and make no attempt to warn him, then only Max will have to be done away with. And you will have proven your loyalty to me and will immediately become my—"

Babette says something muffled which the man doesn't catch.

"What was that?" he says.

"How hot are the fires of hell," says Babette.

"How hot are the what?" says the man.

"Imagine a raging fire ten thousand times as hot as that match burning over every square inch of your body, forever, do you know how long forever is, you do not," she continues in a toneless voice.

"Babette, what are you—?"

"The human mind has no conception of forever, imagine an enormous iron ball the-size-of-the-earth-imagine-that-once-every-hundred-years-a-bird-comes-down—"

"Babette, stop that! Stop doing that!"

"—to-sharpen-its-beak-on-that-iron-ball-now-when-that-bird-wears-that-iron-ball-down-to-nothing—"

"Stop it, I said!"

"—that-will-be-just-the-beginning-of—"

"Stop it! Stop it! Stop it, God damn you!"

He grabs her under the arms, lifts her off the couch, and hurls her against the wall with all his might. She hits with a sickening crack and crumples like a marionette with cut strings, pitching forward and slowly toppling off the sofa onto the floor. A bottle falls off the bar and shatters. The man stands over her, breathing hard, until his flash of rage subsides.

"I'm sorry I did that," he says in a normal voice.

Babette is lying very still.

"Babette, I'm sorry I did that. I don't know what came over me."

The man becomes alarmed at Babette's lack of movement.

"Babette, are you all right?"

The man bends down to look at her. He sees no sign that she has heard him, no sign that she is even alive.

"Babette?"

There is no movement of any kind, not even breathing. He holds his hand in front of her lips. He feels no breath. He picks up her wrist and feels for a pulse. There isn't any.

"Babette!"

He releases her wrist. It bounces limply on the carpet.

"Oh, no, not you, too," he whispers, the tears springing to his eyes. "Oh, don't do this, Babette, please don't die and leave me. You *can't* leave me, not when I've just *found* you, you *can't*."

He shakes her by the shoulders. Her head flops back and forth on her neck.

"You can't die, Babette. You're my one true love. We were meant for each other. You're the one I've been waiting for all these years. You can't leave me now that I've finally found you, now that we're finally together, you *can't!*"

He stares at her closely. He looks into her face. He puts his arms around her and hugs her to his body and begins to sob, rocking her gently back and forth. A horrid, high-pitched keening sound issues from his throat.

96

NAB BUSBOY AS HYENA!
UNEMPLOYED ACTOR SEIZED
WHILE ATTACKING •
TEENAGER!

The Hyena, the killer who has held New York City in a grip of terror for the past several weeks, was caught last night while assaulting an out-of-town teenager, police announced very early this morning.

Stefan Volkening, 38, a part-time busboy and out-of-work actor, was arrested by New York City detectives as he pounced on what was to have been his next victim.

"Well, it's over at last," Chief of Detectives Patrick J. Noonan was quoted as saying. "I am proud not only of the men who ar-

rested him but of every man, on the force, because without their help we could never have done it."

The Mayor, speaking to a crowd of reporters at City Hall, declared: "The citizens of this city can rest easily, knowing that the person known as the Hyena has been caught." The Mayor had high praise for the entire New York City Police Department, declaring: "They have once more demonstrated why we call them New York's Finest."

Volkening, dark and glowering, with what witnesses have described as "vacant eyes," is being held without bail, under heavy guard, for the murders of six New York City women: Linda Lowry, Beverly Rachlin, Virginia Manteuffel, Pamela Marlin, Frieda Winston, and Sharon Hammond—all of Manhattan.

LUCKY NUMBER SEVEN

Pretty Patty Ramsay, 17, of Columbus, Ohio, narrowly missed becoming the Hyena's seventh victim. In New York for a between-semesters vacation, she was walking in the Times Square area when the alleged killer assaulted her without warning.

Luckily, two detectives from the Third Homicide Zone, Det. Max Segal and Det. Salvatore Caruso, had been tailing him. When Volkening grabbed the girl, Segal and Caruso moved in and disarmed and arrested him.

"Everything happened so fast," said Miss Ramsay, the Hyena's would-be seventh victim, "I didn't even have the *time* to get scared. Then the police were there and then it was over. I thank God they were following him, otherwise I might not even be talking to you now."

Asked how she was enjoying her first visit to New York, Miss Ramsay replied, "Well, it's certainly not a dull place to visit."

97

The man slowly releases Babette's lifeless body and lets it sink back to the floor.

He feels an overwhelming sense of loss, a poignant emptiness which seems to touch some ancient memory buried deep in his subconscious mind. He has done a horrible thing. Killed the only woman he's ever loved. Killed the only woman he could ever have loved. You always kill the one you love, he thinks.

He hadn't meant to kill her. He'd only tried to stop

her from saying those things. He couldn't stand her saying those things. He hadn't meant to kill her, though. Was it really his fault that she was dead? It was an accident. Were accidents anybody's fault?

In a sense, it was nobody's fault. In a sense it was *everybody's* fault—his, hers, even Max's. It was Max, after all, who'd gotten her to move in with him in a lustful attempt to deprive her of her chastity. It was Max who stood between them, in life as in death. If it were not for Max, Babette would be someplace else now, alive and well and ready to fall in love with somebody who was morally pure and worthy of her and she would not be lying dead now on the floor of this apartment. Yes, in a sense, in a very real sense, it was mostly Max's fault. Someone had to be punished for Babette's death. Max was the logical choice.

He stands up straight and begins walking about the apartment. He tidies up everything but the broken glass. He aligns all the picture frames on the wall. He closes all the blinds and shades and curtains.

He goes to the circuit-breaker box on the kitchen wall and flips all the switches to OFF, plunging the apartment into total blackness. He takes out his knife and snaps it open. He squats down behind the door and begins to wait.

98

Five weary detectives of the Third Homicide Zone are making notes and sketches, covering their mouths and noses with handkerchiefs, holding the retch back with their teeth and trying not to look any longer than they have to at what used to be Marilyn Middleton.

Her body, dark and swollen with the putrid gases of decomposition, has been slashed and stabbed repeatedly with a sharp metal instrument. The breasts, buttocks, vagina, belly, and face have taken the worst of the slashing. The nude body is lying on its side, half-hanging off an unmade bed. The bed and the floor are encrusted with dark brown dried blood.

Larry and Jerry, noting the position of the body and the placement of various pieces of furniture which seem to indicate that a violent struggle had taken place, speak from behind their handkerchiefs.

"Well," says Larry, "it could be worse."

"Yeah," says Jerry, "she could've been a floater. My first 10-83 in the job was a floater. Also a female. She was all puffed up like a balloon, and when we tried to fish her out of the river she hit something sharp and burst. She exploded all over a brand-new sportscoat I'd just bought that day."

"That'll teach you to wear good clothes on the job," says Larry.

"You know," says Jerry, "for the first time I'm glad that Segal isn't here."

"Segal knew this gal, didn't he?" says Larry, stepping out of the way of the Crime Scene Unit man who is taking his series of flash photos of the body as rapidly as possible so he can get out of the stinking apartment.

"He said he took her to dinner to talk about suspects," says Jerry. "I think he played a little hide-the-salami with her too, which is why I think it's nice he isn't here to see her in her present condition."

The Medical Examiner arrives, looks at the decomposing body hanging off the bed, shakes his head, and clucks his tongue.

"I thought there wasn't going to *be* any more of this," says the M.E. with mock petulance. "I thought the citizens of this city could rest easily now, knowing that the person known as the Hyena has been caught. What's the matter, don't you *listen* when our Mayor speaks?"

"Hey, give us a break, doc," says Larry. "We only collared the sonofabitch last night. This is not what you might call recent work, now is it?"

"Well, just see that it doesn't happen again," says the M.E. merrily and moves over to the bed to make his preliminary examination of the corpse.

99

Max arrives back at his apartment well after 2:00 A.M., feeling exhausted, but terrific, and also a little high after tossing off a few rounds of congratulatory drinks with Caruso. In just a few hours Volkening is going to give the Assistant D.A. a statement about the Hyena homicides, and even if Caruso did happen to be backing him up at the time, it was still Max who had made the actual collar.

He unlocks the door, anxious to wake up Babette and tell her the news and is irked to find none of the locks locked from the inside. Foolish kid, hadn't he told her how dangerous it was to leave those locks unlocked, especially when you were asleep?

Well, it hardly mattered now. If Volkening really was their man—and it was hard to see how he wasn't, especially in view of the details of the various homicides that he began to remember as they were locking him up in his overnight lodging cell—then attractive young single girls in New York like Babette were going to be breathing a lot easier.

Max closes the door behind him and triple-locks it. He reaches for the light switch and flicks it on, but nothing happens. Damn, he thinks, the bulb's burned out. Well, there's a supply of bulbs in the cabinet above the sink.

"Baby, wake up," he calls downstairs. "I've got great news."

Max walks slowly to the sink to get a bulb out of the overhead cabinet, feeling his way in the dark, and crunches a piece of broken bottle under his heel. Surprised that Babette would have broken something and not cleaned it up, he bends down to get it.

At that moment the man lunges forward with his knife, aiming for the center of Max's back. But Max's bending down causes the killer to misjudge his target. Instead of plunging into Max's back, the blade stabs only air. The killer, who is thrown off balance by not having his forward thrust met with flesh and bone, collides with Max and almost falls.

At the precise instant of collision Max is not clear

whether the person behind him is Babette playing a prank or a prowler trying to kill him. But then the man grunts a masculine grunt in regaining his balance and there is no longer any doubt in Max's mind. Max whips out his revolver just as the killer strikes a second time. The blade slashes Max's gun hand, causing him to drop the gun.

Max crouches in the dark, trying to figure out where the next attack will be coming from, trying to figure out who his attacker could be and how he got into the apartment and what has happened to Babette and whether he can find his gun again in time to use it and whether there is any danger of hitting Babette with a bullet if she is anywhere around and if she's not then where the hell is she?

Max passes his hand lightly over the carpet, trying to locate the .38, trying not to make the floorboards creak and give away his position as he moves. Scanning the carpet, he finds only broken bits of bottle, and finally grabs the broken bottleneck as an alternate weapon.

There is no sound from the killer to indicate his position. Max touches his right hand and finds it wet with blood. The wound is worse than he'd thought. He'll have to make his handkerchief into a tight bandage to stop the blood the moment he's gotten rid of the prowler. At the moment Max feels this task to be not beyond his capabilities, despite the disadvantages of being both wounded and gunless.

There is a creak to Max's right. He whirls, the bottleneck outthrust, but fails to connect with his adversary. He circles backward to his right.

Max starts to feel a certain numbness in the slashed hand. He shifts the broken bottleneck to his left and continues lightly patting the floor with his right. The

floor squeaks directly ahead of him. Max tenses, waiting
for the attack, but it doesn't come.

How long has the prowler been in his apartment?
How did he get in? Has he harmed Babette? With sickening clarity Max recalls Babette's premonitions of disaster and her entreaties not to leave her tonight. Why
did he not listen to her after all the evidence he'd had
of her precognitive powers? What a fool he'd been not
to listen to her. If only he'd stayed home as she'd
begged. If only he'd stayed with her and protected
her. If only Babette is still alive and unharmed, he'll
never be so stupid again.

Max's right hand is getting too numb to be of much
use in locating the revolver. He keeps backing up, making occasional creaking noises, trying to feel out the
location of the gun with his foot, and his shoe hits
something awful—a body. He gasps. Babette! Oh no!

He drops the bottleneck and reaches downward. He
touches bare flesh. Her body is still warm—is she still
alive?

He realizes too late that his gasp has betrayed his
position. As he starts to get up the killer attacks again.
This time the knife-blade penetrates Max's left shoulder.
The pain is intense, but Max swings out wildly and hits
his opponent in the torso. Max falls back across
Babette's body, bringing his feet up sharply and catching
the killer in the groin. He hears the man inhale sharply
and curse. Something heavy crashes to the floor. As the
killer slashes out again with the knife, Max rolls to his
left and manages to dodge the blade by millimeters.

Max makes a grab for the killer's legs and succeeds
in sending the man to the floor. But before Max can
press his advantage he gets a kick in the face which
sends him reeling.

Max crouches near the floor, breathing hard. The
wound in his shoulder is throbbing and terribly painful.

For the first time it occurs to Max that he might not win this fight, that if he doesn't he stands an excellent chance of losing his life. It is a concept that is wholly foreign to Max. He has never before even considered the possibility of his own death, being young and strong and having had his natural recklessness coupled so often with good timing and good luck that he just naturally thought he was immortal. The notion that he is pathetically vulnerable after all, that he has in fact been vulnerable all the while he was being reckless and that it is suddenly too late to do anything about it, is almost too much to grasp. Max feels the first true fear he has ever felt in his life.

He is somewhere to the left of Babette's body, trying to figure out what to do, trying to figure out if there is anything he *can* do against this crazed assassin, and wishing vainly that he could locate his revolver and blow the bastard's brains out.

He begins creeping further to his left in slow, crab-like motions, making more squeaking noises in the floor, still patting the carpet for his gun. He hears the sound directly behind him and ducks a beat too late. Searing pain rips across his back. He knows he has been badly stabbed. He tries to crawl away from his attacker, but he is losing strength too rapidly for fast motion. He flails away at his opponent with his fists, but dizziness begins to close in on him.

The blade slashes into his right forearm. He winces with pain, falls backward, kicks out again with his feet, but the dizziness is overpowering him. He realizes he is losing a lot of blood. He senses that he cannot keep doing this much longer, that the end is probably near.

He grabs at his assailant with his left hand and finds his throat, but the effort of strangulation is more than he can manage. His hands falls away from the killer's throat and he feels himself sinking into unconsciousness.

He hears a high, fiendish, hyenalike laugh. It is only then that he realizes who his attacker is and that Volkening isn't the Hyena after all.

Somehow Max had known all along that it wasn't Volkening—the Hyena spent a lot of time studying his victims, whereas Volkening had just grabbed a girl on the street whom he'd never even seen before. It wasn't the right M.O. Max and the others had just chosen to ignore it because they had so much wanted Volkening to be the Hyena and for it all to be over. And now, at least for Max, it really *was* over, but not the way he'd always figured it would end.

The Hyena feels Max slump to the floor, and an animallike sound of victory surges through him. Laughing demonically, he makes his way over to the sink and to the wall with the circuitbreaker box. He fumbles briefly till he finds it, then opens the box and flicks the switches. The room is flooded with blinding light.

The Hyena's eyes become accustomed to the brightness. He sees the results of his handiwork with the knife. Max lies in a spreading puddle of blood about ten feet from Babette's body, but the job is not yet quite complete: Max is still breathing.

The Hyena picks up his knife again, which is sticky with Max's blood. With a smug smile on his face he begins sauntering over to finish Max off, taking his own sweet time about it.

A fleeting, almost subliminal image of a human face. Another fleeting image. A bullet hitting the face. A series of slow-motion images of many tiny bits of blood and tissue and fragments of teeth fanning slowly outward. Then intense light. Then sounds of demonic laughter. Then, gradually, gradually, Babette regains consciousness.

There is a terrible pain in her head and neck and back. There is a lot of blood on the floor. There is the

Hyena standing at the wall, having just turned on the switches in the circuit-breaker box. There is a revolver. There is—oh God—there is Max, lying in a bath of blood. There is the Hyena, picking up his knife and walking leisurely back to Max to finish him off.

Slowly, torturously, as if moving her limbs in a tank of molasses, Babette reaches out for the revolver, picks it up, grips it in both hands, and points it at the killer.

Catching sight of movement out of the corner of his eye, the Hyena turns around and is amazed to see Babette alive, with a snub-nosed revolver pointed at his head. He holds up a hand as if to shield his eyes from glare. He takes a step in her direction.

"Babette," he says. "My only love, my—"

The bullet catches him in the mouth, ending his sentence and his life and spraying the room with fragments of his face.

Averting her eyes from the mess which has fallen to the floor a foot away from her, Babette crawls painfully to the telephone on the end table by the couch, pulls it onto the floor by the cord, and dials 0 for Operator.